Louise Sharland moved to the UK from her native Canada nearly thirty years ago after falling in love with a British sailor. She began writing short stories when her children were little and her work has appeared in magazines, anthologies and online. In 2019, Louise won *The Big Issue* Crime Writing competition, and this is her second published novel.

By the same author:

The Lake

My Husband's Secrets

Louise Sharland

Published by AVON
A division of HarperCollins*Publishers*
1 London Bridge Street
London SE1 9GF

www.harpercollins.co.uk

HarperCollins*Publishers*
1st Floor, Watermarque Building,
Ringsend Road
Dublin 4, Ireland

A Paperback Original 2022

1

First published in Great Britain by HarperCollins*Publishers* 2022

Epigraph on p.vii taken from © *Joyland* by Stephen King 2013

A catalogue copy of this book is available from the British Library.

ISBN: 978-0-00-840336-2

Typeset in Sabon Lt Std 12.5/16 pt by Palimpsest Book Production Limited,
Falkirk, Stirlingshire

Printed and bound in the UK using 100% Renewable Electricity at CPI
Group (UK) Ltd

MIX
Paper from
responsible sources
FSC™ C007454

This book is produced from independently certified FSC™ paper
to ensure responsible forest management.

For more information visit: www.harpercollins.co.uk/green

*For my husband, Nick, whose love and support
helped to make this book possible*

'When it comes to the past, everyone writes fiction.'

– Stephen King

Prologue

The rain fell in great unending sheets, soaking everyone who had dared venture out into the darkness. Guests raced to their cars, trench coats and macs slung across their shoulders, but the wet still soaked through to their posh frocks and dinner suits. The goodbyes had been awkward, hurried, tension hanging in the air like evening mist. They had drunk too much, or not enough, and there was still the journey home to consider.

After their argument in the foyer, he had walked the faded white line in the hotel car park to appease her, eyes closed, arms outstretched, while the rest of the guests watched in weary amusement.

'You don't always have to be the life of the party,' she hissed, her patience frayed. 'I just wish once in a while you could be more appropriate.'

'*Appropriate?*' he repeated, and laughing dismissively, whispered something into her ear that made her pale, before helping her into the car and slamming the door on the hem of her evening gown. The long strip of organza would flutter in the breeze for their entire journey.

He was always lead-footed, but now, with just enough champagne inside him and the certainty of a row, he became reckless. Once free of the hotel security lights, the night became eternal, mud-slicked roads momentarily illuminated by the flash of headlights, then once again engulfed in gloom. There had been an argument about his disclosure, fierce and vindictive.

'You're a bloody liar!' she had cried, but he had said something in reply that had silenced her, then put his foot down.

'Slow down!' she screamed and grappled for the wheel, but he pushed her away, momentarily losing control. Then the sensation of the car sliding sideways, everything in slow motion like a crash test recording – spare change and chewing gum flying past – as the car careened down the gully. Then the astonishment of impact, pop of the airbag, and stench of burning rubber. There was a moment of suspended motion and then the car began moving forward again. In the glow of the headlights, the river below was a twisting serpent approaching fast. Next to her the sound of groans, flailing arms, and pleas. The deep thud of the car hitting water. A fear like no other. She fumbled for the seatbelt, her fingers slick with blood, pushed at the crumpled passenger door, pleading with a God she no longer believed in.

Time was infinite, termless. Finally there were voices, a hand on hers and welcome release. She was eased, or stumbled from the watery wreck – her right leg giving out at the first step – and fell face first onto the wet stony ground.

'*Matthew*,' she pleaded, 'save Matthew!' Then the smell of muddy earth, the rusty taste of blood on her lips and unimaginable pain. The world ending.

1

Ali's back throbbed as the car sped along the narrow roadway towards its bleak destination. It didn't matter how many metal pins were holding her damaged body together, nothing would prompt her to ask the driver to slow down; nothing would stop her from reaching their grim destination. She knew that this road – with its bumps, dips, and unexpectedly sharp bends – would send every damaged joint, tendon, and nerve ending jangling, but she didn't care. She had learned to live with the pain, the morphine tablets easing her on her way.

They had started out early, taking a scenic B-road, and carrying on through Dartmoor, not even slowing to give the wild ponies a second glance. She had insisted they steer clear of tea shops and cafés. Even now, two months after the accident, she was reliant on a pair of unwieldy crutches, and there was still that scar on her cheek. She felt a gentle hand on her shoulder, and a reassuring squeeze.

'You'll be fine,' said her best friend Liz from the back seat.

Ahead of them the road snaked behind rocky tors, the stony layers stacked like gargantuan pancakes. It was still early, yet the sky was an odd, deepening, night-time blue. A gust of wind buffeted the car, and Ali found herself letting out an involuntary squeal of pain.

'We can turn back,' said Dane, their driver and Liz's husband, 'if it's too much for you?'

'No,' she muttered, 'I promised,' and gripping the door handle indicated for him to carry on.

The crossroad appeared out of nowhere, just a rattling signpost pointing left to a single-lane road.

'I can do this,' she said to herself in a private mantra. The prayer beads hanging on the driver's rear-view mirror swung across the windscreen like a hangman's noose.

The place was exactly as she had seen in the accident photos. On one side a steep, fern-covered incline leading towards a romantically named tor, on the other, spiky gorse sloping down towards a dark, twisting river. She stared at the water, willing herself to remember . . . But all that came to mind were the same fragments of memory, terrifying and confused, that had haunted her for weeks: frantic screams, a furore of crunching metal, and the unforgettable stench of burning rubber. Her specialist, Dr Bhogadi, had said that it was likely some of her memories would be permanently shrouded in a haze of shock and post-traumatic confusion.

'There's retrograde amnesia,' he had told her the morning of her release from the neuro-rehabilitation unit. He had been holding a life-size plastic model of a human brain in his hand. 'One can remember some things distinctly, but for those few hours prior to the injury.' He shrugged, suggesting it was all one great mystery. 'Then there's anterograde amnesia,' he continued, 'which involves problems with memory for information acquired after injury. This seems a more significant issue for you.' He pointed his HB pencil at various sections of the model, explaining what parts were responsible for storing previously acquired and newly acquired information.

'Why isn't it grey?' Ali asked.

'Pardon me?'

'The model. Why is it pink and not grey?' She was feeling frustrated, even angry at this inconsistency, 'considering it's referred to as grey matter and all.'

Dr Bhogadi had suggested that maybe they had

done enough for one day and booked her in for another outpatient appointment with the physiotherapist.

She felt a slight jolt as Dane eased the car into a lay-by dotted with sheep dung and daisies.

'Shall I help you out?' asked Liz.

'Just give me a minute.' Ali tried to remember the breathing exercises her therapist had taught her – *in for four, hold, out for four* – when all she really wanted to do was scream. She took a deep breath. 'I'm ready.'

'Good lass,' said Dane in the seat next to her.

Gritting her teeth, she pushed open the door and discreetly placed a hand on her right leg to slide it across the seat and onto the ground. Liz was already waiting, crutches at hand.

'Now you be careful,' she said, gripping Ali's arm to help steady her. 'It's wet and slippery, and there's sheep shit everywhere. I'm right beside you if you need me.' Ali smiled, grateful for her friend's strong arm and supportive words. 'Shall I get the . . .' She pointed to the flowers resting on the back seat, but Ali was already making her way across the road.

'Hold up,' said Dane, placing a hand on hers to halt her progress. 'There's no way you're going down there.' He pointed to the steep path, wet grass, and jagged slices of granite that poked up through the soggy earth. She heard the crinkle of cellophane, and knew that Liz was beside her with the bouquet of red roses and the card that read:

To my darling husband Matthew. Happy birthday, wherever you are.
Love forever, Ali

'Why don't I ask Dane to take them down?' said Liz. She indicated towards the gully, past the boulder still covered with flecks of Black Sapphire metallic paint, to the car's final resting place in the river. Ali closed her eyes, reimagining the crunch of impact, the briefest of pauses, then cold water swirling at their feet. There were other glimpses, half-formed images that seemed to dissolve like fog in sunlight, but nothing she could grasp.

There had been a party to celebrate their third anniversary at a posh country house hotel on the moors, all paid for by Ali of course. The weather had been appalling for weeks, heavy rain resulting in swollen rivers and washed-out roads. Climate change at its worst. Had she and Matthew actually laughed as they negotiated the floodwater lapping onto the bridge near the hotel?

Not so funny now.

Tired, she sat down on a large square boulder by the roadside and ran her fingertips across the moss-covered edges. Below them Dane was negotiating his way down the slippery path towards a small plateau just above the river. A bouquet of sunflowers, vibrant yellow against a dull green background, had already been placed on the ground nearby.

As Liz sat down beside her, Ali caught a waft of her perfume, sparking a memory so painful, so profound, she reeled backwards as if struck.

'I can just about remember you getting me out of the car,' she said, turning to her friend, 'but nothing afterwards.' Liz gave an almost inaudible sigh, clearly anticipating what would be coming next. 'Do you think it will ever come back to me?'

Their heart-to-heart was interrupted by Dane's grunts and quiet curses as he climbed his way back up the slope towards them.

'It looks like Emma got here before us,' he said, indicating to the sunflowers on the plateau below.

'She left first thing,' said Ali. 'I asked if she wanted to wait and come with us, but she was determined to do it on her own.'

Dane and Liz exchanged glances. It was no secret that Ali's daughter Emma wasn't happy about her mother's remarriage three years ago, particularly to a man eight years her junior.

'He's only after your money,' Emma had said the night Ali told her of their engagement, and then added the very well targeted: 'What would Dad think?'

Your father has been dead for seven years, Ali had wanted to reply, but she held her tongue, knowing how hard Emma had struggled following Rory's death. Matthew, too, was sympathetic. 'I won't try and replace your father,' he had said to her, 'just try and be like a sort of friend.'

Emma had laughed bitterly and giving him a razor-sharp glare said, 'Don't you mean older brother?'

'Are you okay?' Liz and Dane were watching her closely. 'We lost you for a second there.'

'I'm fine. It's just all a bit . . .'

'Confusing?'

'That's one way of putting it.' A cold wind blew, and Ali zipped her jacket up to just under her chin. 'There are still these fiery sparks of memory from before the accident: Matthew and me picnicking on the hillside—' she lifted a shaky hand and pointed '—just over there. How he slipped the engagement ring into my plastic glass of champagne.' She blinked repeatedly as if trying to reboot her scrambled brain. 'But when I try to actually remember what happened *that night*—'

'You shouldn't stress yourself,' interjected Liz, once again acting as Ali's fierce protector.

'Her memories are important,' said Dane gently.

'Not if they cause her distress.'

Ali turned away, unable to face their sympathy. 'If only things were clearer.'

11

'It will come,' said Liz. 'Just give it time.'

'But there isn't time!' replied Ali, impassioned. 'Matthew is still out there somewhere – traumatised, injured, frightened. I need to find him, and the only way I can do that is by trying to remember what happened!'

The sky darkened, and in the distance they could see rainfall.

'Better get you back into the car,' said Dane, helping Ali to her feet. 'You're still recuperating after all.'

She frowned at his words. *Recuperating* suggested positive outcomes, getting better. Her bones might heal, the scar would fade, but without Matthew . . .

In the distance the low hum of an approaching car made them turn. It took a few seconds before the black BMW Coupé came into view.

'Christ,' muttered Dane. 'Timing is everything.'

They watched as the driver continued past, oblivious to their stares.

'It's just a car,' whispered Ali, but she couldn't help looking back down towards the gully, to where her husband's car – the exact same model – had ended up in the river – thinking of her and Matthew trapped inside, the sound of rushing water, of wanting to be safely out no matter what the cost. An image flashed in her mind; that secret in the car park sparking a response so primal, so ferocious.

Of her digging her fingernails into Matthew's forearm as she grabbed for the steering wheel.

'Do you think it was my fault?' she asked. 'The accident?'

'Of course not,' said Liz. 'It was just that: an accident. It was dark, the road conditions were terrible—'

'But—'

'No buts,' replied Liz. 'It was a terrible thing that happened.' Her voice was tight with emotion. 'It wasn't your fault.'

Ali smiled weakly, grateful for the words of support even though she could tell her dearest friend in the world was lying through her teeth.

2

'There we go.'

Dane gently eased Ali onto the settee and rested her crutches nearby.

'Cup of tea?' asked Liz.

'Looking at her face, I think a painkiller is what's called for,' said Dane.

Ali nodded. 'There's a packet on my bedside table.'

Liz went to get a glass of water and then sat down beside her.

'How are you feeling?'

Ali rested her neck on the back of the settee. 'There's just so much going on in my head, but none of it seems to make any sense. I have so many questions.'

'Of course you do honey, but I really think you

should try and give yourself a break. Stressing your-self out about it won't do any good.'

'The police said that from the skid marks on the road it was clear Matthew was speeding,' continued Ali, ignoring Liz's advice. 'You and Dane were following right behind us, so you would know.'

Liz seemed unusually interested in the vase of freesias on the coffee table. 'It was dark,' she replied, 'raining. I could barely see your taillights in front of me.'

'But?'

'Okay, yes. It was clear he was going too fast.'

'I should have called a taxi,' said Ali, shaking her head in self-reproach.

'Why does all of this have to be your fault?' said Liz, now plainly angry. 'Matthew was an adult, a grown-up; he should have been sensible enough to know not to drive if he'd had too much to drink.'

Ali was surprised at Liz's uncharacteristic criticism of her husband.

'He did prove he wasn't over the limit though.'

'Do you mean that spectacle of him walking the white line in the car park?'

'He was only teasing me,' said Ali, feeling defensive. 'I did have a few drinks too, you know, a few drinks too many.'

'You weren't driving,' said Liz firmly.

'Maybe I should have been.'

'Maybe if the weather had been better, the roads

less slick,' countered Liz. 'Maybe if the council had done that bloody road resurfacing work like they'd promised.' Ali wasn't used to seeing her best friend this irate. 'And maybe if Matthew hadn't been such an idiot and driving so recklessly, none of this would have happened!'

Ali stared at Liz, shocked by her ire.

'I'm sorry,' said Liz, still obviously upset. 'I'm just so angry with him.'

'It's all right,' said Ali. 'I'm angry with him too.'

Dane emerged from the short corridor that led to Ali's downstairs bedroom.

'Sorry it took so long.' He placed the silver blister pack on the coffee table in front of her. 'I searched everywhere. It had fallen down the side of the bed and I couldn't find it.'

Ali popped a lozenge from its blister pack and, gritting her teeth, reached for her glass of water. Once swallowed, she leaned back, and waited for the morphine to take effect.

'Better?' asked Liz.

'Getting there.' Ali forced a smile. 'I can't thank you both enough for taking me there this morning. I know it's just as hard for you.' She paused, trying to contain the tears. Why did the painkillers always make her so emotional?

'It's all right,' said Liz. 'We're here for you. You know that don't you?'

'I just keep on going over and over it in my mind,

17

the bits I *can* remember,' said Ali. 'Matthew and Emma had a row at some point – that's why she wouldn't ride with us.' She gave a wry smile. 'I know there was nothing unusual about those two falling out.' Her eyes narrowed pensively. She turned to Liz. 'You didn't seem particularly happy with him either. Then there was that messing around in the car park. God, I really shouldn't have let him drive.'

'*Ali.*'

'He said something to me before we got into the car.' Ali glanced past the French doors to the fields beyond, her brow creased in concentration. 'Something that changed everything.'

Tension hung in the room like a waft of cigar smoke.

'Do you remember what it was?' asked Dane.

'I've been trying,' replied Ali, tearfully, 'but I can't, I just can't.'

'You mustn't push yourself,' said Liz, giving her husband a stern look.

'I mean, I remember bits from before reasonably well, scattered, but clear, then just those few minutes afterwards.' Ali tilted her head, almost resting it on Liz's shoulder. 'Of you saving me.'

Liz cleared her throat. 'Do you think those are real memories, or just bits you've put together from your conversations with me and maybe the police?'

'I never considered that,' said Ali, deep in thought.

'That they may not be actual memories, just things I've cobbled together from what I've heard.' She peered at Liz. 'It was you who told me how I got out of the car, and the police about what happened afterwards, wasn't it?' Her eyes widened in recognition. 'The truth is I don't really remember much that happened after the accident at all.'

Liz reached for Ali's hand. 'You mustn't upset yourself. Trying to force things won't do any good.'

Ali pulled at a loose thread on the cushion next to her, watching as it unravelled in one long strand. 'My doctor said there were some things I might never remember.'

'Maybe *not* remembering isn't such a bad thing,' said Liz softly.

'Believe me,' Ali reached for a tissue from the box on the table in front of her. 'I've thought that myself, but if Matthew is out there somewhere – confused, hurt, scared – then I have to try.'

Liz paused, clearly preparing herself for what she was going to say next. 'How can you be so sure that he's still alive?'

Ali was tempted to snap, bite back, but seeing her friend's concerned expression stopped herself. Instead she tapped a finger to her chest and said, 'I can feel it, here.'

'But that's not very . . .' Liz paused, choosing her next words carefully '. . . rational is it?'

'No body,' replied Ali fervently, 'even though

Dartmoor Search and Rescue have been out five times. No real evidence at the scene that his injuries were fatal.' She paused, uncertain if she should continue. 'And then there's the cash-in-hand fund.'

'The what?' said Liz and Dane in unison.

Ali looked away, unable to face her friends' scrutiny. 'I found out that Matthew had been keeping five hundred pounds in cash in the safe box upstairs.' She could feel her cheeks begin to glow. 'He had this idea that he could pay some of the short-term subcontractors working on the holiday let renovations in cash.'

She heard Liz's sharp intake of breath. 'And you let him?'

'Of course not. He'd seen it being done at some sites and thought it would be okay for the occasional one-off job.'

'One-off job?!' said Liz incredulously. 'Had he thought about the implications if the HMRC found out?'

'I know, Liz,' said Ali, clearly upset by having to disclose her husband's transgression. 'It was a dick move, but we talked about it and sorted it out. He never used the cash. I made sure of that. It was there, in the box upstairs, untouched for months.'

Dane, visibly interested in this new bit of information, perched himself on the arm of the settee.

'So what does all this have to do with Matthew's disappearance?'

'The money is gone,' said Ali. 'I checked the box yesterday and it was empty.'

'Oh, Ali,' said Liz. 'Anyone could have taken it: Matthew, Emma, even the workmen who installed the grab rails in your downstairs loo.'

'It was there a few weeks ago.'

'How can you be so sure?'

'Because I went into the cashbox to get some notes for the taxi to my physio appointment.'

'I still don't understand what that has to do with Matthew being missing,' said Liz.

Dane placed a hand on his wife's shoulder. 'What she's suggesting is that Matthew was here, in the house.' He turned to Ali. 'Am I right?'

'He must have been,' she replied. 'No one else knew about the money, not even Emma.'

'This is ridiculous.' Liz was clearly struggling to control her irritation. 'Why would he sneak into his own house and steal his own money? Why wouldn't he just come to you for help?'

Ali took a moment for the dust to settle on Liz's question.

'Maybe he's in some sort of trouble.' Ali realised she was grasping at straws but couldn't help herself. 'Maybe he needed the money for some reason.' There was a sudden shared sense of understanding between the three of them, an unspoken secret. Liz opened her mouth to tell it, but Ali silenced her with a glance. 'We dealt with that problem, Liz, before we got married.'

'So you're saying that Matthew was here,' said Dane, quickly changing the subject, 'in this house within the last two weeks and took the money from the cashbox?'

'We've checked with all the homeless hostels,' said Ali, sounding more and more convinced, 'and the rough-sleeping teams in Plymouth, Exeter and Torbay. If he's not on the streets, then maybe he needed money for accommodation.'

Liz leaned forward, hands on knees. 'This is all so fantastical.'

'Fantastical?' said Ali, affronted. 'Do you think I'm making this up?'

Liz spoke slowly and with great care. 'A month ago you were certain Rory was still alive.'

Ali felt that familiar tingling in her cheeks. 'I get confused sometimes – that's all. Dr Bhogadi said it might happen.'

'Of course it might,' said Liz. 'You've been through a terrible ordeal, not just physical, but psychological as well. Maybe that confusion is what's happening right now.'

Ali gazed at the line of framed photographs on the fireplace mantel.

'No,' she said resolutely, 'I remember.' But even as she uttered the words her confidence faltered.

'But if he's still alive,' said Dane, looking hopeful, 'coming for the cash sort of makes sense. I mean, he may have lost his wallet in the river, or didn't want to use his cash card in case it was traced.'

'Why wouldn't he?' asked Liz, who was evidently angry with her husband for raising Ali's expectations. 'Why wouldn't he want it to be traced?'

There was a crackle of animosity in the room. Ali – tired, confused, and frightened – leaned back and closed her eyes. The last thing she wanted was to row with her friends.

'Ali,' said Liz gently. 'I was with you when you met with the family liaison officer. She said the longer Matthew was missing—'

'I know what she said!' Ali clenched her fists, the knuckles growing white. 'I'm sorry, Liz. I didn't mean to snap at you. She said that the longer he's missing the more likely . . .' She stopped, unable to speak the words. 'But there's still no body, and my Facebook posts have brought up a lot of sightings of someone matching Matthew's description all across the south-west.'

'If that's the case,' said Liz, plainly unconvinced, 'then why wouldn't he come home?'

'I don't know,' said Ali, 'but the police are still monitoring his bank account and credit cards. Why would they be doing that if they thought he was dead?'

The was a long silence before Dane spoke.

23

'There's always hope. Matty was a resourceful ole bugger after all.'

Liz tutted. 'It's been over two months. We need to start thinking about the future.'

'Future,' whispered Ali. 'What future?'

'Oh, sweetheart.' Liz began to cry. 'I know this is awful, unbearable, but things need to be done.'

'Things? What things?'

'Legal, financial.'

'Why are you telling me all this?'

'Because we care about you,' said Liz.

'I'm doing fine,' Ali lied. What she really wanted to say, however, was how late at night she would stare into the darkness wondering, worrying. How her dreams were filled with terrifying images of that night, of the car toppling down the bank, the smell of dead earth and burnt rubber, the sound of water racing past. How every morning she woke up with a gasp of relief knowing that she would be free of those horrors for another few hours at least. How all she could think about was finding Matthew.

'It's not that we're expecting the worst,' said Liz. 'Of course it isn't. It's just that we want to help you prepare.'

'Prepare for what!' said Ali, with unexpected vehemence. 'He's missing, Liz, just bloody missing!' She dabbed the crumpled tissue against her scarred cheek. 'And I don't know what to do to find him.'

Finally giving in to the emotion she had been fighting all morning, Ali began to cry. 'I just miss him, that's all.'

Dane let out a sigh that sounded more like a sob. 'I miss him too.'

Close, but not touching, the three friends came together.

'I'm sorry,' said Ali. 'I know this all sounds mad, but as far as I'm concerned there's more evidence to suggest he's alive than not.' She faced Liz, desperate for reassurance. 'Can't you try and believe that too, for me?'

Liz took Ali's hand. 'Anything for you.'

Dane stood up, his energy shifting the mood. 'That's enough of all this nonsense,' he said. 'We need to stay positive, energised. How about some lunch?'

They sat at the large oak kitchen table, nibbled at cheese and pickle sandwiches, and drank more tea.

'You could do with an online shop,' said Liz, who had taken it upon herself to reorganise the fridge. 'Most of this stuff is out of date.'

'I've been meaning to,' replied Ali, though the thought of scrolling through endless webpages of food made her stomach turn.

'Why don't I do it?' said Dane. 'I do ours, don't I, Liz?'

Liz gave a chuckle. 'Yes, and last week you ordered ostrich steaks!'

Dane gave his wife a wounded look. 'I'm a culinary adventurer.'

Ali found herself laughing for the first time in weeks, and was once again reminded just how grateful she was for Liz and Dane's friendship.

Dane rubbed his hands together in glee. 'I love a good shop. Where's your laptop?'

Ali pointed to the downstairs bedroom.

'Speaking of laptops,' Dane sounded hesitant, as if he was tiptoeing through glass. 'Where's Matthew's?'

'Matthew's laptop?' said Ali, perplexed. 'I thought it was at the office?'

'I don't think so,' said Liz, a tea towel slung over her shoulder.

'It's not here?' said Dane.

'I . . .' Ali could feel her cheeks tingling again. 'I don't know. I don't think so.'

'Do you mind if I have a look?'

'Um, no, of course not.' The warm atmosphere that had brightened the room only minutes before now vanished, leaving Ali feeling as if she was sitting in shadow.

Dane gave her a reassuring smile and Ali listened as he made his way methodically throughout the house. First her downstairs bedroom, then kitchen cupboards and the large island unit, and finally into the lounge and dining area.

'Upstairs?' he asked.

'I'd rather you didn't.' Ali didn't want anyone going into the master bedroom, pristine and preserved for Matthew's return, and it certainly wouldn't be appropriate for him to enter Emma's private space without her permission.

'But—'

'It's not upstairs,' she said decisively. 'I'm sure of it.'

There was a moment of silent exchange between them, only the steady tick of the mantel clock in the background.

'Could it have been in the car with you?' asked Liz, eager to ease the tension.

'No, definitely not,' said Ali. 'We'd just had the car valeted and the boot had been emptied.'

'So where could it be?' Liz and Dane were standing side by side staring at her.

'I don't know,' said Ali, beginning to feel uncomfortable. 'Why would you want it anyway?'

Liz pulled out a chair and sat down beside her. Dane did the same.

'He kept everything on that laptop.' Liz's voice was tense. 'Bank account details, financial records. We need to think about stopping his direct debits, standing orders, that sort of thing.'

'I don't—'

'And if it's missing . . .' said Dane. 'Well, that could be a problem.'

'A problem?'

'You know how terrible he was with remembering his passwords,' said Liz. Ali smiled wryly, remembering her constant invocations to her husband to improve his online security. 'He saved all his passwords to his laptop. If somebody found it—'

'They'd have to know his login,' said Ali.

'Chiefs123,' said Dane and Liz in unison.

'How?'

'His Amazon and Netflix accounts, and almost everything else had the same login – or a variation of.' Dane couldn't hide his look of frustration. 'I can't tell you how many times I told him to change it.'

'Me too,' said Liz.

'And me,' added Ali.

'You can speak to your solicitor about it,' said Liz, sensing Ali's discomfort, 'if that would make you feel better.'

'Why would I want to do that?' Ali knew she was repeating herself but didn't care. On either side of her both Dane and Liz seemed awkward and distraught.

'Just in case,' whispered Dane.

'In case of what!'

Liz placed a hand on hers. 'In case he doesn't come back.'

Ali and Liz met as thirteen-year-olds in the hallway outside the headmaster's office at St Mary's

Catholic Secondary School in Kingsbridge. She had been sent there for wearing inappropriate footwear, a pair of black Dr Martens with yellow stitching she had bought at Camden Market. Liz had been bringing the registers to the secretary's office.

'Nice boots,' she said. Ali had expected a scornful look, but instead was met with an open, friendly smile. 'You're new, aren't you?'

Ali sighed. Her identity, once that of a bolshie North Londoner, had unexpectedly changed to that of *new kid*.

Liz sat down beside her. 'You live at that commune place in Staverton, don't you?'

'It's a shared community,' replied Ali, still not believing the words no matter how many times she said them. It had only been six months since her father, in an epiphany of self-interest, had decided to embrace an alternative lifestyle that included leaving his job as an IT specialist, selling their detached home in Muswell Hill, and moving the family to Devon, to live at Clearwood House.

'What the hell is a *shared community*?' she remembered asking her older brother Graham at the time. What they discovered was a group of ramshackle properties orbiting around an old manor house, and a group of naïve yet optimistic families struggling to maintain them, as well as an ethos of environmentally friendly self-sufficiency.

Even now, her father – an eco-minded widower in his early seventies – still paraded his views, once showing up with placards at a property development she was managing near St Ives. There had also been a brief appearance at her hospital bedside after the accident.

'Ambition is a dangerous stupidity, Alice,' he had murmured, while her brain was still riddled with damage and drugs. Later she wondered if he had ever been there at all.

'Most of the kids from Clearwood go to the Steiner school,' said Liz, clearly curious.

'Not for me,' replied Ali, picking at a piece of gum that had been stuck under the seat. She didn't mention the arguments with her parents, her bunking off, and finally the hunger strike.

'Me neither,' said Liz. 'My mum tried to get me to go there after primary, but I hated it. All the kids smelled like cabbage.'

Ali laughed, grateful for kindness instead of hostility or, even worse, indifference.

'Why don't you come and sit with me at lunch. I'll introduce you to my mates.'

'You sure you want to be seen with the weird kid from the commune?' asked Ali.

'You're not the weird kid from the commune,' replied Liz glancing down at Ali's boots. 'You're the cool kid from London.'

It didn't take long for the small group of girls

to accept her. Liz smoothed the way by telling them that Ali had refused the head teacher's demand to *acquire more appropriate footwear*, and had even sworn at him.

'Why did you tell them that?' she had asked as they emptied their lunchboxes in the bin and then went to stand in the queue for chips.

'Just to make you sound more exciting, dangerous.'

Liz's friends were anything but dangerous. Sweet, friendly, hardworking, and polite, they aspired to rebelliousness, but their happy middle-class existences didn't offer much true motivation.

She went to Liz's house for tea that night and many after, relishing her mother's roast dinners, and home-made steak pies.

'We're vegan,' she had confessed to Liz, one afternoon as they sat eating junk food in front of the telly.

'What's that?' asked Liz, handing Ali another peperami.

'Like being vegetarian only worse.'

By the time they reached sixth form, Ali was spending most weekends at Liz's house. Liz's parents – often escaping to their caravan in Cornwall with her two younger brothers – were grateful for Ali's presence.

One Saturday she and Liz took the train to London and spent the day in Carnaby Street. Liz was mesmerised by the energy and bustle, and Ali found herself dragging her friend from stall to stall. They bought clothes and make-up both knew would have to be hidden from their parents, and that night broke into Liz's parents' drinks cabinet, pouring Tia Maria into their glasses of Coke and topping up the half-empty bottle with tap water.

'To best friends forever!' said Liz, clinking glasses.

'Best friends forever,' replied Ali, and she meant it.

3

Ali waited for Liz and Dane to leave before collapsing onto the settee. After her release from the neuro-rehabilitation unit six weeks before, she had tried to embrace her treatment programme with gusto. Daily physio, meditation, deep-muscle massages – everything to get her *back on track*, as the surgeon had suggested, but back on track for what? Her body felt broken, her mind much the same, and pain and panic attacks had dogged her since she had awoken in intensive care.

'It's good news,' Dr Bhogadi had informed her. 'The MRI scan confirms no major spinal injury . . . There are some minor fractures and significant tendon damage to the right leg which may require micro-surgery, a few titanium pins here and there, but you should be back on your feet within a few weeks.' He clapped his hands together in genuine delight. 'You are indeed a very lucky woman.'

Ali had fought through the post-anaesthetic haze, trying to gather her scrambled thoughts enough to ask about Matthew.

'Is he here? Is he okay?'

There'd been no answer, only a tight smile and a recommendation to get some rest.

An hour later a road policing investigator for Devon and Cornwall Police had arrived along with a family liaison officer. Their expressions serious, they'd explained how just after Liz had pulled her free from the BMW, a freak current had pulled the vehicle further into the river. Specialist officers were searching it even as they spoke, but with the deteriorating weather conditions and river at its highest-ever recorded level, it was proving difficult.

'We're just trying to accumulate as much evidence as possible about what happened that night,' the family liaison officer had said. 'According to Liz, your husband was still inside the vehicle when the car was swept deeper into the river. Can you remember if that was the case?'

Ali looked at the officer, her face distorted in pain, shock, and confusion.

'What are you talking about? He got out. Liz rescued me and then went to help Matthew.' The heart monitor gave a tiny blip of protest. 'The air ambulance came, and the fire crew. He's here now, in the hospital, isn't he?'

Then Emma had stepped forward and taken her hand.

Forcing herself to her feet Ali shuffled her way to the downstairs bedroom where she now resided, the stairs still being too much of a hardship. She reached into the chest of drawers for the large album box. Resting it on the bed, she carefully unwrapped the cream ribbon and lifted the lid. *The Wedding of . . .* read the album cover, also adorned with a slick black and white image of her and Matthew barefoot on the beach. Ali felt a wave of grief sweep over her. She couldn't bring herself to look at all those happy, smiling faces. Matthew in a navy linen suit, and her in a designer tea-length satin dress with hand-sewn seed pearls. Instead, she lifted the album from its resting place and set it carefully on the bed. What she was after was hidden beneath.

The folder felt like a dead weight in her hand, but she still opened it and spilled the contents out on the bed, just as she had done so many times before. Spread out before her were photographs, old and new, and at least a half dozen newspaper articles, some printed from the internet, some clipped from the few tabloids that had managed to make their way into the house after the accident.

MAN MISSING AFTER HORRIFIC CAR CRASH ON DARTMOOR!

She went through the articles one by one, hoping that somewhere there might be a clue, some bit of information that might spark a memory. The articles described her and Matthew as *one of Devon's top power couples, running a property business that ranged from luxury homes in the South Hams to student flats in Plymouth.*

There were photographs of them at events, of her winning *The Most Inspiring Woman in Business Award* at a do that had raised nearly fifty thousand pounds for local charities. Ali ran her fingertip across the scar on her cheek. The woman in the photos, charming, smiling, and overflowing with confidence, was much different to the person she was now. She gave a bitter snort. The Botox she once used to keep her forehead wrinkle-free, was now being employed in a far more practical manner: managing the muscle spasms following her injury. Next to her, Matthew, in his well-cut suit and carefully manicured beard, seemed happy to remain in the background. It was hard to tell there was an eight-year gap between them.

Tired and despondent, she was replacing the items in the folder when a bit of loose paper fluttered to the floor. Ali carefully reached down to retrieve it, her leg aching in protest. It was a newspaper clipping of her and Matthew's wedding announcement. *The bride wore . . .*

She met Matthew after finally agreeing to go for a drink with Liz and Dane at a pub near the river. It was nearly four years since Rory's death, and it had become clear to Ali that the couple were determined to try and get her dating again. As Liz handed her a second G & T, Dane approached, a tall, good-looking bearded man in tow. Standing side by side, the two men could have been brothers.

'Ali can I introduce you to Matthew?'

Matthew kissed her cheek and bought her another drink. They talked about business, Hope Farm, and the loss of his mother only a few months earlier. When Ali finally took her eyes from his, she discovered Liz and Dane had moved to a table by the window and were watching them surreptitiously.

'It's a set up,' she said to Matthew, 'isn't it?'

He smiled and ran his finger across the inside of her wrist.

'Only if you want it to be.'

Still doubtful if she was ready for another relationship, Ali decided to change the subject.

'So you and Dane met up in the army?'

'Joined up when I was nineteen,' he said. 'Thought I was a hard man,' he continued, his tongue loosened by too many porn star martinis, 'but I was useless, always getting in trouble, getting things wrong. If it wasn't for Dane looking out for me, God knows what would have happened. Where he went, I followed.'

He gazed past her, his thoughts far away in a desert somewhere.

'And you didn't stay in?'

'Got out as soon as I could,' he replied, 'but Dane loved the thrill, loved the risk.' He turned to the couple and held up his glass. 'We stayed in touch though.'

Matthew was funny, charming, attentive. When he asked her to dance, slipping his hand around her waist and letting it rest just above the curve of her bottom, she felt an excitement she hadn't experienced since her days with Rory, but Matthew was eight years younger, and she was cautious; the love for her late husband still governing her every move. There were also plenty of pretty young things floating around the pub that night who were probably a lot more suitable for him. *So much for being a South-West Woman of Influence*, she thought to herself as she reapplied her lipstick in the bathroom mirror.

He was waiting for her by the bar where he told her about his job as a maintenance manager for a public services company and the fact that his most recent relationship had ended some months before.

'She wanted marriage and babies,' he whispered, 'but I want someone with ambition.'

They drank, flirted, and danced very close, but later when he asked for her number, Ali became uncharacteristically coy.

'We're probably not right for each other,' she said, thinking of the derogatory terms used for older woman – younger man relationships. She refused his offer of another drink, but was convinced to join him outside for a cigarette.

'I don't give a shit what other people think,' he said in response to another of her comments about their age gap, and in one swift movement leaned forward and kissed her. His hand slipped around her waist and then up along her ribcage, one thumb circling her nipple through the thin material of her summer dress. She insisted they leave separately, but when his car pulled up at Hope Farm, she felt her heart rate quicken. They drank tequila, smoked a joint, and made love on the kitchen table before moving to the bedroom where they spent most of the weekend.

By the time Emma came home from her weekend away, the house was aired, sheets changed, the love bites on her neck covered with concealer – and Ali was already in love.

Now she slipped the items back into the folder, placed it in the box with the wedding album, and returned everything to that special place in her drawer. Reaching for her laptop she logged into her *Find Matthew Penrose* Facebook account, and like every day this week, began searching through the messages detailing possible sightings.

Seen a bloke just like him in Okehampton at the Spar shop buying a six-pack of Strongbow.

Sure I spotted him walking arm in arm with a lush blonde in St Ives. Sorry babes.

Don't you think it's bloody well time that you accepted he's dead, you delusional cow?!

The sound of tyres on gravel pulled Ali's attention away from her computer screen. Emma's Audi was pulling up. Was it five o'clock already?

By the time Emma walked into the kitchen, Ali had packed away her laptop and was sitting at the table with two cups of tea and a plate of bourbon biscuits.

'Hi, Mum.' She leaned over and kissed her mother. Sitting down she took a sip from the mug in front of her and nibbled on a biscuit. 'Thanks, I needed that.'

Ali waited a few minutes, attuned to the signs of her daughter winding down. 'So, how are things?' she asked, trying to sound as casual as possible.

'All ticking along nicely,' said Emma in the careful tone she had been using since her mother's return from hospital.

'I should really come in, you know.'

'Not yet, Mum. You know what Dr Bhogadi said. Another month or two more at least. Liz and I can handle things perfectly well until then.'

'But—'

'You're still getting all the monthly reports, and Liz and I swore on our lives we would tell you if anything came up you should be aware of.' She smiled sweetly at her mother. 'I spend most dinnertimes filling you in on work anyway.'

Ali gave an inward sigh of relief. She wasn't sure she was ready yet to face the office she had shared with Matthew for the last three years, with its signed Exeter Chiefs shirt on the wall and empty coffee cup probably still containing a few dried remnants of Dolce Gusto. She was glad Emma, who at twenty-two had already been in training to become a project manager, was up to helping out. Along with Liz as acting company director and the rest of their dedicated staff, they had managed to reassure Dartmoor Properties' clients that it was business as usual.

'I'm really impressed you've been able to step up like this, Ems.'

Emma appeared pleased by her mother's compliment. 'It's nothing, Mum, really. Liz is doing all the hard work. I'm just helping out.'

'More than helping out. Liz tells me you're great with clients, especially the students.'

'It's not that long since I was one myself,' said Emma. She tapped a finger to her forehead. 'I know how they think.'

Ali smiled in return, but Emma's reference left a pause in the conversation. Ali swirled the flecks of tea leaves around in the bottom of her mug, her mind wandering. Just over a year ago Emma had unexpectedly dropped out of university. Ali hadn't even been aware that her daughter had left her course until she accidentally opened a Student Finance England letter that had been sent to Hope Farm. As with most things she had tackled it head on.

'Mum?' Emma was rightly surprised to see her mother turn up at her student digs in Plymouth. 'What are you doing here?'

Ali held out the Student Finance letter. 'What do *you* think?'

They had walked to a nearby pub and ordered two G & Ts.

'Why didn't you tell me you had dropped out of uni?'

'I didn't drop out.'

'According to this letter you did.'

'Like I said, I didn't drop out.' Emma's voice was stern, defensive. 'I completed my second year and just decided not to do a third.' She took a long sip. 'I was going to tell you.'

'Bloody hell, Emma, it's December.' Ali tried to

control herself, but her voice had risen by nearly an octave. 'You've been out of university for nearly three months, and you didn't tell me? Is it because of that idiot Jason?'

Jason was Emma's first serious boyfriend. They had met as first-year students on the Accounting and Finance degree at the University of Plymouth, and just as Ali and Rory had, got very serious, very quickly. Towards the end of the year, however, it became clear that Jason wasn't interested in monogamy. Emma had wept, wallowed and wailed, but at the start of her second year, seemed to get over it.

'Will you keep it down please,' said Emma, glancing around in embarrassment. 'I know people.'

Ali finished her drink and signalled to the waiter. 'Two more please.' She waited until he left before carrying on. 'Why didn't you tell me you were struggling?'

'I wasn't struggling,' replied Emma with a confidence that bore a striking resemblance to her mother's. 'I just didn't want to do it anymore.'

Ali's tone softened. 'Was it anything to do with losing your father?'

'Oh for God's sake, Mum . . . not that again.' But something about the way Emma hesitated seemed to undermine her denial.

'Five years isn't that long a time you know.'

'I know what you're going to say next, and *no,* I *do not* need to see a counsellor.'

'But leaving your course in your second year and not telling anyone?' Ali tried to hide the hurt in her voice. 'Not telling me?'

'I'm an adult, Mum.'

'I'm not quite sure you've been behaving like one.'

'If this is going to be all about you telling me what an idiot I've been then I'm just going to—'

The waiter returned with their second round and both women sat silently while he cleared away their empties.

'I just wish . . .' began Ali, then cut herself short. This wasn't about her, it was about Emma, and as much as her proud, stubborn daughter might refuse to admit it, Ali suspected the loss of her father and her break-up with Jason were major factors in her decision to drop out of university. The last thing she wanted was to alienate her vulnerable daughter further; more than anything she just wanted to help. 'I realise that you're an adult, and I should respect your decision, but . . .'

'I appreciate that, Mum, really I do, but I've made my decision.'

Ali opened her mouth to reply, then seeing her daughter's determined expression closed it again. There would be no point in arguing. She also knew Emma wouldn't be comfortable with mollycoddling or trite platitudes, so instead deferred to her usual, more practical approach.

'You're still going to have to pay back your student loan you know, and find somewhere else to live.'

'I know.'

Ali sighed, knowing full well that what she was going to say next would have a significant impact on her business, her marriage, her life. 'And you're going to need a job.'

Emma started in admin, helping with bookings and general paperwork. After a few months Ali decided she had the makings of a solid project manager and asked her to shadow Matthew who she had appointed to that senior role not long after they married. Ali had hoped Matthew and Emma's trips scouting for property development opportunities would bring them closer; instead they would return home after a long day on the road both sullen and disgruntled.

'Honestly, Ali, she's such hard work,' Matthew would say to her in bed at night. 'I know she's been through a lot, losing her dad and all, but she won't even give me a chance.'

'Just try and be patient,' said Ali, unsure what advice to offer, if any. Emma's barely contained hostility towards Matthew – *'don't you ever dare refer to him as my stepfather!'* – had begun to tint their relationship in darker, unexpected layers. She had also grown especially protective of her mother.

'I spoke to Grandad,' Emma confessed a few days after Ali and Matthew's engagement announcement. 'He says you should get a prenup.'

'You spoke to your grandfather?' Ali had replied incredulously. 'The man who boycotted your father's and my wedding, wouldn't attend your christening, and who has tried to undermine almost every aspect of my business for the past twenty years?'

'Not undermine,' replied Emma gingerly, 'he just wants you to be more environmentally aware.'

When told of this new development, Matthew was sanguine, unaffected.

'We've got our own plans for the future,' he said, and signed the prenuptial agreement without protest.

Emma's increasing animosity towards Matthew, along with a clear aptitude for working with students, made Ali decide to task her with client interface on student rentals, while Matthew continued to focus on the company's growing portfolio of holiday properties. For a time, things eased off. The summer and autumn months were busy, productive, and for a while peaceful. Then as Christmas approached, everything seemed to change. Emma grew increasingly distant and preoccupied. Most nights she stayed with friends, but when she did come home – normally only for some food and a change of clothes – she went straight to her room, only deigning to offer Ali a few curt words, and ignoring Matthew altogether.

Ali had tried to talk to her, ask her what was going on, but all Emma would say was that it was personal. It certainly didn't seem to be due to work. Emma's success at turning over student rentals was exemplary. No complaints, only accolades.

In the two months since the accident, however, her daughter's demeanour had brightened. Ali tried not to attribute it to Matthew's disappearance – that would be too unbearable. She dreaded to think their relationship was so awful that Emma had cheered up in his unforeseen absence, but she did seem a lot more confident and at ease. Maybe it was more to do with helping to run the company under Liz's mentorship than anything else. Ali could see how close Emma and Liz had become, how hard Emma worked for Liz's approval, and felt an unwarranted pang of envy. As much as she tried, she could never emulate Liz's calm, easy-going demeanour. She had spent too much of her life fighting, but she also understood that it was what Emma needed right now.

'Mum?' Ali could see Emma watching her closely. 'You okay?'

'Just thinking.' Ali gazed towards the French doors that opened from the kitchen-diner onto the garden and the wide expanse of fields beyond. In the distance the tip of Dartington Hill nudged the sky. A breeze blew, ruffling the curtains, and bringing with it the sweet, dusty smell of freshly cut hay. Since leaving the rehabilitation unit, Ali had spent most of her time in this open-plan space, sitting at the large oak table, staring into the fields beyond, or moving back into the kitchen to gently press her sore leg against the warmth of the Aga.

'Ems?'

'Yes, Mum.'

'Do you think I'm mad for believing that Matthew might still be alive?'

Accustomed to the question, Emma walked over and knelt beside her mother.

'Of course not.'

'Because I do believe it, you know, with all my heart.'

'I know,' replied Emma, 'but it's been nearly three months, Mum, and not a single sign of him.' Ali could hear the tension in her daughter's voice. 'Why would he do that to you?'

Ali lifted her cup of tea, and seeing it was empty, put it down again. 'I don't know.'

Emma, plainly upset, would not let it go. 'I mean not to tell his own wife he was alive?'

'I know what you're thinking,' said Ali, 'what everyone is thinking.'

'If he was swept away . . .' Emma's voice softened, and referring to her mother's frequent argument about Matthew's disappearance added, 'there may never *be* a body.'

Emma's words were like arrows rooted in Ali's chest.

'There were those Facebook sightings.'

'A couple of people saying they've seen someone who may or may not look like a tall, dark bloke in his mid-thirties? Not quite definitive, is it?'

'Do you want him to be dead?' said Ali, her composure lost at last. 'Is that it?'

'Of course not.' Emma's tranquil compassion only made Ali feel worse. 'I just care about you.'

Ali, still caught up in the turmoil of pain, loss, and guilt, wasn't listening.

'If only I didn't have a go at him—' her words were frantic, '—about him messing around in the car park.'

'It was an accident, Mum.'

'Everyone keeps on telling me that, saying how I wasn't responsible. How it was the weather, the roads, even the fact that Matthew's car had new tyres.' She laughed at the absurdity of the last comment. 'But it doesn't make me feel any better.' Seeing her daughter's worried expression she paused. 'I'm sorry, honey; I know I should be focusing on other things. My recovery, my *wellbeing*, and I've still got a business to run.'

Emma took both her mother's hands in hers.

'Liz and I have got everything in hand.'

'And the rest of the team?'

'They're all hurting, but okay.'

Ali began to sob. 'Oh God, Emma.'

'It's okay.' Emma embraced her mother and held her tight. 'It will all be okay.'

'I miss him.'

'I know.'

'Not just Matthew,' said Ali, her voice heavy with remorse, 'your father too.'

Ali and Rory bought the derelict old barn and surrounding acre as twenty-two-year-old self-confessed entrepreneurs. Pooling together their incomes from Rory's job as a builder, and Ali's as a receptionist in the small construction firm where they first met, they also included donations, family loans, and the small life insurance pay-out Ali had from her mother's premature death from breast cancer. Rory, always with an eye for a deal, knew a bargain when he saw one.

'Thirty thousand pounds, Ali,' he murmured into her ear as they lay burrowed under the duvet in their freezing cold flat. 'The land alone is worth twice that.' The seller, a retired farmer with arthritis had warmed to Rory's charisma and plans for the future. 'I told him we were getting married,' he added, warming his hands on her thighs, 'and that the barn was going to be my wedding present to you.' She had immediately untangled herself from their embrace so she could look him in the eyes.

'And are you?'

'Am I what?'

'Going to ask me to marry you?'

Weekends, evenings, and every moment they weren't working in their day jobs – or their second jobs as a bartender and waitress at a nearby pub – involved clearing, chipping away at, and prepping the dilapidated building for its reincarnation as a split-level, four-bedroom, open-plan barn conversion.

'Spread over 1,000 square feet of living space with mainly ground-floor living and stunning views of the South Devon countryside,' he would whisper to her, as they made love against an old seed drill that sat smack in the middle of what one day would be their lounge. Rory, ever the entrepreneur, later sold the rusting heap – *a vintage farm implement* – for three hundred pounds.

Even with all their hard work and wheeling and dealing, they were still unable to afford both building materials and rent on their flat. Eventually they moved into one of the barn's barely habitable rooms, covered the gaps in the walls and windows with plastic sheeting, and spent their evenings huddled around an old paraffin heater they had found at a car boot sale. It was cold, dirty, frustrating, and demoralising, but Ali had never felt happier.

They were just making serious headway when she got pregnant with Emma. Renovations, full-time jobs, and a new baby made for a tense relationship and overwhelming workload, but they had persevered.

'Good old days,' said Ali, running her fingertips across the antique oak dining table that cost nearly as much as their deposit on the barn, but it was said without much conviction.

4

Ali watched from the kitchen window as Emma warmed up for her regular after-work run, smiling as her daughter stretched her hamstrings, marvelling at her strength and flexibility. Before the accident she would often go running with Emma along the river path and past the small twelfth-century cemetery at Dartington. Now all she could do was watch and wait. She wasn't sure if her body – damaged and dented – would ever be able to run along that route again. Emma waved and headed out, her long stride taking her to somewhere Ali couldn't possibly follow.

She poured herself a glass of wine and started the tea.

'The one thing I *can* do,' she muttered to herself. She popped two pies in the oven, threw together a green salad, and even attempted a celeriac mash, finished with some truffle oil she and Matthew had brought back on one of their trips to Tuscany. Feeling restless, she emptied the clothes dryer and folded the T-shirts, jogging bottoms, pants, and socks. At the bottom of the pile was a baby-blue T-shirt. One of Matthew's that must have been hidden in the bottom of the laundry basket. Ali held it to her face and inhaled deeply. It no longer carried his earthy scent, but instead smelled of washing powder and fabric softener. She rested the T-shirt over her shoulder like a sleeping child, and gripping the banister tightly for support, carefully made her way upstairs.

She rested her fingertips on the door handle to the master bedroom, unsure whether she had the strength to enter. It had been weeks since she had last been in this space, thinking for some bizarre reason that it would bring bad luck. Now, as she studied the luxurious expanse of windows and wood, en suite, and velvet-covered chaise longue at the end of the bed, she forced herself to break the spell.

'There is no magic,' she muttered, 'and all the bad luck has already happened.'

She opened the doors to the built-in wardrobe and put the freshly laundered T-shirt in a top drawer. Glancing up, she scanned her expensive workwear, designer blouses, trousers, and a chocolate-brown leather jacket she'd had made especially. She took it from the hanger and slipped it on, relishing the rich, tarry scent. She'd had one very similar made for Matthew as a birthday surprise, and he had laughed good-naturedly at the thought of them having matching apparel.

'Preparing us for old age, Ali?' he had teased, but she could tell he was pleased.

She peered over to his side of the wardrobe, expecting to see the rich glow of dark leather. There were suit jackets, blazers, a trench coat, but nothing resembling the jacket she was wearing. She pushed aside the clothing, frantically searching for the missing garment, her only reward an empty cedarwood hanger.

'It was here a few weeks ago,' she said out loud. 'I know it was.' She went through the wardrobe again, taking all the clothes off the hanging rail and laying them on the bed, emptying the drawers and searching behind the rows of shoes. Matthew's favourite leather jacket was gone. Beginning to feel desperate, she searched the spare upstairs bedroom, office, and – feeling slightly guilty – Emma's room. Then she made her way downstairs to the wet room and even the front entrance hall. Nothing. She sat on the hallway shoe storage bench, her heart pumping, sweat trickling past her temples and sliding underneath her chin. At some point in the last two weeks someone had come into the house and taken Matthew's jacket. She was certain of it.

'Mum?' called Emma from the kitchen.

Ali took a moment to wipe her face and collect herself. She knew she'd have to approach Emma carefully about the missing jacket, if at all. She carefully eased herself to her feet. Her frenzied search, lifting the heavy coats and blazers from the rail, and scrabbling through the shoes at the bottom of the wardrobe, had left her feeling achy and weak.

'I'm here,' she replied and pressing her hand against the wall for support, made her way to the kitchen.

Emma's face was slick with perspiration.

'How was your run?'

'Good,' said Emma, untying her laces. 'Jesus, Mum,' she said as she stood up again, 'you're as white as a ghost. Are you okay? Do you need to lie down?' Any thoughts of asking Emma about the missing jacket were cast aside as Ali was helped to a kitchen chair and a glass of water placed in front of her. 'Do you need a painkiller?' asked Emma. 'Should I call the doctor?'

'I'm fine, sweetheart, honestly.'

'And are you sure you should be drinking?' asked Emma, spotting Ali's half-empty wine glass next to the cooker.

'It's alcohol-free, love.'

The thought of drinking anything that tasted

even vaguely like wine was still too much for her. That night both she and Matthew had had a few glasses – not over the limit, but close. Maybe if she hadn't insisted he drive her home . . . That recollection was like a flare, searing through her brain. She and Matthew had argued in the car park. He told her something that exploded on the car journey home, but what was it? As their guests said their goodbyes, kissing and embracing them, they had both put on fake smiles and false bonhomie, Matthew even slipping his arm around her waist for good effect.

She and Emma ate in silence with the occasional banal comment about the weather, and Emma glancing up at her mother every so often, asking if she was all right.

The discovery of the missing jacket had sent Ali's imagination spinning, and as much as she tried to contain her wandering, worried thoughts, she could not.

'Emma,' she said, pushing away her half-eaten plate of food, 'what did you and Matthew argue about that night?'

Emma paused, her fork frozen in mid-air.

'I don't know what you're talking about.'

'The night of the accident. Matthew went outside for a cigarette after dinner, and I saw you arguing with him.'

'It was nothing, Mum.'

'Evidently that's not the case,' replied Ali, 'because when he came back to the table for dessert he was in a terrible mood.'

'Was he now?'

'So what were you arguing about?'

'Is that what's got you so worked up?'

'I just want to know.'

'What didn't we argue about?' Emma stood up, her chair scraping across the floorboards, and reached for their plates.

'You didn't answer my question.'

'That's because instead of this ridiculous obsession with trying to remember what happened that night, you should be concentrating your energies on getting better.'

Ali let out a shaky sigh. 'Easier said than done, and with Matthew missing—'

'Presumed dead.'

'Missing!'

'Christ, Mum. I know you'd really like to believe he's still alive somewhere out there, but there's been no record of him using his credit cards or mobile phone, no mysterious John Doe hospital admissions.'

'And no body!' exclaimed Ali, repeating her desperate reasoning. 'How can he be dead if there's no body?'

'You need to focus on getting better—' Emma's voice was clouded with impatience '—on a positive future, not losing yourself in the past.'

'Don't you understand?' said Ali, feeling angry and impatient. 'If I don't know what happened I'll be forever stuck in the past, always wondering, always going over and over in my head if I was responsible for what happened that night.'

'You are *not* responsible for whatever happened to Matthew that night,' said Emma, her voice serious. 'I can promise you that.'

5

When Ali woke the next morning Emma had already left for work. She made her way into the kitchen, ignored the herbal teabags that had been left out for her, and made herself an espresso in the pricey coffee machine she had bought Matthew for Christmas.

She gazed up at the barn's whitewashed vaulted ceiling with its ancient timbers and thought once again of Rory.

Dartmoor Properties, the company they had started only as a means of getting trade prices for materials for their barn conversion, had slowly but convincingly transformed into something true. Now, after twenty years of operation, it had an annual turnover of nearly five million pounds. The early years of the company had been exhausting yet exhilarating. She and Rory had worked all the hours, buying and flipping cheap properties, risking everything they owned, including their beloved Hope Farm, on deals that could make or break them. They survived on adrenaline and the promise of a rich future.

When Emma was born midway into their acquisition of a dilapidated Victorian townhouse, Ali simply strapped the new-born to her chest and breastfed her through meetings with the builders. Rory's daring and self-belief took her to new places. *'This is the first day of our best life!'* he would say, as exhausted and bleary-eyed from another sleepless night, she would start cold-calling prospective clients. *'We can leap the hurdles and break down the walls standing between us and our exciting futures,'* he would proclaim, and when she argued exhaustion would add, *'Don't play the victim to the circum-stances you created!'* How about *we* created? she remembered thinking, but Rory was her light, her truth, her strength.

When he pushed her, she responded; when he challenged, she grew brave. *Great things never come from comfort zones,* she would say to herself as she submitted yet another eviction notice in order to flip a property. There were Post-it Notes scattered across the small space in the corner they had used as an office. *Don't stop when you're tired. Stop when you're done!* And the unbearably ironic: *Sometimes later becomes never.*

Later became never for Rory however, when a month after his thirty-fifth birthday he began to experience chest pains. He brushed it aside as the after-effects of a bad cold, but when Ali found droplets of blood speckled across his pillow like Valentine's Day confetti, she insisted he see the doctor. There were scans, tests, consultations and finally a prognosis.

'Lung cancer,' the consultant said bluntly, 'asbestos-related.'

'Asbestos?' said Ali, recalling the barn demolition, dust and debris everywhere, how lax they were with wearing masks, Emma in a baby pen just outside.

'Not the barn, honey,' said Rory, gripping her hand, his fingers like ice. 'That was eighteenth century, safe as houses.' He chuckled to himself and then began to cough. Even this soon into his illness he was struggling to breathe. 'It was the outbuildings. I did most of the work when you went to visit your father, remember?'

Ali had an image of Rory as she was reversing the car out of the dirt drive, shirtless and in his favourite faded Levi's, tearing the corrugated iron from the roof of the 1950s garage.

Sipping a second cup of espresso, Ali watched the mist slowly rising from the fields beyond the kitchen window.

'All that hard work,' she muttered, 'all that sacrifice. Now I can't even make it up the stairs on my own.'

For the last few months, she had existed in a sort of shadow realm of pain, guilt, and apathy. Her visit to the accident site yesterday, no matter how upsetting, seemed to have jarred loose some of those feelings, like freeing a pebble from her shoe. While she didn't feel particularly brave or determined, she did feel the beginnings of some sort of purpose. Maybe it was time for her to start moving again. Forwards or back, at least it would be motion. Picking up her mobile she booked a taxi and went to have a shower.

Ali arrived at the offices of Dartmoor Properties just before the eleven o'clock huddle. She could smell fresh coffee and heard the sound of nearby laughter.

'Pass me a maple glaze,' came a familiar voice. Ali made her way into the meeting room to find her employees tucking into a box of Krispy Kreme doughnuts.

'Ali!' Liz leapt up from where she was sitting at the head of the table. 'What are you doing here?' As if seeing a spectre, the rest of the team stared open-mouthed at her before quickly joining Liz in getting to their feet. Along with Liz there was client services manager Amita, Richard – a marketing graduate who dealt with online bookings and social media – their repairman Darren, and a spotty-looking teenager Ali had never seen before. Most surprising of all was the figure standing by the window.

'Dane.' Ali couldn't contain the surprise from her voice. 'Just visiting?'

For the briefest of moments his eyes narrowed, but then he gave her his usual open, ready smile.

'Dane's been helping us with the upkeep on some of the student flats,' said Darren. 'Only temporary. A few jobs to do over the Easter hols is all.'

Ali was aware that things hadn't been going so well for Dane recently in the small financial services business he had started after leaving the army seven years ago. *Feast or famine,* Liz had once told her. There had been payday advances to Liz once or twice in the last two years, and Ali had wondered if some of that was down to Dane's business skills. Maybe she would try and find something more permanent for him at Dartmoor Properties. He had been so helpful setting up the office when they'd moved to new premises last year, and when Matthew came back, he would probably need plenty of support. If Dane was working permanently for Dartmoor Properties, he could help him settle back in. She would ask Liz about it.

'I'd best be off,' said Dane, glancing at his watch. 'I've got to collect some plyboard from the building merchants.' He stepped forward and kissed Ali on the cheek. 'It's great to see you back in the office, Als.'

Buoyed by Dane's support, Ali resumed her attention to the task in hand. 'Sit down, everyone, and relax. This isn't an inspection you know.' There were chuckles of relief, and her five colleagues regarded her warmly. 'Amita,' she continued, 'Emma tells me you've got engaged. That's wonderful news. Congratulations. You should be getting a little something in the post in the next day or two.'

'In the post?' said Amita.

'Well, I know you and Amir are looking at houses, so I hoped a gift card would be suitable.'

'Oh, Ali, you shouldn't have.' The young woman's deep brown eyes glistened.

'Well, we are a family after all,' said Ali, hoping her forced attempt to sound cheerful rang true. 'And who's this?' she said, focusing her attention on the young man sitting next to Darren.

Darren cleared his throat. 'This is Stevie, our new apprentice.'

'Very nice to meet you, Stevie,' said Ali. 'Liz never told me we were taking on an apprentice.'

'Stevie's been helping with general upkeep on some of the holiday properties,' said Darren. 'It was all agreed with Matthew before he, well . . . before the . . .'

'Hoping to be a painter and decorator one day, ma'am,' said the teenager, picking up the slack. Ali could almost hear the sighs of relief in the room.

'Well good for you, Stevie.' She tried her best to sound supportive, encouraging, but felt a sudden, profound sense of dislocation. Even these tiniest of changes made her feel like she was out of the loop, useless. A hush settled and she could feel everyone watching her, their sympathy overwhelming. Her bad leg tingled, and her scar itched. She had spent a lot of time this morning covering it with a special concealer so all that could be seen was a thin line across her cheek, almost as if she had fallen asleep on a piece of dried spaghetti. Then she had done her hair and chosen one of her best outfits. Dark wool, well cut, and with lapels that could slice through ice. Standing in front of the mirror that morning, she could almost begin to see the woman she once was.

'Your timing is excellent, Stevie,' she said, 'because there is a special reason I wanted to come in and see you all today.'

She heard the sound of footsteps behind her.

'Mum.' Emma sounded both pleased and concerned. 'What are you doing here?'

'Emma, I'm glad you're here. I was just about to tell everyone the news.'

Emma's brow creased. 'What news?'

Ali glanced around the table at the wide-eyed worried faces.

'Don't look so frightened, everyone.' She gave a smile that was probably too large. 'I've decided to give everyone a bonus for all the hard work you've been doing since . . .' She found herself unable to complete the sentence. 'Well, since I've been away.'

Met with silence, she gazed around at the stunned, frozen faces. 'Isn't someone going to say something?'

'That's wonderful news.' Liz was clearly taken aback. As acting MD, it would have been no secret to her about just how much of the company's capital was tied up in upcoming projects. 'What a delightful surprise.' She gave Emma a worried look. 'I guess we'll have to work out some of the details.'

'The funds are available.' Ali didn't mention that the money was coming from a pot of private financing she was planning to give Matthew for a proposed buy-to-rent project in Torquay. 'And I'd really like to reward you all for your loyalty and dedication over these last few difficult months.'

She could feel tears settle under her eyelashes,

but blinked them back. Ever since the accident it seemed as if she had lost a layer of skin, both literally and figuratively, as if that hard shell she had so carefully constructed after Rory's death, had been excruciatingly peeled away by Matthew's loss.

'Oh, Mum,' said Emma, clearly struggling herself.

Ali smiled at the circle of sad faces staring back at her.

'Cheer up, everyone.' She laughed. 'Onwards and upwards!'

The onwards and upwards line was a long-standing joke at Dartmoor Properties, as along with all his general property development work, Rory had become particularly expert at building staircases.

'Onwards and upwards,' replied the team, sounding slightly too cheerful.

Ali could sense Liz scrutinising her closely. She knew she could see the droplets of perspiration that dotted her forehead and her right hand shaking, just one more after-effect of her injuries.

'It's great to see you in the office, Ali, just fantastic, but I reckon we're okay to handle things for another week or two while you get back to full form. Aren't we, gang?' There were supportive nods all around. 'And speaking of handling things, I reckon we all should get right back to it, don't you?'

There was a murmur of agreement and the team hurried from the room, buoyed by Ali's visit and the promise of an unexpected bonus.

'Are you sure now is the right time to be handing out money?' said Liz, her voice laced with concern.

'I just wanted to thank everyone,' replied Ali, 'be a part of the team again.'

'And you will,' said Emma. She poured her mother a glass of water from a jug on the table and handed it to her. 'God knows everyone wants to see you back. They talk about you all the time you know. "*I wonder what Ali would think of this. I know we need to push harder because Ali would have done.*" We all feel your presence and support, even when you're not here.'

Ali smiled at her daughter in admiration. Only seven years since the death of her father and she had risen from the tragedy with strength, determination, and compassion.

'I'm proud of you, Ems.'

'I'm proud of you too, Mum, but right now, I think you need a painkiller and a good lie-down.'

They travelled home together in silence, Emma occasionally glancing Ali's way.

'The bonus thing was a surprise.'

'It was desperate, ridiculous.'

'Of course it wasn't. Everyone has been working

so hard, and to be honest they *have* been feeling a bit worried. The bonus is a good thing'

'Worried,' said Ali, her highly tuned business radar on alert. 'About what?' Emma shrugged. 'Tell me.'

'Just stuff I overheard, you know, that the business might fold, or you might sell up.'

'Sell up. Why would I do that?'

Emma paused. 'Because of all the uncertainty around Matthew, and the strain the project costs this new build is putting on the company.'

'I know.' Ali had sensed the uneasiness in the room. 'But you can reassure everyone that everything will be fine. The project is still on course, even *with* Matthew being away.'

'Away?' said Emma. 'You don't seriously believe everyone thinks he's just away do you?'

'Emma, please.'

'And even if he is *away*, it's not like he'll be able to step straight back into work, is it?'

'I—'

'I mean there's the question of where he's been, what he's been doing, and why he's been deliberately hiding from everyone.'

'I don't think hiding is quite the right word.'

'What would you call it then?' Emma's old hostility towards Matthew had obviously not been muted by recent events. 'No contact for months, not even to his seriously injured wife?'

Ali looked out of the window at the landscape speeding past, desperately trying to collect her scattered thoughts. 'Maybe there's been more to all this than you realise.'

'What do you mean by that?'

Ali was unaware she had spoken her thoughts aloud. 'It's nothing, Emma, nothing.'

They spent the rest of the journey in silence, Emma's doubts and Ali's anxiety filling the widening gap between them.

6

Ali had insisted Emma drop her off at the house and go back to work. The gentle drizzle that had started while they were in the car had now changed into a steady downpour. She stood in the front drive, her crutches embedded in gravel and mud, considering how best to navigate the simplest of tasks, getting into her own home. Since the accident she had grown to hate the large step up to the front door. That and trying to negotiate bags and crutches invariably ended up with her stumbling her way into the foyer. She had already knocked over the umbrella stand twice.

Instead she decided to take a small pathway dotted with stepping stones and tufts of thyme and mint, which led to the French doors at the rear of the house. She jangled the latch on the wrought-iron gate that enclosed the back garden. It tended to seize, and Ali knew a few good rattles would free it, Emma had learned to manage it, but Matthew was forever struggling. She chuckled, recalling the jangle of metal followed by her husband's curses. *'This bloody thing, Ali!'* She would laugh, make her way to the gate and in one swift movement undo the latch. *'Easy if you know how,'* he would say before embracing her. She had been meaning to have it fixed, but something about that moment when he would smile at her helplessly from the other side of the gate had made her love him all the more.

Once inside she stripped off her soaking coat and muddy shoes, and changed into a pair of cashmere joggers and top. Then she lay down on the settee, covered herself in a throw and scrolled once again through the Facebook group replies before falling into a fitful sleep. When she woke a few hours later the room was deep in gloom. She stood up in a futile effort to ease the tingling in her leg, then spotted the half glass of water and packet of painkillers that were still on the coffee table from when Dane and Liz dropped her off the other day. Lifting the tablet to her lips she caught sight of herself in the gilded mirror over the fireplace. Her face appeared deathly, and at some point her make-up had been brushed off, exposing the thin red line of her scar.

'No,' she muttered, and dropped the tablet where it bounced off the table and onto the floor. 'I near to stay clear-headed.'

She heard a soft tap on the front door and then a key turning in the lock.

'Ali?' called Dane. 'It's me.' She heard him enter the foyer, the ruffle of a coat being hung up by the door, and the soft thud of boots being placed on the mat. 'I hope you don't mind me letting myself in,' he said as he made his way down the hallway and into the lounge.

'Not at all,' she replied. 'That's why I gave Liz the key.' After the accident, and with Emma working late most nights, she had given Liz and her brother Graham front door keys in case of emergencies. 'What on earth have you got there?' she asked, pointing to the large carrier bag he was holding.

He grinned sheepishly. 'Liz made food.' He handed her the bag. 'Veggie lasagne, sweet potato curry, and some rice. There's even chocolate brownies.'

'She really shouldn't have.'

Dane ran his fingers through his soaking hair. 'She worries about you, Ali.'

'I know.'

'I worry about you too.'

'It was nice to see you in the office today,' said Ali, changing the subject.

'Just helping out a bit here and there,' he said hastily. 'You don't mind, do you?'

'Of course not. I always appreciate it. Fancy a cup of tea?'

'No thanks. I can't stay long, but there is something I wanted to talk to you about.'

'Oh?'

'What you said about Matthew yesterday, about him still being alive.'

'It's okay if you don't believe me.'

Dane stepped closer. 'That's the thing, Ali, I do believe you.'

'What?' A small surge of adrenaline rushed through Ali's body, warming her cheeks. Could someone really be on her side?

'It was like you said . . . There's no body; Matthew was a strong swimmer.' He rubbed his jaw thoughtfully. 'I've seen your postings on Facebook, all the replies.'

'The police think I'm desperate.'

'Well it is sort of weird for someone to go missing like that.' Ali could see that he was struggling with what he had to say next. 'Was Matthew in any kind of trouble?'

Ali's eyes widened. 'Trouble?'

'You know.' Dane shifted awkwardly. 'Had he started trading again? Gotten himself in difficulty?' He shifted slightly. 'If we found his laptop we'd know for sure.'

'No!'

'Hey now.' Dane seemed taken aback by the

strength of her reply. 'I didn't mean to upset you, Als, it's just that—'

'We got through all that,' said Ali, her voice wavering. 'Matthew and me. It made our marriage even stronger.'

'I know you did, and I know how much he loved you, how much you loved each other.' Dane squeezed her arm. 'I was there on the beach with you both the day you got married, remember. I've never seen him so happy.'

'We *were* happy,' said Ali, nodding. She tried to force away a memory that would not fade. 'And when we lost the baby he was so wonderful.' She felt her equilibrium falter and the room begin to spin.

'Easy now,' said Dane, grabbing her by the elbows to steady her.

'Do you really think it's possible?' She rested her head on his shoulder. 'That Matthew's alive?'

'Of course I do,' said Dane decisively. 'And I'm going to help you find him.'

'There's something you should know.'

'Is it to do with the missing money from the cashbox?'

'Yes and no,' replied Ali, and seeing Dane's confusion forced herself to carry on. 'His leather jacket is missing too.'

'The one you had made for him? The one he wore everywhere?'

'It was in the wardrobe a few weeks ago,' she

said, her voice rising in excitement, 'and now it's gone.'

'Are you sure?'

'Positive!'

'Which means,' said Dane, encouraged by Ali's conviction, 'that he must have come for it!'

'He must have!'

The two friends embraced, united in their mutual belief that their friend and partner was still alive.

'We need to get organised,' said Dane, 'do a recce on the most recent sightings!'

Ali collected her laptop and headed towards the kitchen. 'You'd better come with me.'

She waited until Dane was seated, and then reaching behind the microwave, retrieved a document that had been deliberately hidden there. As she unfolded it, Ali could see that Dane recognised it immediately.

'It's a map of the south-west,' he said intrigued. Ali flattened the crinkled edges against the surface of the table. 'But why all the red circles?'

Ali placed her laptop next to the map and lifted the lid. 'Every red dot,' she replied, 'indicates a sighting.'

'Of Matthew?' said Dane, looking impressed.

'There was one in Bristol a few weeks ago.' Ali scrolled, indicating to the Facebook page, 'and then a few days later in Tiverton.'

Dane gazed at her in wonder. 'Is this what you've been doing? On your own, at home?'

'Someone's got to find him.'

Dane placed both hands on the marble-topped island and studied the annotated map carefully. 'We should check out some of these sightings,' he said, tracing a line with his finger from one red dot to another.

Ali felt her heart race. Was someone at last taking her seriously, was someone going to help?

'I was planning to start next week,' she said, her excitement building.

Dane pointed to her crutches. 'You shouldn't drive yet. I'll go.'

'But I have to do something.'

'We need to expand to other platforms,' said Dane, folding the map and sticking it in the inside pocket of his jacket. 'Twitter, Instagram.'

'I can do that,' said Ali. 'I've got contacts all over the south-west. I can ask them to share.'

'Good thinking.' Dane placed a hand on her shoulder, his finger brushing the curve of her neck. 'The thing is, Ali . . .' He cleared his throat. 'It may be a good idea if we don't mention anything to Liz about this.'

Ali frowned. 'I'm not so sure—'

'You know how protective she is of you, particularly since the accident.'

'Yes, but—'

'She'll try and convince us to stop,' said Dane. 'Insist I stop.'

'But—'

'I know it feels wrong not telling Liz, God knows I do.' Dane's voice softened. 'But do you want to find him or not?'

'Of course I want to find him.' Ali's earlier excitement now changing to unease. 'But not telling Liz . . .?'

'I'll make you a deal,' said Dane. 'As soon as we find something concrete, we'll tell her, okay?'

Liz considered Dane's suggestion carefully.

'And if she asks, we tell her the truth straight away.'

Dane held out his hand. 'It's a deal.'

Ali reluctantly shook on it. Liz was her dearest friend in the world, and they had no secrets. Was she really willing to sacrifice that for what could only be described as a long shot?

'There is one more thing,' said Dane.

'Yes?'

'If I'm going to be travelling across the south-west, maybe having to stay in hotels—'

'You're going to need some money.'

'I'm sorry, Als, I know it's awkward.'

'It's fine,' said Ali, 'just fine. I'll transfer some money into your account.'

'Better make it cash,' said Dane, looking increasingly guilty, 'because of Liz and all.'

'I'll get a taxi to the bank tomorrow.'

7

With Emma out with friends, Ali was left alone with her ongoing apprehension and, since Dane's visit, increasing anticipation. Was she finally going to find Matthew? She pushed aside the creeping guilt she felt about not telling Liz and resumed her search of Facebook sites, hoping for more sightings, but the pages were silent.

Frustrated and anxious, she made her way back up the ash-and-glass staircase Rory had so lovingly built, to the master bedroom. Opening the wardrobe doors, she scanned the designer dresses and tailored suits, hoping Matthew's leather jacket had mysteriously reappeared, but the cedarwood hanger was still empty.

She sat on the bed and ran her hand across the pillow where Matthew should be sleeping. Reaching into his bedside table she removed a bottle of Paco Rabanne *1 Million* and gave the room a spritz. The top notes of mint and blood mandarin filled the air, and for a moment time had no meaning.

'*Pregnant?*'

Matthew had been standing by the fire in his Gieves and Hawkes suit, looking like the lord of the manor – or the lord of the barn conversion, at least.

'I know it wasn't planned,' said Ali, sipping on her mineral water, her mouth dry. 'I mean me, having a baby, at forty?' He gazed into the fire, his expression unreadable. 'I know you said you didn't want children.' She wanted to add something light-hearted like '*all the best laid plans and all that*', but didn't have the courage.

He put his whisky glass on the mantel and moved towards her. She stepped back, uncertain but not afraid. Now only inches apart he placed his hand on her stomach and smiled.

'A baby,' he whispered, '*my* baby.'

She had never loved him more. When she lost the baby four months into the pregnancy he had been stalwart, supportive. Just before Christmas they had discussed trying again.

The buzz of her mobile jarred her back to the present.

Hey sis, exhausting day in Exeter doing an effing huge audit and then three-car pile-up on

*Haldon Hill means traffic to Exeter is backed
up for at least three hours. Fancy offering your
bro a bed for the night? I'll bring pizza! xx*

Ali replied to the text, got up, closed the wardrobe doors, and went back downstairs.

When Graham arrived she had wiped her eyes, touched up her make-up, and put a couple of beers in the fridge.

They ate pizza, drank beer and talked about everything but Matthew. Finally, when they were settled on the settee, a fire blazing, Graham tackled the ghost in the room.

'So, any news,' he said, 'on Matthew?'

Ali nibbled on her lower lip. She had considered telling him about her and Dane's plan to visit the sighting locations, but decided against it. He, like Liz and Emma, had become particularly protective of her since the accident, and she wasn't sure he would approve of what she suspected he would refer to as a wild goose chase.

'Any updates from the police?'

'I spoke to the family liaison officer a few weeks ago.' Ruth the FLO from Devon and Cornwall Police had been keeping her updated on the investigation. 'It's still being treated as a missing persons case.'

Graham sipped his beer. 'And that's a good thing?'

'Of course it is.' She wasn't sure where Graham

was going with his questioning, but had a strong feeling where it would end up. 'It means they still believe he's alive too.'

Her brother couldn't hide his scepticism.

'And are you still seeing your counsellor?'

'Now and again.'

'Because bereavement is a complex thing.'

She gripped her beer bottle, her fingernails tearing at the label.

'I am not bereaved, because Matthew is not dead.'

'*Ali.*'

'Please, Graham, don't.'

His dark eyes held hers. 'I saw Dad the other day,' he said, changing the subject.

Ali focused her attention on the lip of her beer bottle. 'How is he?'

'The usual,' said Graham. 'Fighting the man, the establishment, the system.'

'And who is he pissing off to do that this time?'

Graham chuckled. 'Everyone. He's developed a sudden interest in hacktivism.'

'What?'

'Hacking as a form of civil disobedience.'

'Christ, as if his normal acts of civil disobedience aren't enough.'

Graham chuckled. 'Do you remember when he chained himself to the fence at that pig farm and it got in the Totnes news?'

'I never heard the end of it,' said Ali. 'Kids at school were making pig noises at me for weeks.'

Graham laughed again. 'Just one more reason why I had to learn to fight.'

Ali reached across the table and squeezed her brother's hand. Having an activist father who didn't care who he upset, as well as being one of the only openly gay boys in sixth form, certainly didn't make for an easy secondary school experience for him.

'How are things with David?'

'On and off.' He sighed. 'Mostly off.'

'Maybe it's time to move on.'

'For both of us?' he asked.

They sat in uneasy silence, each absorbed in their own doubts.

'So what was this big audit you were doing today?' asked Ali, desperate to brighten the mood.

Graham cleared their plates away and clicked on the kettle.

'Can't say much,' he said, dropping peppermint teabags into their cups, 'but major fraud at a rather prominent south-west business.'

'Oooh,' said Ali, her voice tinged with mirth. 'Is this when being an accountant gets exciting?'

Graham grinned at his sister. 'Being an accountant is always exciting.'

They drank tea and ate the carrot cake Graham had bought from the bakery on the high street.

'I was hoping to see Ems tonight,' he said, as they both prepared to go their separate ways to bed: Ali to her downstairs room, and Graham to the guest bedroom upstairs.

'She does her best to try and spend some nights at home with me,' said Ali, 'but she's young. She should be out with her friends having fun.'

Graham hugged his sister goodnight. 'You've both had a pretty hard time of it.'

'We all have,' she replied, not playing at resilience for once.

'I just wish I could do more,' said Graham. 'Living two hours away means I can't always be by your side when you need me.'

'You're doing more than enough,' said Ali, 'and Liz and Dane are just down the road.'

'They're a godsend,' said Graham.

'They are,' agreed Ali, 'they really are.'

That night, Ali lay in bed and reached for her mobile phone. Searching through her video files she finally found the one she was looking for. It was taken by Graham on the afternoon of their wedding reception in Grand Cayman. She, Matthew, Dane, and Liz, were all sitting at a large table with a beautiful floral centrepiece, glasses of champagne in their hands. The men's ties had been loosened and top buttons undone, and Ali had taken down her updo so that her hair fell in soft curls around her shoulders. They were all slightly drunk, tired but elated, their closeness apparent.

Matthew reached an arm around Ali's shoulders and kissed her cheek, declaring her *the most beautiful bride in the world*, and both Liz and Dane grinned in agreement. The camera panned left, and Emma came into shot. She looked lovingly at her mother but when her gaze shifted to Matthew, her smile had grown tight.

'To the happy couple,' came Graham's voice from behind the camera.

'The happy couple!' came a chorus of replies. The image wobbled, Graham evidently lifting a glass himself.

Her mobile rang, awkwardly fusing the sounds of the wedding party and her ringtone. She checked the caller ID and grimaced.

'Dad,' she said, trying to stop the edge from creeping into her voice.

'Alice.'

She waited for what would come next. A diatribe, manifesto, or condemnation? That was his usual form of communication. Maybe, just for once it might be a check on how she was doing. It wasn't long before her hopes were dashed, however.

'I see your company has purchased some holiday properties in Woolacombe.'

'I'm fine, Dad. The leg is healing well, though

I'm still experiencing some memory loss, thanks for asking.'

'Don't be facetious, Alice.'

'Is that why you rang?' she said, not bothering to hide her irritation. 'To offer up another lecture on how I'm stealing homes from the locals?'

'Aren't you?'

'I run a property development business, Dad. That's what I do, and for your information we only purchase seaside properties that are listed as inhabitable and will need a complete renovation, not ones that can be moved into straight away.'

'But you're still listing them as holiday lets.'

'Yes, I am,' she replied firmly.

Never one for ambiguity, her father got straight to the point. 'I'm worried about you.'

'I'm perfectly—'

'Emma tells me you have some ridiculous notion that Matthew may still be alive.'

Ali's earlobes grew warm.

'Well, thanks as always for being so sensitive, Dad.'

'Alice, please.'

For a moment she was tempted to tell him about the Facebook sightings, the map and her and Dane's plan of action, but she resisted, knowing full well that it would only be dismissed as some sort of misguided fantasy.

'I think I hear Emma's car in the drive, Dad, I'd

better go.' Before her father could reply she ended the call with a quick goodbye and a promise to visit soon.

She woke the next morning to the smell of frying bacon and the sound of laughter.

She dressed and made her way into the kitchen where Graham was flipping pancakes and Emma making coffee in the DeLonghi.

'Mum!' Emma left her barista duties and stepped forward to give her a hug. 'Uncle Graham is making breakfast!'

'So I see.' Emma's face was filled with such happiness that for a moment Ali forgot her worries. 'Cappuccino for me please, maestro.'

Emma gave her mother a mock salute. 'Extra chocolate on top?'

'Yes *please*!'

Ali settled herself on a stool at the island. Graham was watching her, his expression loving yet sad. She gave him the practised smile she had cultivated for just such occasions.

She indicated to the pan in his hand. 'I hope they're blueberry.'

'Of course,' he said, and leaning over kissed her cheek, 'anything for you.'

8

Imagine that the air around you is imbued with a calm white light. The light of healing. As you inhale, imagine this loving light entering your body, into your bloodstream and bones . . .

'What a load of old bollocks.' Ali reached over and turned off the meditation app on her mobile. Her counsellor had recommended it to help clear her mind, but Ali was increasingly using it to try and probe her distorted memories of that night, to spark them back into life. Sometimes, just sometimes, if she relaxed enough, there were moments of absolute clarity, but at other times her mind was cluttered with uncertainty, and she could get nowhere with it – like today. Since her trip to the office the other day, however, and Graham's recent visit, it was beginning to feel as though she was slowly returning to the land of the living, instead of existing in that shady in-between place where she remained helpless and afraid – and she wanted to keep progressing in that direction. She had to bring back the memories of that night, if she had any hope of getting the answers she so desperately desired.

Clearly, though, meditation wasn't going to work for her today, so instead Ali texted the family liaison officer who had been handling the case. Within minutes she received a reply suggesting they get together for a coffee and chat.

'Not here.' She tapped in her response to the FLO's text. 'Dartington? I could do with getting out.'

They met at the café on the twelve-hundred-acre estate that was based around an ethos of arts, ecology, and social justice. They sat by the window drinking their lattes and gazing at the sparrows darting amongst the picnic tables, hoping to find a soggy morsel of cake or bread.

'Thank you for coming, Ruth,' said Ali, shifting her sore leg on the hard edge of the seat.

'I've been trying to reach you for two weeks, Ali. I've left messages, voicemails.'

'I know, and thank you.' She closed her eyes and tried to force some calm. 'I was worried you were ringing to tell me that you were scaling down the search.'

'Why would we do that?'

Ali thought back to the recent comments from both Liz and Emma about Matthew's disappearance. 'Because of the fact that there's been no trace of him for nearly three months.'

'But you are getting hits on your Facebook page.'

'Are you following that?' said Ali intrigued. 'I was under the impression you thought that was just foolish desperation on my part.'

'Nothing is foolish in a search for a missing person,' said Ruth, 'and you have every reason to feel desperate.' Ali let the words sit with her for a bit. The FLO should be her closest ally in her search for Matthew, but something about Ruth's scrutiny, as sympathetic as it was, made Ali feel guarded, afraid. 'Has anything else of interest come up?'

'Just what you've seen online,' replied Ali. She wasn't about to tell her that she and her best friend's husband were involved in a secret plan to find her husband. There was a moment of awkward silence between the two women, each waiting for the other person to speak.

'I know things have been awful for you, Ali, but I did want to reassure you that the search for Matthew is still ongoing.'

'You mean for his body, don't you?' She had read the recent online news article about the Dartmoor Search and Rescue Team taking out cadaver dogs.

'We have to explore every avenue,' said Ruth gently. 'Considering the nature of the accident, the time since it occurred.'

'But you've seen the responses on my Facebook page,' said Ali, thinking Ruth, like almost everyone else was just one more naysayer.

'There are a lot of homeless men in their mid-thirties out there, Ali. Just because a few people think they may have seen him doesn't mean that—'

'What does it mean then?' Ali hadn't meant to raise her voice, but her frustration with Ruth had been slowly simmering ever since she had first suggested creating a missing persons Facebook page. 'I'm sorry. I shouldn't have spoken to you that way.'

'It okay,' said Ruth. 'I know this must be difficult, and as I said we're investigating every possible lead.'

Ali pressed two fingers against the centre point between her eyebrows. 'I had a few questions.'

'Yes.' There was no judgement or impatience in Ruth's voice, only openness and understanding.

'I've been trying to remember that night.'

'That's good, Ali, really good.'

'It was raining so hard, and the river, I'd never seen it that high.' Ruth listened intently. 'Matthew was driving too fast – we all know that – and I remember yelling at him to slow down, but he wouldn't . . .' Ali trailed off unable or unwilling to articulate what happened next.

'According to witnesses, the BMW was travelling at considerable speed.'

'But he wasn't over the alcohol limit.'

Ruth peered at Ali over the edge of her coffee cup. 'There's no way to be sure of that without a breathalyser or blood sample.'

'But I wasn't over the limit and I'm sure he only drank as much as I did.'

Ruth regarded her kindly. 'You *were* over the limit, Ali. The blood samples taken at the hospital revealed that. I told you that the first time we met, remember?' There seemed to be just the tiniest hint of censure in the officer's voice. 'But it's not an issue because you weren't driving.'

'But I should have been.'

'What?'

'Matthew and I agreed that I was going to drive home that night, but I ended up having one or two glasses of champagne too many.'

'So he drove instead?'

'He assured me he was fine, but I should have known better. I should have insisted we get a taxi or ride with Liz and Dane.'

'Why didn't you?'

'I tried, but for some reason he wouldn't. We argued

about that too, and something else—' she screwed her eyes tight in concentration '—something much more serious.'

Ruth sat up a bit straighter. 'Can you remember what it was?'

Ali glanced at the FLO. 'I really wish I could.' She closed her eyes in a fruitless effort to concentrate. 'He had been in a strange mood all evening. Liz too. Then there was a fall-out with Emma after dinner.' Ali paused. 'They were always falling out, but this time it seemed pretty serious. She refused to come with us and insisted on riding home with Graham.'

'Emma told me she had a go at Matthew about drinking too much.'

'You spoke to her?'

'It was important to determine if it might have been a contributing factor.'

'A contributing factor to what?'

'To the subsequent argument you two had in the car park.'

'I don't understand.'

'Is it a possibility that the argument Emma had with Matthew led on to the one you had with him?' Ruth spoke slowly, concisely. 'And that argument carried on into your car journey home.'

Ali tried to push away the image of her and Matthew speeding along the darkened roadway. Of the car weaving back and forth across the road, the look of absolute fury on his face, his lips curled back exposing white teeth in the dark. How she screamed and grabbed for the steering wheel to try to stop him. She could feel Ruth studying her closely.

'I don't remember.'

'Are you sure?'

Ali clenched her hands together tightly. 'Right now I'm not sure of anything. I mean, for a second I think I might remember something, and then I realise it's just what you, Emma, and Liz have told me.' She pressed her fingertips against her temples. She hated lying to Ruth, but until she could unscramble her memories to determine what was a real recollection, not a reported one, she wasn't saying anything. 'I thought I remembered that Dane had to force open both car doors, but it was you that told me that, wasn't it? And then all my memories of what happened afterwards are from Liz or Emma.' Ali gripped her thigh, feeling the reassuring pulse through the thin material of her leggings. 'It's just all so confusing.'

Ruth leaned in a little closer. 'I need to ask you something, Ali. And I need you to think carefully before replying.'

'I'm tired, Ruth. I just want to go home.'

'It's important.' The officer's voice while still gentle and reassuring had a touch of urgency to it.

'If it helps to find Matthew.'

'Thank you.' Ruth's disposition shifted from casual to professional in a matter of seconds. 'Do you remember undoing your seatbelt at any time during the journey, or after the accident? It must have been undone in order for you to get out of the vehicle.'

Ali thought for a moment. 'I don't remember. I thought Liz undid it when she pulled me out.'

'Liz says not, and we don't think Matthew would have been able to undo his seatbelt either.'

'What?'

'You're aware Matthew's car was forensically examined.' Ali gritted her teeth, the word 'forensic' creating a jolt of fear in the pit of her stomach. 'The condition of the vehicle, particularly the driver's side, suggests that there was a good chance Matthew would have been incapacitated after it first ended up in the river.'

'Incapacitated?'

'Unlikely to have been able to undo his seatbelt and escape the vehicle on his own.'

'Oh.'

'I know this is upsetting, Ali, but I made a promise to you the first time we met. Do you remember what that was?'

Ali exhaled. She hadn't realised she'd been holding her breath.

'That you would always be open and honest with me.'

Ruth smiled. 'Always.'

'So you're saying that Matthew would have been unable to escape the car on his own when it went into the river?'

'That's what the forensics suggest.'

'But if the car was that damaged, maybe the seatbelts were, too. Maybe they came undone on their own.'

'Examination of both seatbelts and mechanism indicates they were both still in full working order after the crash.'

'Why didn't you tell me all this before?'

'This is confidential information, really only for a Coroner's Court.'

The thought of Coroner's Court made Ali feel ill.

'So let me get this straight,' said Ali, trying her best to process the information Ruth was telling her. 'We know that Matthew was still in the car with me when it first when into the river.'

'Both Liz and Dane confirmed that,' said Ruth.

'And when Liz got me out . . .'

'Matthew was still in the car then too.'

Ali nodded, remnants of previous conversations with both Liz and the FLO now coming back to her. 'And Liz sent Dane to get torches, and Emma to get the first aid kit from their car.'

'You were bleeding heavily from that wound in your thigh.'

'But Matthew was conscious. Talking.'

'You remember that?'

Ali's eyes widened. 'I remember.'

Ruth sat forward. 'Go on.'

'It's hazy, but after Liz got me out, she went back to the car to help Matthew. He was talking to her, distressed, but talking.'

Ruth nodded in concurrence. 'Liz told us she was trying to keep him calm, that he seemed safe.' Ruth frowned, and Ali noted the irony of her words. 'She was more worried you might be bleeding out.'

'And she left him?'

Ruth placed her hand on Ali's. 'It was a judgement call. How was she to know that a freak current would pull that car into the river?'

'And that's when Matthew went into the water?' she said, ignoring the FLO's last comment.

'That's what we're trying to find out.'

Ali gave a shaky sigh. 'No wonder Liz feels so guilty.'

'Has she told you that?'

'No, but I can tell.'

Ruth waited a few minutes for Ali to collect herself before returning to their earlier conversation. 'So when I asked about Matthew's seatbelt—'

'How it could have come undone, right?' A gasp of hope seemed to fill Ali's lungs. 'Maybe he wasn't as badly injured as everyone thought.'

'Ali—'

'I mean if Liz says she didn't undo his seatbelt

then Matthew must have been able to undo it himself, and if he was able enough to do that, then he must have been able enough to survive going into the river!'

'That is not what I meant.' Ruth's voice was calm. Ali realised she must have to address unrealistic expectations like this from loved ones all the time. 'What I meant is that we are still looking into other possibilities about how Matthew's seatbelt came undone.' She leaned a little closer. 'That's why I'm asking you again to try and remember everything that happened while you were still together in the car. Could Matthew have undone his seatbelt before the car went off the road, or had he even put it on in the first place? Could it possibly have been undone during your argument—' she studied Ali's face intently '—or something else perhaps?'

Ali regarded the family liaison officer with growing unease. Her questions were becoming more specific, and more disturbing. 'Are you suggesting that I did it?' she said. 'That I undid his seatbelt?'

'Maybe you were trying to help him escape the vehicle when Liz arrived.'

Ali closed her eyes, and a moment of clarity emerged. Her lying on the riverbank, blood from the injury to her face seeping into her mouth, the deep thunder of water as it rushed past, the sound of tortured metal as the BMW was dragged deeper into the river.

'Why are you doing this to me?' said Ali, now near tears. 'Why are you blaming me?'

'This isn't about blame,' said Ruth. 'This is about trying to determine what happened that night, for your sake as much as anyone else's.'

Ali let out a slow, steady exhalation. 'There is one thing I *can* remember. Something that I haven't told anyone.' Even though she could see Ruth was hugely interested, Ali also knew the FLO was too experienced to let on. Instead, she waited patiently for Ali to continue. 'I can confirm to you without question that I did not undo Matthew's seatbelt.'

'And how is that?'

Ali hugged her arms close to her body to stop herself from shivering. 'Because I wasn't the least bit concerned about helping Matthew.' An anguished sob escaped her lips. 'I was only interested in saving myself.'

She was expecting to see judgement on Ruth's face. Instead, she was met with understanding and kindness.

'It's more common than you think.'

'Things were just happening so fast,' said Ali, losing herself in the emerging memories of that night. 'We were sliding across the road, and then down into the gully. Then we hit the boulder. God almighty, I'd never felt anything like it in my life. If it wasn't for the airbags God knows what would have happened, but the car just kept on going.'

Ruth's tone became urgent. 'Go on.'

Ali leaned forward, her head almost touching her knees. 'We must have hit a patch of gorse or something, because the car bumped, rose up and slowed for a second, then it was going downhill again.' Ali stifled a sob and forced herself to carry on. 'I could see the river in the car headlights. The water was so high, racing by so fast, and we were heading towards it. Even in all that chaos I knew I had to get out. I must have undone my seatbelt and tried to get out before Liz came to help.' She paused to suck in a mouthful of air. 'I can't swim, Ruth. I abandoned Matthew because we were heading towards the river, and I can't swim.'

Ruth reached into her pocket and handed Ali a small packet of tissues.

'And you've known this all along?'

'Sort of.' Ali wiped the tears from her cheeks and blew her nose. 'It's like the memories were all puzzle pieces that didn't quite fit together, until now.'

'In my experience that's certainly a common after-effect of trauma,' said Ruth, 'and while I'm no doctor, I'd imagine a head injury too.'

'That still doesn't excuse me abandoning him.'

'You didn't abandon Matthew. Had you not been so seriously injured, I'm sure you would have done everything in your power to free him.'

'Do you really believe that?'

'Of course I do.'

'But if he was able to undo his seatbelt himself, wouldn't that—'

'As I said—' Ruth's voice was firm '—that appears doubtful. The more likely scenario is that his seatbelt was already undone, or came undone at some point, causing him to slip into the water.'

Traumatised and tired, Ali rested her head in her hands.

'We're doing everything we can to find him, Ali. I promise you that.' Ruth squeezed Ali's shoulder. 'Thank you for being honest with me today. That information will be very helpful to our continuing investigation.'

The words *continuing investigation*, reiterated Ali's earlier worries that the FLO wasn't just here to support her, but to scrutinise her as well.

A dreadful suspicion hit Ali like that boulder in the gully. Did the police think that she might have been responsible for undoing Matthew's seatbelt, resulting in his slipping out of the car and into the river? A flicker of recognition burned through her brain like a moor fire, crackling through her synapses. That whispered secret he told her before getting into the car, spreading like poison through her bloodstream. Her cheeks flushed with fury, screaming at him as they pulled out of the car park and all along the narrow road that bordered the gully. Matthew laughing at her, putting his foot down. Her pounding her fists against his arm, grabbing the steering wheel screaming, *'It's a lie. It's a lie!'*

She turned to Ruth and without thinking said, 'Was the dashcam in the car when you recovered it?'

9

Ali returned home from her meeting with Ruth, emotional, exhausted, but with a renewed sense of hope and vigour. If she and Liz were both pretty certain they hadn't undone Matthew's seatbelt, and it was still in full working order, then the only way he could have been freed from the vehicle was to have taken it off himself, despite Ruth suggesting he wouldn't have been able to do so on his own. Ali made a mental list of her argument: He was alive and still conscious when the car first went into the water; his airbag had gone off, hopefully mediating his injuries; he was fit, strong, and an excellent swimmer, and often went wild swimming in the Dart, so he would have known how to handle the cold water and currents.

'He's alive,' muttered Ali. 'I know it.'

She logged onto the Facebook page to check for any updates, but there were no new sightings. She sent Dane a carefully worded text asking if he could stop by to have a look at the broken gate. They'd agreed a code earlier – Ali would text asking for help with DIY at Hope Farm, or even a lift to the physio. That way if Liz came across it she wouldn't be suspicious. Once again she was overwhelmed with guilt and self-loathing. How could she so blatantly lie to her best friend? Almost immediately after sending the text her mobile rang.

'Hey, Ali.'

'How are things?'

'Nothing in Weston,' said Dane, referring to Weston-Super-Mare. Ali could hear noises in the background. Traffic, a jackhammer, and the beep of a lorry reversing. 'But that's to be expected. I'm certain I'll have more luck when I head towards some of the smaller towns.'

'Are you staying along the coast?'

'For a bit,' said Dane. 'I thought I'd try Minehead next and then maybe inland a bit.' He paused, and Ali thought she could hear him sucking in air. Had Dane taken up smoking again? 'Maybe Tiverton.'

'There was that sighting in Taunton a few weeks ago.'

Dane acknowledged her comment with a small click of his tongue. 'It does feel like he's moving closer to the A38.'

'Closer to home.'

Somewhere in her periphery Ali heard the sound of a key in her front door.

'Ali, it's only me!'

'It's Liz,' she said to Dane, her voice panicky.

'Just stay calm.' He sounded nervous himself. 'As if we've never spoken.'

'I'm not sure I can do this.'

'It's too late,' said Dane. 'We've gone too far now.'

'Ali?' called Liz. 'Where are you?'

'I'm in the kitchen,' replied Ali to Liz, and then to Dane said: 'I've got to go.'

'Don't tell her anything, Ali.'

'I won't. I promise. Bye for now.'

She'd just replaced her mobile to her jeans pocket when Liz entered the kitchen.

'Hello, my darling,' said Liz, giving Ali a hug. 'What have you been up to?'

Ali pointed to the laundry room, to where she had just rushed in and opened the washing machine door.

'Sorry, Liz, I was just doing the laundry.' When had she gotten so good at lying?

'I was on my way home,' said Liz, 'and thought I'd drop in to say hello.' Her hair was damp and her nose bright red. 'It's bloody freezing out there,' she said, placing her hands against the Aga to warm them. 'Who'd have believed it's nearly Easter?'

Ali reached for two wine glasses and the half bottle of prosecco from the refrigerator. She wasn't going to be able to get through this without a little alcohol.

'I know you're driving, but you can have one glass with me, can't you?'

'Just a small one.'

Ali poured them both a small glass of wine, and they sat at the dining table watching the wind whip through the trees.

'Everything okay?' said Liz, picking up on her friend's uneasiness. Ali thought back to Dane's words from only a few minutes before. *We've gone too far now.*

'I had a meeting with my family liaison officer today,' said Ali, knowing that distraction was the key to avoiding disclosure.

'Ruth?'

'You know her?'

'The police spoke to everyone who was there that night as part of the accident investigation,' said Liz. 'It was while you were still in hospital.'

Ali imagined her brain as a series of Jenga blocks, each with their own label. *Before the accident, accident, after accident.* Slowly but surely they were fitting themselves together to make an overall picture. There was, however, one notable gap in her wooden tower of recollection.

An awful lot had gone on while she was in hospital that she still didn't know about.

'Ruth and I were talking about seatbelts.'

'Seatbelts?'

'How they could have come undone that night.'

Liz seemed to be mystified. 'What do you mean?'

'She asked how Matthew's seatbelt could have come undone.'

'Did it worry you, her asking questions?'

'No, why do you ask?'

'Well, she worried me when she asked about the accident,' said Liz, 'all friendly and smiley at first, but underneath a Rottweiler.'

Ali began to laugh. 'That's exactly how I felt.'

'Just doing her job I suppose.'

'I suppose,' said Ali, 'but this seatbelt thing has left me really confused.' She looked at Liz. 'Did *you* undo Matthew's seatbelt?'

Liz opened her mouth to reply then stopped.

'Liz?'

'I wasn't really focusing on Matthew to be honest,' she replied finally. 'Maybe if I had been more diligent. Maybe if I hadn't left him in the car—'

'You did the right thing.'

'But if I had gotten him out maybe he'd still be alive today.'

Ali gritted her teeth. 'He *is* alive. I'm sure of it.'

There was a moment of awkward silence between the two.

'Had I known the current was that strong, that it would pull the car deeper into the water I would have done something,' continued Liz, her voice heavy with regret. 'The truth is, Ali, I was only thinking about saving you.' She paused to wipe away a tear. 'Just the way you saved me.'

Ali considered Liz's words, a deep reflection of a friendship that began nearly thirty years before, and which had encompassed the joy, heartbreak and violence of both their lives.

Liz's first serious boyfriend, Bobby, was a farm labourer. He drove tractors, forklifts, HGVs, and beat her senseless every Saturday night. The two friends had lost touch in that difficult period since leaving sixth form and starting life, and Ali – pregnant, lonely, and desperate to see her best friend again – had begun searching for her, finally ending up at Liz's parents' house in Kingsbridge.

'I've seen the bruises,' Liz's mother said to her in between sobs, 'but she refuses to leave him. Sometimes that girl's sense of loyalty is just too ridiculous.'

She eventually found Liz working at a bookies in Camelford.

'Ali!' Liz seemed thinner, smaller, defeated. 'What on earth are you doing here?'

'Can't I take my best friend out for lunch?'

By dinnertime she had helped Liz pack her bags and return home. Six months later Liz was working part-time for an estate agent, and part-time for Rory and Ali, helping them to grow the business. She was also the only person Ali considered as a godparent to Emma. Their friendship grew even stronger, and Liz became one of the family. When Dartmoor Properties had grown enough to employ full-time staff, Liz was the first one they hired. Ali and Rory even loaned her the deposit for her first flat. When a few years later she met Dane and fell in love, Ali couldn't have been happier. A little suspicious of Dane's laddish ways at first, she soon grew to like, even respect him. After all, it would be Dane, some years later, who would introduce her to Matthew.

'It wasn't your fault, Liz.' Ali felt grateful to finally be able to support her friend again. Since the accident it had been pretty one-sided. 'I never blamed you and never will. You were just trying to do your best.'

Liz reached her hand across the table and Ali grasped it. She was trying her best to move forward, God knew she was, but there still seemed to be so many hurdles in the way. Her recovery from surgery, anaesthesia, trauma, the heavy painkillers she still relied on, and the not knowing what happened to Matthew, all made for a concoction of indecision that traversed her entire life. The only thing that was keeping her from falling even further into hopelessness was Liz, Emma, Graham, and her determination to find Matthew. She reached for the bottle of wine. 'Top-up?'

Liz held her hand up in refusal. 'As much as I'd love to stay and chat, I really should be getting home.' She held up her mobile phone. 'Dane's away on business in Bristol but he'll be calling me later.'

The mention of Dane made Ali flush with guilt. Here she was asking her best friend to be truthful about the night of the accident while she was knowingly keeping secrets.

'I could stay a little bit longer if you need me to,' said Liz, misconstruing Ali's rueful expression.

'Honestly, Liz, I'll be fine.'

Liz's mobile buzzed. 'I've really got to go. I'll give you a ring when I get home to make sure you're all right. Maybe we can do something together this weekend?' She leaned over and kissed Ali on her unscarred cheek. 'Dane's going to be away again, meeting some old army buddies up north.'

'That would be lovely,' replied Ali, knowing full well Dane was planning to visit some of the places in North Devon where Matthew had been spotted. She waited until Liz had left before emptying the last of the wine into her glass.

'You'd better be worth it, Matthew,' she muttered, for the first time questioning her husband's motives.

10

Ali sat alone in the lounge, watching the dying embers of the fire fade from crimson to black. She heard Emma's car pull up and a few minutes later the back door being opened. There was the sound of keys being tossed onto the countertop, the refrigerator door being opened, the pop of a cork, and the gentle glug of a wine glass being filled. Then she heard the steady thud of her daughter's shoes on the hardwood floor as she made her way into the lounge.

'Jesus, Mum,' said Emma, 'you scared the life out of me. What are you doing sitting alone in the dark at this time of night?'

'I was waiting for you.'

Emma switched on the overhead light, dimming it so the room was bathed in soft ochre. Spotting the empty bottle on the coffee table she said, 'You didn't neck that on your own did you?'

'Of course not. Liz came by.'

Emma seemed uneasy. 'What did she want?'

Something in Emma's tone spoke of anxiety and repressed anger. Had she and Liz fallen out? Ali sincerely hoped they hadn't. Right now, Liz was the only person holding her fractured family together. She watched as Emma took a long sip of wine, nearly emptying her glass. 'Are you okay, honey?'

'Long day, that's all.'

'Everything all right at work?'

'Everything's fine.'

'Because if there's anything—'

'I said everything was fine!'

Ali stared at her daughter, both hurt and surprised.

'I'm sorry.' Emma sat down on the settee beside her mum. 'It just all gets to me sometimes.'

'What does?'

'The chaos that seems to be our lives.'

Ali regarded her daughter sadly. 'It will get better sweetheart.'

'A few years ago, I might have believed that. Ever since Dad died it just feels like everything is just so . . . uncertain.'

'Life is uncertain, honey.'

'Thanks for the pep talk, Mum.'

Ali gently pushed aside a lock of hair that had fallen across Emma's face. 'You know what I mean.'

'I just feel like I'm waiting for the next crisis.' She rested her head on her mother's shoulder. 'I was just starting to believe that maybe things would be all right.' She pointed to Ali's crutches, a stark reminder of what had recently befallen them. 'But then I see those.'

Ali kissed Emma's forehead. 'I'm all right, darling; safe.'

'For the moment.'

'Oh, Ems.'

'I still think of that night you know, all the time.' Ali knew Emma had been in the car with Graham, following Liz and Dane, that she had seen the car go off the road, and along with the others had skidded down the bank to try and rescue them. 'Maybe if I had stayed,' she said, 'got him out of the car while Liz was seeing to you—'

Ali had already anticipated her daughter's next words would be something along the lines of, *'He would still be alive today'*, but couldn't bear to hear it. Of course he was still alive. She and Dane were searching for him. She pushed her battered brain to a different place, to try to remember if she had asked Emma about the seatbelts. Surely someone must have. She opened her mouth to speak, but seeing the tortured expression on her daughter's face thought better of it. What Emma needed right now was reassurance, not more questions.

'It was raining, sweetheart – dark, dangerous. Liz wanted you safely out of the way, and I'm glad of that.'

Emma exhaled deeply and seemed to relax. 'Did Liz tell you about the new business?'

'New business?'

Emma grinned proudly, displaying the two dimples that Ali rarely seemed to see these days. 'The Assadorians want to speak to us about a commercial property development.'

The Assadorians were a Plymouth-based family of Armenian property owners, very powerful, very connected.

'You're kidding me.'

Emma gave a knowing smile. 'You didn't know I went to school with the youngest daughter, Mariam, did you?'

'You what?'

'All through sixth form we used to go for sneaky smokes behind the cricket pavilion.'

'And you just approached her?'

'She's ambitious like me, Mum.' Emma took a final sip of wine. 'And she also has a bit of a parental legacy to contend with.'

'Your father you mean?'

'All those Post-it Note things. *Opportunities don't happen. You create them! If you dream it, you can*

118

do it! God there were a lot of exclamation marks in my life.'

'Your father was one big exclamation mark.'

'Anyway,' continued Emma, unwilling to talk about Rory, 'she's asked me to look for locations for a boutique hotel project somewhere along the coast.' She gave her mother a shy smile. 'I may need your help getting my head around the building regs for the South Hams.'

Ali felt a wave of excitement flood through her. 'I'd love to help. Matthew and I were looking at a few commercial development possibilities in Salcombe as well as a private property for us. I may still have the estate agent brochures.'

'Just holiday lets right?' said Emma, confused by her mother's words. 'Not hotels.'

'Well, we were thinking of expanding beyond just lets.'

'Expanding?'

'Along the lines of what your friend Mariam mentioned, boutique hotels, luxury Airbnbs, that sort of thing.' She smiled to herself at the thought of her and Matthew sitting up late into the night, drafting their plans on the back of sheets of old wallpaper. She was sure she still had them stored away somewhere.

Emma's voice was tense. 'But that would take hundreds of thousands of pounds of investment.'

'We were just thinking about it.'

There was a long pause. 'Did Liz know?'

Ali felt unexpectedly defensive. 'We weren't anywhere near advanced enough in our planning to discuss it more widely, honey.'

'But you *were* planning to tell her.'

'Of course we were. I wouldn't keep anything from Liz.' Ali immediately recognised the irony of her words. She and Matthew had discussed telling Liz about their plans, but he had convinced her against it – *'wait until we have something more concrete, Als'* – and then there were her more recent clandestine plans with Dane. When had she become so secretive? Next to her she could sense Emma's brain whirring.

'But you didn't put any money into it?'

'No, Ems, like I said it was only in the planning stages.'

Emma let out a sigh of relief. 'Thank God for that.'

Ali felt a stab of resentment. 'What do you mean by that?'

'Oh come on, Mum, you know how bad Matthew was with money.'

'I don't think that's quite fair.'

'I know you double-checked his paperwork, redid his estimates, and Liz was constantly on at him about his invoicing.' Emma's expression was patient, kind, but there was an edge to her voice.

Ali knew that her daughter and husband hadn't

really gotten on, but she hadn't realised Emma held this much resentment for Matthew.

'I was aware of that, honey; we were working on it.'

'Not hard enough.'

'What on earth do you mean by that?'

Emma grunted. 'He's not the man you thought he was.'

'Of course he is,' said Ali, acutely aware of her daughter's use of the past tense. 'He's kind, supportive, funny, and loving, and yes he did have some problems managing his online trading business, but we addressed that.'

'Might as well call it online gambling the way he played the odds.'

'What do you know about it?' Ali's precariously managed self-control had started to fail her. 'What the hell do you know about anything?' She felt unexpectedly upended by Emma's astute assessment of Matthew's money problems, and all the trauma that she had so carefully placed in that *don't deal with it* part of her brain, began to bombard her already fragile senses. The death of her beloved Rory and now Matthew's disappearance felt like fissures running through the delicate fibre of her psyche. The blood rushed to her brain and her heartbeat raced. She felt terrified, desperate, never seeming to be able to fill her screaming lungs. Normally she could discreetly manage these attacks, dosing herself up on medication and hiding away in her bedroom, but with Emma here there was no escape. The dark mantle of despair engulfed her, and she was falling.

'Mum!' cried Emma. 'What is it, what's wrong?'

'Panic. Attack,' gasped Ali. Emma grabbed her mother and took her in her arms, held her tightly and caressed her scarred face, whispering to her as if she was a small child.

'It'll be all right, Mum. It'll be all right.'

Finally, Ali felt herself begin to return to normal. The palpitations had eased, and her vision had cleared so that she was no longer looking at the world through a narrow aperture. Seeing her daughter's anxious face, she longed to reassure her. 'I'm fine, Emma.' Her throat was dry, so dry. 'The doctor warned me that something like this might happen. Post-trauma stuff.' She glanced past Emma to the pictures on the mantelpiece. Emma as a baby, teenager, and a reluctant bridesmaid at her wedding to Matthew. A black and white photo of Rory standing in the long grass behind Hope Farm holding his infant daughter in his arms. She and Liz at the Women in Business Awards, raising their champagne glasses in celebration. Graham at his university graduation, only Ali by his side. Every image was a lifeline, an anchor that kept her from being washed away by a swirling whirlpool of fear.

'I'm sorry for what I said about Matthew.' Emma

exhaled deeply and Ali could feel the warm puff on her neck. 'He was your husband and you loved him. I should have respected that.'

Ali paused, relishing the warmth of Emma's cheek next to hers. 'I know it isn't easy for you, Ems, that you don't really get on.'

'No, we didn't.' The finality of her words made Ali flinch. Emma sat up and slowly ran her hand through her long hair, twisting it around her finger, just as she used to do when she was a child. 'I'm sorry, Mum. I didn't mean to be so abrupt. I'm just under a lot of pressure at the moment.'

Ali found herself defaulting to her habitual role of solution-finder. 'What kind of pressure? I thought you said things were fine?'

'Everything *is* fine!' Emma's anger was back, but this time driven by something more primal. She rested her head in her hands and began to cry. 'Sometimes I just worry.'

Not for the first time Ali wondered if putting her daughter in a role of such responsibility, even with Liz at the helm, had been unfair. Maybe it was just too much too soon. Just because Ali managed it at twenty-two, didn't mean Emma could.

'If it's too much for you—'

'It isn't,' replied Emma, still apparently upset. 'Just because I have a bad day doesn't mean I can't cope.'

'Of course not. That's not what I meant.'

'So what *did* you mean?' said Emma, sounding spiky.

'I meant, Ems, that I worry about *you* just as much as you worry about *me*.'

Emma gave a wry laugh. 'I don't think that's possible.'

'Oh, darling.' Now it was Ali's turn to hold her daughter close. 'I'm sorry this has been so hard on you.'

'If you could only just accept that Matthew is gone,' said Emma, speaking openly for the first time, 'it would make it all so much easier.'

Ali sat back stunned. 'Is that what this is all about? You're trying to get me to admit Matthew is . . .?'

'Say it!' Emma shouted. 'Just say it.'

'I can't,' said Ali. 'I won't.'

'*Not until there's a body*,' parroted Emma.

Ali fought the urge to strike back. She could see the distress on Emma's face, could hear it in her voice. It was clear now more than ever that she wasn't the only one who had been suffering.

'Why don't you go to bed,' said Ali, struggling to cope with her jumbled emotions. 'You look exhausted. We can talk more tomorrow.'

Emma's face crumpled into sadness. She opened her mouth to speak and for a moment it appeared as if she was going to divulge something more, but just as quickly shut it again. Her secret would not be shared, not yet anyway. She kissed her mother goodnight, and wandered towards the stairs.

'I'm sorry, Mum,' she said, 'for speaking so harshly. I just want things to be back to normal again.'

'I know,' said Ali. She wanted to offer her daughter words of comfort and reassurance, but she had none. Until she knew what had happened to Matthew nothing would ever be normal again.

She waited until Emma had made it upstairs and she heard her bedroom door shut before reaching for her mobile phone. It was clear to her now that Emma's behaviour wasn't just motivated by resentment or anger; it was all driven by fear, pure and simple. It was after midnight, but she knew her brother, a night owl like herself, wouldn't mind the late communication. *We need to talk,* she texted. *It's important.* Then after pushing send, she sat watching the final spits and sputters of the fire.

11

Ali lay in bed, watching sunlight slowly settle on the pillow next to her. She could hear Emma moving around the kitchen, first the kettle, then the refrigerator door. There was the sound of a teaspoon clattering to the floor, then a curse. Ali thought about getting up to try and speak to her, to revisit, even resolve some of the issues she had so carefully side-stepped last night. Instead she reached for the painkiller on the table next to her, a precursor to almost any activity first thing in the morning, and swallowed it dry. Then she waited for Emma to leave. Some things were just too painful to deal with first thing in the morning.

She made a small tick in the row of boxes on her pain management schedule which she kept next to her bed, did her physio, showered, and then got dressed. Determined to greet her brother looking at least half decent, she put on a denim dress and awkwardly tried to slip her bad leg into a pair of tights.

'Damn it!' she cursed, after another failed attempt, and instead opted for a pair of loose cotton trousers and a top.

'Increased mobility will come, Alice,' Dr Bhogadi had said to her at one of her follow-up visits. Ali changed the subject, unwilling to discuss her fear that she might never walk properly again, with even this most expert of people, but he would not be side-tracked. 'With time and effort, you will be . . .'

'Almost normal?' she had interjected, but he had not replied, only squinted at his notes and muttered something about expectations.

Yesterday's conversation with Ruth and all the issues it had raised, as well as last night's disturbing exchange with Emma, had seemed to compel her into some sort of action. What that action might be she wasn't sure yet. Maybe it was time to change her routine, or in fact create one.

She studied her face closely as she applied the special concealer to her scar. The thin line was fading nicely, and she hoped, as the plastic surgeon had suggested, that it would be almost unnoticeable by Christmas. She shifted slightly to study her profile. She was a good-looking woman, always had been, her chestnut hair, dark eyes and olive skin hinting at the Mediterranean ancestry on her mother's side. She had lost weight since the accident, making her cheekbones and jawline slightly more angular and defined. She appeared closer to Matthew's age than her forty-three years, and had once held that knowledge with pride. She added mascara and a slick of lip gloss, then put on the diamond stud earrings Matthew had bought her as a wedding present. By the time Graham arrived an hour later she was sitting at the kitchen table with a carafe of coffee and a plate of cinnamon buns in front of her.

There was the familiar sound of a key turning in the front door.

'Ali?'

'In here.'

She heard Graham make his way from the front door, down the corridor, and into the kitchen.

'Something smells good.'

Ali pointed to the cinnamon buns on the table. 'From frozen I'm afraid.'

'Still home-baked,' he said, leaning forward to kiss her cheek.

'Thank you for coming over at such short notice.'

'No problem, I'll probably be commuting back and forth on this Exeter job for the next few months. You look fantastic by the way.'

'I thought I'd make an effort,' Ali joked, 'for my brother and all.'

'Give yourself a break,' said Graham. 'Shit. I'm sorry, Als,' he said contritely. 'The last thing you need is someone lecturing you in self-care after all you've been through.'

She gave a wry grin. 'Don't worry about it. It's hard to know what to say sometimes, and even harder to know how to reply.'

'There's always the old adage—'

'Fake it till you make it, bro?'

'It got us through Dad's vegan shoe period, didn't it?' Graham tapped a finger to his chest. 'And anyway, you're speaking to the poster child right here.'

'You definitely made it.'

'After a bit of a bumpy ride,' he replied, 'and anyway this isn't about me.' He reached for a cinnamon bun and took a bite. 'Why the midnight message?' he asked, wiping icing from his chin.

The previously bright morning became stormy. Rain lashed against the windows and trees bent in submission to ferocious winds.

'You're shivering,' said Graham.

'I'm finding it's all catching up with me a bit.' Her unsettling conversation with Emma last night was still weighing heavily on her mind. 'Could you do me a favour,' she said indicating to the area beyond the kitchen, 'and grab my pashmina from the back of my bedroom door?'

Graham smiled and wandered down the short corridor, returning a minute later with the pashmina, which he carefully placed around Ali's shoulders.

'I've seen your meds chart,' he said gently, then a bit more sternly, 'which you're not following.'

'I promised myself I'd try and be off the heavy stuff by October. I don't want to turn into some sort of pathetic addict.' She blushed at the realisation of what she had just said. Graham's prescription drug issues had been addressed many years before. 'Oh God, Graham, I'm sorry. I didn't mean—'

'It's all right,' he said. 'Those days are long gone.' He gazed past her into the lounge. 'Why don't I make a fire and we can sit ourselves down and talk?'

'That would be lovely,' said Ali, pulling her pashmina more tightly around her shoulders.

It took a while for Graham to get the kindling lit, but it wasn't long before he had a fire blazing and they both settled down on the settee.

'So what's the story?'

Ali took a moment to get her thoughts together. 'I was speaking to Emma last night.'

'I gather it was something serious?' said Graham. 'To warrant such an urgent-sounding text.'

'There's something going on, Graham, at Dartmoor Properties. I don't know what it is, but something's just not right.'

Graham placed his second cinnamon bun of the morning back down on the plate. 'Not right how?'

'She kept on making all these veiled references to money and finances.' Ali twisted her wedding ring nervously around her finger. 'I went into the office on Tuesday.'

'You what?'

'Just to say hello, and also to tell the staff I was going to give them a bonus for all their hard work.'

'*And?*' Graham pressed, apparently unsure of where the problem lay.

'They were lovely of course, all of them.'

'But?'

'Liz seemed worried when I mentioned a bonus, and later Emma mentioned something about business dropping off.'

'And has it?'

'A bit,' said Ali. 'Our regular customers have stuck with us, but new business is unusually slow. Maybe they're worried about an incapacitated MD and a missing project manager. We've got a big project coming up, but we won't see any revenue from that until the end of the year at the earliest, so money is tight.'

'You've had slow periods before,' said Graham reassuringly. 'You'll come out of it.'

'I've checked the online accounts,' said Ali, slowly

working her way towards the reason for their meeting, 'but I'm still having trouble concentrating. My eyes get tired.'

Graham sat for a moment, silently studying her face. 'You want me to look at the books, don't you?'

Ali cleared her throat. 'I'm just concerned there's stuff going on that I really need to know about, but they're all trying so hard to protect me that no one dares speak it.'

'You mean Liz.'

'And Emma. Last night she seemed close to telling me something, but then stopped.'

Graham's brow furrowed in concern. 'About the business.'

'Partly.' Ali wasn't going to openly tell Graham that her daughter's vitriol was squarely aimed at Matthew. 'And I'm not suggesting there was anything *dubious*.' She said the word with extraordinary caution, like sparks on her tongue.

'But you are concerned.'

'Both Liz and she have taken on a lot since the accident, too much in fact. Emma's been working late almost every night.'

'You think it's too much for her?'

'A little,' replied Ali. 'She's really risen to the challenge of the last few months and I'm proud of her, but I've seen what stress and overwork can do to a person.' She thought of Rory working all through the night, the endless cans of Red Bull, and the dark circles under his eyes even as he was laid out at the funeral home. 'I want to protect her, Liz too.'

'But if they're saying everything is all right—'

'The thing is, Graham, everyone seems so intent on trying to shield me that I'm worried important issues are not being communicated.' Ali set her jaw tight. 'This is my company. I'm not afraid to have difficult conversations if I need to, particularly if that means supporting my daughter and my best friend.'

'It's nice to see the old Ali coming back.'

'I wouldn't go that far.'

Graham stood up, and walked towards the French doors. 'What exactly should I be looking for?'

'I'm not sure.'

Her brother shot her a knowing look.

Ali gave a resigned shrug. 'Emma said something last night about invoicing.'

'Invoicing?'

'Maybe Liz hasn't been able to keep up with the billing, maybe Matthew's suppliers needed paying but no one could find the paperwork.' Graham appeared startled by his sister's unexpected candour. 'I lived with the man for three years. He was amazing with getting a deal done, but when it came to paperwork . . .'

'Accountancy can make or break a business, Ali.'

'Don't you think I know that?' she said forcing herself to stay calm, pushing back the fear. 'I just need you to check that everything is all right.' Ali realised that now more than ever she needed to be truthful. 'I can get my head around the fact that we may be struggling a bit at the moment. That's happened before and we've gotten through it, but it's the not knowing that's worrying me. I rebuilt this company almost single-handedly after Rory died, and I could have so easily given up. God, I wanted to give up, but I didn't. I fought on, and on, and on.' Graham's back was still towards her, but she could tell he was listening closely. 'Dartmoor Properties has been the one constant through all the shitty things and all the great things that have happened in my life. I don't want to lose it.'

'And I assume you don't want Liz and Emma to know,' said Graham succinctly.

'This is one thing I can do for them,' said Ali. 'Get an expert in and take some of the pressure off.' Her expression grew serious. 'I don't want them to think I don't trust them.'

Graham slowly made his way back to Ali and sat back down beside her. 'I'll need all your logins for the accounting software program.' He rubbed a hand across his jaw. 'Who has access?'

Ali felt a sense of relief at the fact that Graham had agreed to take this on.

'Me, Liz, Emma—' she made an odd sort of gulping noise '—Matthew.'

Graham placed an arm around her shoulders. 'I'll do everything I can to help. I promise.'

12

Ali spent the next few days checking Dartmoor Properties' workflow schedule on the online planner. Easter was fast approaching and there would be a heavy turnover on the holiday properties from now on. There were also always small maintenance jobs to do on the student lets during unoccupied periods. Everything seemed to be in order, but Ali had an odd niggling feeling, as if there was something she had missed. If only her attention wasn't being pulled elsewhere.

She visited her Facebook page once more, making a list of all the sightings of Matthew in the last month – their days, times, and locations. Maybe there was a pattern that she and Dane could use to track him down. They certainly seemed to be centred around weekday evenings and town centres. She'd had a text from Dane only yesterday to say he would be spending a few hours in Barnstaple at the most recently reported sighting, but hadn't yet heard back from him.

'Where are you, Matthew?' she muttered. 'And what on earth do you think you're doing?'

The sound of her mobile buzzing wrenched Ali's attention from her laptop screen.

'Ruth.' Ali's throat felt so tight that she almost couldn't speak. 'What is it?'

'It's about the dashcam.'

Ali felt her heart rate quicken then calm. Every phone call from the FLO was an emotional jolt. If they had found the dashcam with audio they may have been able to download the recording, including any conversations from within the vehicle. She wasn't absolutely certain she wanted to hear what went on in the car that night, but knew it was essential to determining Matthew's current whereabouts.

'The forensic vehicle examiner has confirmed that no dashcam was recovered from the vehicle.'

'But there was one.'

There was a pause. 'He suggested it may have been swept away.' Ali's mind went to that dark place – mud, blood, rushing water, and fear. 'With the shattered windscreen and the speed of the current—'

'Just like Matthew was swept away?'

'I'm sorry, Ali. I didn't mean to upset you.'

'It's fine, Ruth. I did ask.'

'And you're sure the dashcam was in the car that night?'

'Positive.'

The family liaison officer made a small *hmm* sound. 'Maybe it's something to look into a bit more thoroughly,' she said almost absent-mindedly. Then realising who she was speaking to added, 'Are you all right?'

'It's hard to feel let down by anything anymore.'

'I know, Ali, but things will get better.'

I doubt it.

She spent the rest of the afternoon on the settee covered in a tartan throw. The dampness of early spring seemed to creep in through the polished floorboards and settle into her bones. Too tired to make a fire, she lay wrapped in the throw, watching the rain-battered windows and hoping for sleep. Finally, near dinnertime, she wandered into the kitchen, her right leg dragging slightly behind her, and removed the packet of painkillers from the cabinet. Shuffling her way to the kitchen island, she popped one from its foil sarcophagus, watching as it skidded along the countertop, the bright orange tablet a sunburst on the grey marble. She placed it on her tongue and washed it down with the cold dregs of this morning's cup of tea, then returned to the safety of her chequered nest. She was just nodding off when she heard a knock on the front door and a key being slipped into the lock.

'Emma, Liz, or Dane,' she said in a soft voice. 'Who is stepping through the keyhole this time?'

Seconds later a red-faced Graham hurried his way into the living area.

'Graham, what are you doing here?'

'Ali,' he said breathlessly, 'I tried to call. I need to speak to you.'

'What on earth is so important you had to come all the way from Exeter to tell me?'

Graham regarded her with concern. 'Are you all right? You look pale.'

Ali shrugged. 'Bad morning.'

Graham's face was etched with pain. 'I'm sorry, Ali, but it's going to get a lot worse.'

He made them both a pot of tea and sat beside her. Taking his laptop and notebook out of his briefcase, he laid them on the table in front of him, along with a red pencil.

'I did some in depth investigation into the financial management of Dartmoor Properties going back to when Matthew was first appointed project manager.' His expression became serious. 'The records indicate he negotiated the purchase of three holiday flats in Woolacombe last spring as well as another property in Salcombe for your private use just before Christmas.' He peered at Ali over his spectacles. 'Is that correct?'

'It is,' said Ali uncertain as to why Graham had decided to use Matthew's appointment as project manager as the starting point for his investigation.

'There are associated expense receipts entitled "business lunch" from a Michelin-starred hotel in Cornwall,' continued Graham pursing his lips in a way that Ali knew meant he was annoyed. 'Three hundred pounds, Ali, for lunch!'

'I signed that one off,' replied Ali unperturbed. 'He got us a contract to source and redevelop a residential property in Cornwall for a rather prominent London-based celebrity. The deal is worth over two hundred thousand pounds for the company, and the publicity will be priceless. I think the three-hundred-pound initial investment was worth it, don't you?'

Graham gave her a look and then carried on speaking. 'Then we have the invoices.' He reached for his laptop, then decided against it. 'They were all over the place, very little detail, many of them handwritten. No centralised auditing system, poorly archived. What was Liz thinking?'

'Liz?'

'As office manager she should have been on top of this.'

Ali gazed at the framed wedding photo on the mantelpiece – the image of her and Matthew on their wedding day, suntanned, smiling, happy.

'Matthew insisted on handling his own paper-work.'

'Or not handling it,' said Graham, his voice thick with censure. He leaned closer. 'I've found some-thing, Ali, something quite concerning.'

'To do with Matthew?'

'Whatever he was up to with the project accounts suggests he was either terrible with finances or very clever with them.'

Ali felt herself bristling. 'What do you mean *whatever he was up to*?'

Graham gave a huff of frustration. 'His records are so disorganised it will take me weeks to figure them out.'

Ali thought about all the reminders she had to create for her husband on his mobile phone. MOT and car tax, insurance renewals, dentist appoint-ments – everything had to be logged into his calendar with notifications. Even then she still had to regularly check the spreadsheet she kept for his personal admin in order to remind him.

'His organisation skills weren't always the best, but his project work . . .' Why did she feel the need to constantly defend her husband? 'He pretty much negotiated the purchase of the holiday homes single-handedly. Some we kept on, some we renovated and sold. We made enough on those to cover most of our annual wage bill.'

'I'm not saying he wasn't talented, Ali,' said Graham, his tone cautious. 'How he got that deal on your place in Salcombe I'll never know.'

'He had a way of bringing people around,' said Ali. She was aware of her brother watching her but didn't elaborate.

She wasn't about to tell him about Matthew's tendency to use the hard sell to get what he wanted, how he'd pushed a vendor, a recent widow, to close only two days after her husband's funeral. Maybe that's what he and Emma had argued about the night of their anniversary dinner. *Business is business, Al,* Matthew used to say, sounding more and more like Rory every day.

'The renovations on those student flats . . .' Graham referred to his notebook. 'Kitchen floor, new bathroom tiles, replacement window frames.'

'Yes,' said Ali. Of all the jumbled things in her brain, she could remember that. 'The work was done over the Christmas holidays when the students went home.'

Graham opened the lid on his laptop, tapped the power button and an accounts payable summary came into view. 'According to your monthly project plan you outsourced the work to an external maintenance firm: JDS Property Services?' He pointed his biro at the screen. 'If I can draw your attention to this payment dated the 14th of December last year. It's for eight thousand pounds to cover renovations to properties on Eustace Road, Mutley Plain, Plymouth.'

Ali felt unnerved by her brother's use of formal language.

'No one's on trial here,' she said, trying to lighten the mood, but seeing her brother's serious expression added, 'Are they?'

Graham didn't reply.

Ali tried her hardest to focus, to concentrate. 'We have them on a retainer, normally for short-notice jobs, out-of-hours stuff, emergency repairs. They also manage larger projects like the student flat renovations if Darren's busy with other work. I imagine I'll be subcontracting them for the Cornwall job. You met the director, Mark Burns, at our engagement party.'

'Got on quite well we did,' said Graham. 'And you also pay them a monthly fee—' he pointed to a payment schedule from nearly a year before '—to the account listed here? JDS Property Management Services?'

'Two hundred pounds a month retainer fee minimum, sometimes more, for emergency call-outs to ensure they'll be available to do repairs or maintenance at short notice.' She could see her brother's sceptical expression. 'It's not a waste of money,

Graham. If there's a water leak in the middle of the night at one of our luxury holiday lets, or a student cuts through a gas pipe, and it has happened believe me, we need to ensure we can get someone there within an hour or two. We also top that up monthly depending on the work they've been doing. With our expansion into the seaside holiday lets it's been a godsend.'

Graham pointed to the screen once more. 'You can see here retainer payments of between two and five hundred pounds in October, November, and December of last year.' He scrolled back a bit further. 'And at the end of December an additional fee of two thousand pounds for electrical and gas safety testing for a number of properties.'

'Yes, yes,' said Ali, growing impatient. 'We needed the safety certifications for the students lets. We normally do that over the Christmas period when the flats are empty. Really, Graham, what's your point?'

Graham leaned back, pressed his hands together, and stared at the ceiling. 'You know, Ali, the older I get the less and less I believe in coincidence.'

For a moment she thought her brother had lost his mind. 'What on earth are you talking about?'

'It just so happens a colleague of mine in Bristol was recently having a moan about the state of his daughter's student accommodation. She's studying

Commercial Photography at Plymouth College of Art.' Graham ran his thumb and forefinger down along his beard. 'The kitchen flooring was lifting, bathroom tiles were cracked and mouldy, and the windows – well the poor girl was near freezing to death because of the state of the windows. Promises were made of course, but nothing has materialised from the property owner.'

'And where are you going with this?'

'The student in question resides at 17B Eustace Road, Mutley.'

It felt as if someone had reached into her chest, grabbed her lungs and was squeezing them hard. 'I don't understand,' said Ali, but of course she did.

'Payments were made, Ali, significant ones, but the repair work to the student flats never took place over the Christmas period, or any period for that matter, and the monthly retainer payments from October last year onwards never actually went to your subcontractor, JDS Property Services. Even more concerning, it may be the case that the electrical and gas checks on the student flats never actually took place.'

'What?'

'I took the liberty of calling Mark this morning. We had a couple of glasses of Glenfiddich at the bar at your and Matthew's engagement party and stayed in touch. He's even sent a couple of clients my way.'

Ali was afraid to ask but had to. 'And what did he say?'

'I was very discreet of course, but he told me that JDS Property Services received a letter from Dartmoor Properties at the end of October last year. It stated that you were suspending the maintenance contract for an indefinite period, and would no longer require their emergency call-out service, as well as the fact that you had decided to keep any further maintenance work in-house.'

'In-house?' said Ali. 'With only Darren and some spotty apprentice!'

'As I said,' replied Graham, 'the contract was suspended, and the company has not had any further engagement with Dartmoor Properties since October.'

Now the true enormity of what her brother was saying hit her. 'Which means we shouldn't still be paying the monthly retainer fee.'

'But more significantly—'

'The December invoices were fakes!'

'Which brings me to another problem.'

'Oh God, what next?' Ali made a feeble attempt to get to her feet, but her bad leg was unsteady, and she found herself gripping Graham's shoulder for support. He took her hand and gently coaxed her back down onto the settee.

'You're going to need to sit down for this next bit.' He pointed for a third time to the computer screen and Ali started to shiver. 'Someone went into your online bookkeeping site and changed the account payee name of JDS Property Management Services to just JDS. They knowingly changed the details so it would look like you were paying the retainer fee and invoices to the legitimate company.' He dropped his voice slightly. 'Then they transferred that money into an online bank account not connected in any way to Dartmoor Properties.'

Ali's mouth dropped open. It was a moment before she could speak. 'So this was no accident or administrative error.'

'It was deliberate and calculated,' said Graham sternly. 'It's also pretty clear that whoever falsified the invoices had a detailed knowledge of the workings of Dartmoor Properties' accounts payable methods. They knew that the retainer payments would have been rolling ones, like a direct debit for your car insurance or mobile phone. No need to check on them until you're thinking about changing providers.' Ali could hear the strain in Graham's voice. 'They also would have probably known that you don't have that much to do with the student flat side of the business, so wouldn't have been keeping an eye on those accounts.'

'Everyone knows I deal with the luxury rentals end.' Ali struggled to control her increasingly panicked breathing. 'I get it, Graham, I get it.

Whoever has been stealing from me works for Dartmoor Properties. No mystery there. The question is who?'

Graham exhaled heavily, making a small wheezing sound. 'That *is* the question.'

'Why are you so oblique?' Ali snapped. 'If you know who is doing this then just bloody tell me!'

Graham let out a heavy sigh. 'The thing is, Ali – I haven't detected any further false invoices since that last one in December.'

'So whoever was stealing has stopped.'

'Or has been made to stop.'

It came to her then, sudden and alarming, like a lightning strike in the dark.

'And the retainer payments?' she whispered. 'Are they still being transferred into the fake account?'

'The last retainer payment was transferred from Dartmoor Properties into the dummy account on the 2nd of January of this year. No further fraudulent payments have been made since—'

'Since Matthew went missing!' Ali felt as if a large hole had opened up beneath her. 'You're suggesting that my husband has been stealing money from my company since last year?'

'I'm not suggesting anything,' said Graham grimly, 'just telling you the facts.'

Ali could feel her heartbeat race and her lungs contract. 'The facts being that someone has been stealing money from me, and that this stealing has miraculously stopped since my husband went missing.'

'Don't you think it's time to—'

'Until there's a body, Graham, he is still bloody missing!' Ali paused for a moment, forced herself to take a sip of coffee to ease her parched throat and settle her clattering nerves. Somewhere in the swamp of all her panic and anxiety, clarity resurfaced.

'If it *was* Matthew why would he be stealing a measly twelve grand, and why would the direct debits have stopped in January?' She could tell from Graham's expression he had been thinking the same thing. 'He didn't know the car accident was going to happen. If he was getting away with it since August, why would he suddenly decide to stop in January?'

Graham cleared his throat. 'Maybe he had paid off whatever it was that needed paying off.'

'Two hundred pounds a month for three months is not quite worth risking everything for, is it?'

'Plus the false invoices of course. Twelve thousand pounds is a significant amount of money.'

Ali was not daunted by her brother's words. 'He's just secured a deal for over two hundred thousand pounds; twelve grand is a pittance.'

'Not if it was to cover a debt he didn't want anyone to know about.'

It all clicked into place and Ali felt her heart sink. 'You think he was still trading, don't you – that he stole the money to pay off his losses.'

'He did have a bit of a history of poor judgement when it came to his online investments, and from what you told me his debts in the past were usually around that amount.'

'That was mostly *before* we were married, and his judgement wasn't always poor.'

'But then why the prenup?'

'You know why.'

Only a few months after their engagement Ali discovered Matthew had been running a small 'side interest' as he called it, in the form of a financial services company called Taran Holdings. The term *financial services* was used loosely, however, as Ali soon learned he was dealing in foreign exchange trading, a risky venture that involved buying foreign currency at a low exchange rate in the hope of selling later at a profit when rates rose. The investment capital required was significant.

'You promised you would stop!' she had yelled after stumbling across the forex site on his laptop a few weeks before their wedding. 'I told you before it's a fool's game, just another form of online gambling.' She pointed to one of the articles in the side bar. 'They even call it spread betting!'

'It's not a fool's game if you're winning,' he

replied. Turning the laptop towards her, Ali was astonished to see a balance of forty thousand pounds' profit in his account.

'Put it in the bank, Matthew,' she pleaded. 'Do not, and I mean it, *do not* roll it over.'

'I earned that money,' he replied calmly, and pointing to her engagement ring added, 'Paid for that rock didn't it?'

It took her less than two seconds to pull the engagement ring from her finger and throw it at him. 'Close the account, Matthew, or the wedding is off!'

'For Christ's sake, Ali!'

'I will not have my integrity or that of my company compromised by someone who's involved in dodgy trading!'

'Dodgy trading!' Matthew's face was crimson. 'I'm good at this, really good!' His irate tone changed to one of gentle persuasion. 'We could use the money I make to fund further development for the company, further growth.'

'That's only if the trading goes well and you're actually making money, not losing it.'

'I do make money!'

'Not always,' said Ali, referring to the five grand she had lent him not long after they first met, as well as the two grand she had given him a few months later. 'There's always a risk you'll lose everything.'

'I paid you back all that money,' he said, grasping the inference, 'with interest. But none of that matters, does it? All Ali Jones, local superstar businesswoman really cares about is the bloody company that she and her saintly first husband built!'

Ali waited a few minutes for Matthew to cool down before speaking.

'Why do you keep feeling you have to prove yourself?' she said. 'I love you and believe in you. Together we're going to make Dartmoor Properties even better.' She strode past him to the fridge where she poured them both a shot of ice-cold vodka. 'I'll make you a deal. You give up all the online trading and I'll make you a project manager.'

'What?'

'Project manager at Dartmoor Properties. If you're as good as you say you are, you can leave that maintenance manager's job you so despise and the trading, and come and work with me.' She watched his expression change from anger to ambition in the two seconds it took him to down his vodka. 'Close your forex account and I'll make you a project manager with double the annual salary of that money trading crap of yours, and without the risk.' She watched him weigh up the options, but he was no fool. Every trader had their bad days, and his profits were more often than not overshadowed by loss. 'You can use all those forecasting skills of yours to help us make Dartmoor Properties even more successful.'

He had opened his mouth to reply, but she raised an index finger and stopped him. 'And if you're so keen on investing, maybe you could actually make some good use of that dirty money.'

'It's not dirty,' he had argued, 'it's legitimate profit.' But by the end of the evening she had gotten her way. Matthew had agreed to give up foreign currency trading and use his forty thousand pounds along with nearly triple hers to invest in more property.

'Maybe a holiday place for us?' he had ventured, as they lay in bed together after celebrating their agreement.

'Maybe,' she replied, 'but there is one more thing.' She sat up on her elbow to look at him. 'If I ever find out that you're still trading, successful or not, the marriage will be over.'

Now back in the present with her brother regarding her – God she hated being pitied – she bit back. 'I don't believe it,' she said. 'He promised. We had an agreement.'

'I really didn't want to have to show this to you,' said Graham. He clicked onto a hyperlink that led directly to the login page of Dartmoor Properties' accounting software, and typed in the password Ali had given him. 'I checked the login details on the software program to try and determine who had changed the client information from JDS Property Management Services to just JDS.'

'Where the payments had been redirected to?'

'Exactly.'

Ali's voice was tiny. 'And?'

Graham scrolled back three months. 'The 14th of December, 6.49 a.m.' Ali leaned forward to study the screen. A payment for eight thousand pounds from company funds had been approved and transferred to an online client account entitled JDS. 'Do you see it?' said Graham. At first Ali thought he meant the transaction itself, but then realised he was directing her to the final column, *Transaction Approved by* . . .

'M J Penrose,' she whispered, 'Matthew.'

There was a moment of absolute silence – time standing still – as the full impact of what Graham had just shown her took effect.

'This wasn't impulsive or reckless,' he said despondently, 'and it was no accident.'

'*No*,' muttered Ali, weakly, 'he wouldn't.'

'I'm going to have to look into things further.' Graham sounded both angry and sad at the same time. 'The company finances, I mean.'

Ali pressed her icy fingertips against her blazing cheeks. 'Not yet.'

'It's really a matter of urgency that I check that the fraudulent activities don't extend beyond JDS Property Services,' said Graham. 'For all we know there could be thousands more pounds of missing money.'

'Liz would have spotted it,' said Ali, trying her best to sound convincing.

'Would she?' replied Graham, obviously not impressed by the office manager's skills. 'What we really need to do is speak to the bank . . .' he paused briefly '. . . and possibly the police.'

Ali regarded her brother with dull eyes. 'I need to think about it,' she said. 'We've only just re-established client confidence, and Emma's been developing an impressive new business stream. Then there's the Cornwall project, which we're already well into planning, including applying for a rather hefty bank loan to cover the initial outlay. A scandal of this sort will only undo everything we've worked so hard for.' She envisioned herself standing on top of a crumbling cliff face. 'What good will dragging everyone through more heartache and scandal do?'

'This isn't something that can be ignored!' growled Graham, 'or even worse swept under the rug.'

'Why not?' countered Ali. 'This is my company and my responsibility. I make the decisions. If what you say is true and Matthew betrayed me, then it's up to me to fix it.'

'And the misappropriated funds?'

'The losses I can deal with.'

'You're not seriously going to bury this are you?'

'If I can't bury my husband, at least I can bury this.'

'Bloody hell, Ali! And if there's more missing money, then what?'

Ali reached for her cup of coffee and downed the last cold mouthful. 'Why don't you let me worry about that.'

'This is insane. You need to go to the bank, to the police.'

'You can tell me what to look for.' She folded her arms resolutely. 'I'll come to you if I find anything irregular.'

Graham was nearly speechless with exasperation. 'This isn't about preserving anyone's reputation,' he said, plainly trying to control himself, 'but about protecting your business.' He reached forward and folded down the laptop lid. 'I also have a legal if not ethical responsibility to report any corporate fraud to the authorities.'

Ali looked away. 'I need to think.'

'Think about what?' said Graham. 'Someone's been stealing from you, Ali, and it's looking pretty conclusive that it was your husband.'

'I know,' she replied, unable to argue against his words, 'but before I go to anyone with this I want to make absolutely certain he was responsible.'

'And how exactly do you propose to do that?'

She paused before answering, knowing that Graham – like almost everyone else – thought

Matthew was dead. Mentioning the Facebook sightings, the leather jacket, the plan she and Dane had created would do no good. 'I'm going to find that money, Graham, so help me God.'

13

Ali promised Graham she would take action regarding the stolen funds immediately, but the shock of the revelation had left her anxious and uncertain. It was another two days before she could build the courage to act. There was also the very clear need to look into her husband's fraud with the utmost discretion. Nobody else could know. That would require careful planning. When Emma mentioned she was meeting an old friend for dinner in Exeter, and was thinking about making a weekend of it, Ali was all for it.

'That way you can have a drink without worrying about having to drive,' she said, knowing how sensitive her daughter was about the subject since the accident. It was undoubtedly manipulative, but

Ali had something important to do, and she needed absolute privacy to do it.

'Are you sure you'll be all right on your own?' said Emma as she put her overnight bag in the boot. 'Do you want me to ask Liz to check on you?'

Ali resisted the urge to tell her daughter that she was not an invalid, but instead offered a more tempered response. 'I'll be fine, honey, you go and enjoy yourself. I've got everyone on speed dial if I need them,' and then almost shooing her away added, 'you could do with a break.' She had a mission after all, one that frightened yet reinvigorated her.

She had handed over her office key to Emma not long after the accident, so now had no choice but to go through Matthew's things to try and find his spare one.

She hadn't touched his bedside table in the three months since the accident, but had insisted the cleaner made a special job of polishing it each week. She sat down on the bed and gazed out of the window. Late afternoon was shifting into evening and hints of another storm stained the dusky sky. She placed both feet firmly on the carpet beneath and slid open the drawer. For a moment the smell of aftershave weakened her resolve, but she forced herself to carry on.

'I can do this,' she whispered. Inside Matthew's

bedside table she found an old watch, some receipts from nights out with his mates, his Exeter Chiefs season ticket, nail clippers, expensive moisturiser, and – tucked into a thin silk bag – a sleep mask. Ali gave the bag a shake and heard a soft jingling sound. Removing the mask from its delicate casing, she slipped her hand inside. Her fingers gripped something cool and angular. She withdrew the mystery item to discover a standard-looking keyring. Attached to the split ring was a plastic square, within it a black and white striped image of the Cornish flag, the word *Kernow* written across it in white.

Her brow furrowed. This wasn't the spare office key Matthew normally used; she had found that resting on top of his silk pocket squares almost immediately. The keyring itself was scratched and battered, but the key appeared relatively new. Was it for an old flat? A lock-up? She slipped it and the mask back inside their protective sack, and was about to shut the drawer when she noticed something in the back corner of the drawer. Reaching into the dark recesses she pulled out a black faux croc business card wallet. This tacky item was nothing like the handmade leather one she had bought Matthew when he started as project manager at Dartmoor Properties. She opened it, uncertain of what she might find. Inside were some cheap Vistaprint-type business cards. She slipped

161

one out, expecting to see details from his old maintenance manager's job, but instead was shocked to be confronted with the horribly unexpected.

Taran Holdings – Foreign Currency Trading and Investment
Company Director Matthew Penrose

She stared at the business card, her emotions slowly transforming from surprise to despair, then in fury flung the wallet onto the bed, the cards splaying across the sheets like a messily dealt poker hand. They seemed new, not leftovers from four years before when he was still trading, when he had promised to stop trading. She reached forward, picked one up, and methodically began tearing it into pieces, letting them flutter to the floor. She did the same for the remaining six cards, ending up with a dusting of white cardboard flakes all over her feet.

'They're just old business cards,' she said, 'a memento, nothing else.' But she felt shaky and unconvinced. Was what Graham had suggested true? Had Matthew kept on trading even after he had promised to give it up? Had he gotten himself into trouble, into debt? Was that the reason for his stealing money from Dartmoor Properties? It would certainly explain his anxious behaviour leading up to the accident, as well as the fact that every time she asked him what was wrong, he had either snapped at her or tried to change the subject. Then there was the drunken conversation some months before between her and Liz at a spa weekend in Cornwall. Liz, not always the most jovial of drunks, had commented on the expensive watch Matthew had bought Ali as a birthday present.

'Why is he buying you that sort of bling when he seems to be continually in and out of debt?' Liz had complained. 'It took him ages to pay Dane back the three grand he borrowed.'

Shocked, Ali had pressed for more information, but Liz had fallen asleep and could not be roused until the next morning, when she appeared to have forgotten the conversation altogether.

'No!' she yelled, the force of her conviction swirling the paper fragments at her feet. 'I won't believe it until I have some proof.' The problem was the harder she fought for answers the further it seemed to drive her towards a certainty she wasn't willing to face. Maybe the truth just wasn't something she could handle. She felt an acute and agonising ache in her heart, and with it the realisation that no matter what Matthew had done, she still loved him – as she had done ever since the beginning.

Ali hadn't expected to see Matthew again after their first weekend of debauchery, but a month later he showed up at Liz and Dane's 'It's Nearly Summer' barbecue wearing a gaudy Hawaiian shirt and a knowing smile. They greeted each other politely and chatted as if they were casual acquaintances. Finally, after a few drinks and a slow dance, things grew more serious.

'I tried to ring you,' he said.

'Work has been pretty crazy.' She spoke quietly hoping no one else would hear. 'And as much as I enjoyed our previous time together—' Matthew grinned boyishly at her careful choice of words, and once again she felt herself being taken in '—there still is—'

'That age thing.'

'It *is* a thing, Matthew.'

He grinned in bemusement. 'Like I said before, you don't seem to be the kind of person who cares what other people think.'

'I don't.'

Grabbing her hands, he pulled her towards him. 'Then prove it.' She could feel the warmth of him, could smell his cologne. The world around her had gone quiet; the air seemed to still. She leaned forward and kissed him, ran her hands up his torso and linked them behind his neck. Around them there were resounding cheers and the sound of clinking glasses. Ali thought she heard someone call out, *'It's about bloody time!'* She looked over to see Liz and Dane smiling at them. She felt enclosed in friendship and love, a community. Ever since Rory had died, she had felt isolated, alone, afraid. That night Matthew came back with her to Hope Farm and stayed.

Their relationship was joyful, playful, fun. He wasn't demanding of her time, knowing that business was her first priority, but encouraged her to look for other things in life. Not long after they had started living together he had spotted one of Rory's old Post-it Notes that had slipped under the refrigerator. *Invest in Your Dreams,* it read. *Work Hard Now!!!*

'Wow,' he had exclaimed, a slight smile on his lips, 'three exclamation marks.' Ali had reached for the small square of paper, but Matthew had crumpled it in his fist and thrown it in the bin. 'Some things just don't need to be saved, Ali.'

He spoke little of his own job except to say that it wasn't stretching him. He spoke little, too, of his own background except to say that his father left when he was fourteen, and as Ali already knew, his mother had passed away earlier in the year.

They married the next January, a beach wedding in the West Indies, a dour Emma as her bridesmaid, Liz, Dane, and Graham as witnesses. Within a month she had appointed Matthew as her project manager. At night they would talk through their workday. Matthew – always attentive, always keen – slowly began to make suggestions.

'I was thinking about something along the south coast maybe Salcombe way,' he said, referring to the second home they had agreed to invest in together.

Ali had glanced up from her laptop. 'Salcombe? That's got some of the highest property rates in the country.'

He stepped forward, shut the laptop lid, and kissing her neck. 'Why don't you let me look into it?'

Ali was certain all the office workers would be gone by seven but still decided to wait another hour just to be certain. When she arrived, the car park outside Dartmoor Properties was empty, but she still got the taxi driver to pull up outside the IT company opposite.

'Wait here,' she said, handing the driver a twenty-pound note. 'There'll be two more of these when I'm done.'

Pulling up the hood of her jacket, she hobbled her way to the front entrance. She had left her crutches in the taxi, but didn't fool herself into thinking that anyone seeing a tall woman limping heavily across the tarmac wouldn't know it was her. She crossed her fingers that the door code hadn't been changed, entered the numbers for Emma's birthday, and gave a sigh of relief when she heard the lock click open.

Once inside, and cautious of mobile security guards, she avoided turning on the lights, choosing instead to use her iPhone torch to navigate her way to her office. She reached into her pocket for Matthew's key. Through the glass panel she could see the framed wedding photo of her and Matthew placed inelegantly on a filing cabinet. Emma must have moved it when she had started using Ali's desk.

Once inside her office she went to the desktop PC and logged on. She could have accessed the accounts from her laptop at home, but she wanted to be here, at her own desk, in control. She was growing tired of the constant attempts to keep her from her work. God, she was fed up with the patronising tones that seemed to accompany every communication to her. Whether it was from her daughter, brother, best friend, or doctor, they all sounded the same. *Forget about work and focus on getting better . . .*

'*The brain is like a muscle,*' Dr Bhogadi had once said to her, and in his charming way of attributing gender to different parts of the body added, '*when we use her, we feel joyous, but like any muscle, she also needs recovery time, rest.*' He had tapped the back of her hand. '*Be gentle with her.*

Did none of them realise that Dartmoor Properties was so connected to who she was that it was impossible for her to step back? In fact, stepping *up* to the challenges that her company might be facing was the main thing that was keeping her going.

She ran her fingertips across the wireless keyboard, rested her hand over the mouse just as Matthew would have done. She wanted to be here, sitting in this seat, using the very PC he may have used to steal from her. There seemed to be a perverse logic to it all, but a logic nonetheless. She tapped in the password Matthew used for their Netflix account. Chiefs123, and wasn't surprised to see that it worked here too. He was either incredibly naïve or incredibly lazy, perhaps a bit of both.

'This is where it started,' said Ali, settling back in the seat, 'and where it will end.'

Once in, she logged into the online accounting software and went straight to the monthly retainer payments, scrolling back to the autumn of last year. She could see that the two-hundred-pound monthly fee normally paid to JDS Property Management Services had indeed been re-routed to JDS just as Graham had said, but that the payments had stopped in January. She clicked on the little square of dots for more information. The login dates and times were listed, as was the account name of the person who had made the changes: Matthew. She could also see that funds had been paid into the false account for work on the student flats that hadn't actually been done. Becoming increasingly convinced now that Matthew was responsible, she opened the Payees tab.

'Where exactly did my money go?'

It didn't take long to find the sort code and account number of the dummy JDS account. Ali knew there was no way the bank would confirm if it was Matthew who owned it, so instead she googled *sort code checker*, entered the numbers and discovered it was an online personal account, untraceable unless she brought in the bank and police, something that she was not willing to do. Alone in the darkened office, her features illuminated by the cool neon light of the PC monitor, she felt her determination begin to crumble.

'Oh God, Matthew,' she sobbed. 'Why?' Somewhere in the back of her mind she had hoped she'd gotten it wrong. She couldn't deny that on paper her husband had sometimes appeared like a dubious choice: younger, impulsive, and the ongoing suggestion that his side venture, even though it was under the supposedly legitimate title of forex trading, was still just online gambling. No matter what everyone else thought, however, Ali knew better. It had been Matthew who had suggested expanding beyond cottages on Dartmoor to the more lucrative coastal areas, closed the deals, and got the properties at a steal. It had been Matthew who had negotiated the purchase of the house in Salcombe, currently being rented as an Airbnb for nearly two thousand pounds a week, and it was Matthew who had introduced Ali to a number of influential clients whose wealth extended into the millions.

'We're taking Dartmoor Properties to the next level!' he had announced the morning of their third anniversary. Dressed only in his boxers, and light-headed from their champagne breakfast, he'd bounced his way towards her on the bed before dropping to his knees, kissing her toes, and slowly working his way upwards. As she'd run her fingers through his dark curls, moaning softly, an image of Rory standing at the bottom of their newly installed oak staircase yelling, *'We're taking Hope Farm to the next level,'* came into her mind.

14

It was after nine by the time she arrived home. Firstly she went to the chest of drawers, and, after lifting the wedding album from its box, laid it on the bed, followed by the folder containing the articles about Matthew's disappearance. Beneath that was an A4-sized padded envelope. Tired now, she sat on the edge of the bed, the package cushioned in her lap like an artefact. It was a few minutes before she was able to slip it open and reach inside. She let her fingertips glide past the smooth paper of Rory's death certificate and carry on to where she knew, nested in the bottom corner, was a small blue box. She placed it carefully on the bed next to her and slowly lifted the lid. Moonlight glimmered through the window illuminating the pair of simple, matching wedding bands – nothing like the ones she and Matthew had commissioned from a bespoke jewellers in Plymouth. She tugged the platinum wedding and engagement rings off her finger, letting them fall onto the bed. Plucking the simple gold band from its plastic pillow, she placed it on her finger to where it had sat so comfortably until her engagement to Matthew four years before.

Relishing the obscurity of darkness, she struggled her way upstairs. Maybe it was the uneven shadows or her shifting mental state, but even though she was moving upwards, for some odd reason it felt as though she were descending downwards into a great, dark hole. The sensation made her giddy and she was forced to stop and grip the banister for support.

Entering the master bedroom, she went to Matthew's side of the bed, and taking a plastic shopping bag from her cardigan pocket, began emptying the contents of his bedside table drawer. Into another bag she emptied his socks, boxers, and workout gear, but tackling his row of suits in the built-in wardrobe was just too much for her. She glanced at the spot where his leather jacket should be suspended, but once again the hanger was empty. Tired and shaky, she felt her bad leg give out, and found herself collapsing onto the bed. The absurdity of the situation struck her, and she began to laugh, all the heartache and fury emerging into hiccups of bitter, ironic mirth. It wasn't long before her giggles shifted to tears, and she found herself thumping the pillow in fury. 'I won't believe a word of it until you say it to my face, you bastard!' Finally spent, she forced herself to her feet and after limping her way to the hallway closet, threw both bags of Matthew's things into the space behind the laundry basket. Then she followed the darkened corridor to Emma's room.

Emma's return home was supposed to have been temporary, just a stopgap after her recent flat let had ended – *just to get a deposit together, Mum* – but had extended to nearly a year. Then with the accident and Ali's injuries and mobility issues, there had been little question of Emma leaving home. Ali had tried to encourage her daughter to live her own life.

'I'll be all right on my own,' she'd told her many times. *'You should find a flat, get back out there.'*

'Not until you're better, Mum,' Emma would reply, and Ali remembered feeling an extraordinary sense of relief at her daughter's words. Always independent, sometimes to the point of isolation, she knew now more than ever how much she needed her daughter's help, not just to navigate the slippery staircase and polished wooden floors, but also the fear, pain, and increasingly frequent panic attacks. The thought that Hope Farm, once her sanctuary, her lifeblood, could have transformed into a prison, and a dangerous one at that, only further reinforced her fear and sense of loss.

She ran her fingertips across the hand-knotted throw and lifted the bottle of expensive perfume from the dressing table. The scent of bergamot tickled her nostrils, bringing with it images of Emma dressed for a night out, Ali zipping her up, tucking a wayward tendril of hair into her ever-present messy bun, and adding a final spritz of perfume. What had happened to all those wonderful moments? Once they had been close, spending hours together talking about life, love, and everything – Ali the wise mother, Emma the eager and receptive daughter. A palpable distance had grown between them since her marriage to Matthew. She had hoped Emma coming to live with her and Matthew would have offered a pathway to reconciliation and understanding, instead it had only seemed to intensify the divide.

After Emma's return to Hope Farm last year, there was rarely a night that both she and Matthew were in the house together that didn't include an argument.

'*It's not your business, Matthew!*' Emma would yell. '*Stop acting like you own it!*'

'*It's not yours either,*' he would reply glibly, '*not yet anyway, and a lot can happen to change all that.*'

She had glanced from him to her mother.

'*What the hell does he mean by that?*'

Ali had changed the subject, not willing to share the discussions she and Matthew had recently had about him becoming a partner. Matthew had helped to expand her thinking to new places, grown Dartmoor Properties in ways she never could have imagined. Before they met, the business had begun to grow stagnant, Rory's old approaches becoming outdated in the increasingly digital nature of the property development world. This was reflected in limited growth and a worrying, diminishing revenue. Since Matthew's lead on expanding the company into seaside holiday rentals, and hiring a social media and marketing manager, a new energy had seemed to embody the company. Not long before Christmas Matthew had done a presentation to staff entitled *Time to Grow*, using the analogy of an ancient oak to represent the potential different strands of Dartmoor Properties.

'We have the roots,' he said, directing his laser pointer to the established high-end rentals, 'and we also have our trunk – student flats – but what about the new shoots?'

Across the table Ali could see Emma roll her eyes.

'Without new growth,' Matthew continued, 'the entire organism withers and dies.' *A bit of a grim analogy*, Ali remembered thinking at the time, but his suggestion that holiday flats would offer a year-round income at relatively low cost seemed to go over well. 'People staying for a week or two aren't going to complain about one dodgy radiator.' He was standing akimbo in front of the pull-down screen and Ali thought he had never seemed so sexy. 'We can plan short maintenance periods in between lets, which will allow us to continue to gain revenue as we develop the properties to a higher spec, and in turn a higher rental fee, but that doesn't mean we're going to ignore the luxury end of the business.' He put down his laser pointer. 'To that end Ali has an important announcement to make.'

The news about the Cornwall deal had caused a ripple of excitement throughout the meeting room. She had been pleased to see the looks of stunned admiration on her staff's faces, pleased also that her husband had proved himself so worthy.

The shriek of a fox jolted Ali back to the present, back to her daughter's darkened bedroom in which she was trespassing. It was getting late, but there was still one more thing she had to do. Hobbling over to the steel and reclaimed wood laptop desk, she switched on the light. She ignored Emma's MacBook Air that sat on top, and instead reached into the top drawer, searching for the higher spec MacBook Pro that had been Matthew's laptop, hoping that Emma had been using it. The drawer was empty. Dane's search the other night through the rest of the house had been fruitless, and Liz was right when she said it wasn't in the office at Dartmoor Properties. Ali gave a huff of frustration. That laptop contained confidential company information; information that could help her find the missing twelve thousand pounds. It was also probably one of the last things Matthew had touched before he went missing.

Switching off the light, she made her way down the hallway and back downstairs. She sat on her bed staring at the full moon through her bedroom window. For the last three months she had been in a stupor of pain, grief, and loss. The shocking discovery of Matthew's fraud had heightened it to an almost unbearable degree, but like all the other sorrow in her life she kept it well hidden in that secret place that was hers and hers alone. What was twelve thousand pounds in the grand scheme of things, and more importantly, was she really prepared for all the secrets that finding it would reveal?

'It's just money,' she muttered, knowing full well that the insurance pay-out on Matthew's written-off BMW would cover the missing money in a heartbeat.

Her mobile vibrated on the bedside table next to her.

'Dane.'

'Sorry to call so late.' His voice sounded echoey, as if he was speaking to her from inside an empty room.

'Is it about that sighting yesterday?'

'Last week it was Minehead, now Barnstaple.' His voice was low, hushed. Was Liz nearby? 'He's working his way home, Ali.'

She had wondered the same thing, but hadn't dared to speak it aloud. According to the most recent sighting, it appeared as if Matthew was working his way back to Totnes along the south-west coast. Her mind flew to Ruth and where the police were in all this, but then recalled the FLO's recent comments about understaffing and manpower shortages in Devon and Cornwall Police.

'Just not important enough,' she muttered.

'What?'

'Nothing,' she replied. 'Where next?'

'Could be anywhere,' replied Dane. 'Dulverton, Okehampton.'

'I'm—'

'Don't even say it,' interrupted Dane. 'You're still not well enough to drive that distance. Leave it to me. When I find Matthew we might just need a little man-to-man to get to the bottom of what this has all been about.'

Man to man, thought Ali. *What about husband to wife?*

'Okay,' she said finally, 'but I want to be kept updated, and if you find him, hang on to him until I get there.'

'Promise,' said Dane. She could hear Liz's voice in the background. Was he in the bathroom, the garage? 'Gotta go.' And then the phone went dead.

15

She was standing naked on a rocky tor. Around her slivers of granite jutted out from the earth like shards of broken glass. Moonlight crept out from behind clouds, bathing the landscape in inky light. She was walking fast, almost running, her back and bad leg perfect, unaffected. Ahead she could see a soft spiral of grey smoke. She raced towards it, her body strong and agile. Thick grey mist enveloped her. As she stumbled past creeping rushes, she found herself sinking to her waist in cold, boggy earth. 'Matthew,' she called, 'are you here?' Next to her the water churned and bubbled. Something was making its way up from the muddy depths towards her . . .

Ali woke with an agonising inhalation, as if a gross intake of fresh air could somehow erase the oneiric image, of her silent scream as Matthew's decaying, putrid body floated to the surface, of empty eye sockets, and silver elvers slipping in and out of his fleshless face.

'God almighty.' It had been over a week since her last nightmare, and none had been as horrific as that. Maybe it was the painkillers she had taken before bed that had caused such terrible night-time hallucinations. She glanced at her bedside clock: 3.15 a.m. She doubted she would get back to sleep tonight. She was just considering getting up to make herself a cup of tea when she heard a soft jangling sound float in through her open window, then a more aggressive clank. Was someone trying to get in through the side gate? Had Emma decided to come home instead of staying over at her friend's house? A gust of wind blew fiercely, causing the branches of the wisteria to tap against the window in a strange, unsyncopated rhythm.

She strained to hear the sound of footsteps on gravel, or the gentle grating sound of a key turning.

'Emma?' She tried to call, but her voice was insignificant, strangled. 'Is that you?' A sudden burst of rain splattered against her bedroom window, drowning out any other identifiable sounds. A moment later the rain eased, and the night resumed its silence. There was the creak of old wood, this time inside not out, and Ali felt herself paralysed with fear. She reached past her bedside table to where her crutches lay leaning against the wall. Her fingers slipped and her sticks went crashing to the floor, the thud of aluminium on wood reverberated throughout the ground-floor rooms. Another creak of the floorboards. The first step on the staircase.

She forced herself to sound brave, challenging. 'Emma, is that you!' There seemed a moment of absolute silence, of stillness so complete it was as if sound had never existed. Then footsteps coming closer. She sat up. A figure – tall, broad-shouldered, featureless – filled the doorframe. The tarry scent of leather filled the room.

'Who's there?' Her fingers fumbled for the light switch, but she was awkward, too slow. 'Matthew,' she called into the silence, 'is that you?' Another gust of wind rattled the blinds momentarily calling her attention. When she peered through the darkness back to the doorway, the figure was gone.

She forced herself to her feet, her leg protesting in agony, and limped her way down the corridor to the kitchen. She felt a rush of cold air at her feet. The French doors were wide open. The curtains fluttering in the breeze, made a loud flapping noise like sails in a storm. She scanned the darkened room in terror, then in a moment of resolve shuffled her way to the kitchen island and grabbed a six-inch blade from the knife block.

'This is my house!' she screamed, but the only response was silence.

'It looks like nothing's been disturbed,' said the young PC, taking a gulp of tea. They were sitting at the kitchen table, the pink notes of dawn just beginning to brighten the horizon. 'No footprints outside either.'

'There's gravel in the front and a patio in the back,' said Ali. 'I should think it would be doubtful there would be any footprints, don't you?'

The repeated narrative from the two young PCs: *Are you sure you didn't just leave the doors open when you went to bed? Easy enough done, you know,'* had left her feeling both angry and frustrated, and then them repeatedly asking, *'Are you sure nothing's missing? Would you like to look again?'* suggesting that unless something had been taken then no break-in had occurred.

'We'll make a full report of course,' the ginger-haired PC declared, a tattoo of a dragon snaking around his bicep, 'but there's not much to go on, particularly if the door hasn't been forced.'

They had explained in much detail how a forced entry offered an enormous insight into the perpetrator. *'Modus,'* said the darker-haired PC, who was evidently struggling to grow a decent beard. 'Tools, that sorta fing. Pop that in the database, and voilà, we'll get at least a half a dozen perps.' Ali had tried to follow his verbal shorthand as well as his dubious enunciations, but had quickly given up. 'Best fing you can do is to have a nice little double check before you go to bed. Make sure all the doors are locked securely.'

'I didn't imagine it.'

'Those painkillers can cause some pretty trippy dreams.' Ginger had obviously spotted the Sevredol on the bedside table when he went to check her room. 'I had some when I put my back out. Used to dream there were aliens trying to come in through the bathroom window.'

'They kill the pain, not my common sense,' replied Ali, tersely. Finally, seeing she was getting nowhere, she decided to send the police on their way.

Yes, a report would be filed, and yes, they would contact her FLO to tell her what had happened. *'But remember, love, a good double check before bed, got it?'*

How was it that these young men could make her feel so old? Is that how she now appeared?

She showered, dressed, checked her meds schedule, and took a painkiller. Then slowly, methodically, made her way around the house. She started with the garden. There were no footprints or toppled plant pots, no bent-back or broken twigs, suggesting someone had run haphazardly through the garden in the middle of the night. The police officers were right when they said the French doors hadn't been forced. Aside from some bird droppings on one of the panes they seem to be as good as new.

She made her way back inside, scrutinising the ochre-coloured floorboards for any marks, scuffs, or dirty residue, and inwardly commended herself for watching all those forensic investigation documentaries on the BBC. She checked the artwork and first editions on the bookshelves, and the Welsh dresser where she found her grandmother's silver still pristine and untouched. She was feeling stiff and sore after being up most of the night, but knew there were still one or two more places she had to search. She considered the staircase. The thought of struggling her way up those slippery steps made her heart sink, but one of Dr Bhogadi's proclamations unexpectedly came to mind. *'Mobility is the cure.'* He had said it to her often enough. *'Keep that beautiful musculoskeletal machine of yours moving, Ali, and all will be well.'*

She checked Emma's bedroom first, still thinking that her daughter might have snuck into the house last night and was sleeping peacefully, but the police constable had checked all the upstairs rooms and found them empty.

Next door, the small office was immaculate, the air still, the cashbox empty. She entered the master bedroom. A quick glance around indicated everything was as it should be, but something felt odd, different. She went through the wardrobe

184

and checked the small built-in safe where she kept her expensive jewellery and passport. Then she went around to the side of the bed to where the remnants of Matthew's torn-up business cards still lay scattered across the floor from a few days before.

Her attention was caught by the light's reflection on a large scrap of card. She leaned over to take a closer look and felt her stomach clench. Placing her hand on the bed for support, and with agonising slowness, she bent over and picked it up. Impressed on the pristine white card was the tread mark of a shoe, the pointed arch of its toe.

Ali eased herself down on the bed, then almost immediately forced herself up again. Had someone been in this room last night and left a shoeprint on that piece of card? It *was* a shoeprint, wasn't it? Her gaze fell to the bedside table, to the drawer that lay open. She glanced back to where she had just been seated, the soft indentation of her buttocks on the duvet. Had Matthew sat there last night, going through his things, searching for something? What on earth could he have been looking for? Money, credit cards, his season ticket? Most of those she had gathered up and thrown in the back of the linen cupboard along with the rest of the items in the drawer.

She hurried out the room returning seconds later

with the shopping bag of Matthew's things which she emptied onto the bed. Pocket squares now wrinkled, Chiefs ticket, moisturiser, cologne – tick, tick, tick went her mental list. In increasing frustration, she began throwing the items aside. Sunglass case, nail clippers. 'What the hell were you after, Matthew?' Her fingertips brushed across silk, and she remembered the sleep mask with its secreted key. She grabbed the soft case, shaking out its contents. The Kernow keyring sat on the pillowcase in front of her.

'Is this what you were looking for?' she whispered in amazement. 'This shitty little thing?'

She spent the rest of the day worrying about the key. Was it connected to Matthew going missing, his secret trading, or something else? A flat for a mistress, or series of mistresses, a garage full of stolen goods? Her speculations became more and more absurd as the day wore on, and she found herself becoming increasingly doubtful. Had last night really happened, or as one of the police officers suggested, had her bewildered brain simply created it? She had been so certain of that figure in the doorway, but now, with sunlight streaming through the kitchen window, and the sound of birdsong in the meadow, it seemed more like hallucination than truth.

'Am I losing my mind?' she whispered.

The ping of a text pulled her from her dark ruminations. It was from Liz.

Emma asked me to check on you this weekend, but Dane and I thought it would be much more fun if we just show up at yours with a home-made curry! See you at seven?

Ali replied with two thumbs up, grateful not to have to spend any more time alone at Hope Farm than necessary. Forcing calm, she changed into a favourite floral dress, and put some more prosecco in the wine fridge as well a couple of reds for Dane. Maybe what she needed was to get pissed and forget about things for a bit.

She was just making a jug of Pimm's when she heard a key slipping into the lock, then the thwack of the door being held back by the safety chain. For a moment her heart jolted.

'Ali?' It was Liz's voice. 'Are you there?'

Ali approached the front door and could see two familiar silhouettes through the frosted glass.

Ali undid the chain and opened the door.

'Why the chain?' said Liz. 'No one will be able to get in if there's an emergency.'

Ali tried to laugh off her friend's concern. 'Just old habits – nothing to worry about.'

She had considered telling Liz the moment she walked in about the break-in, but something about the way those two young PCs had spoken to her, dismissing her as helpless, misguided, drug-addled, had made her reluctant to tell anyone. She was also completely fed up with coming across as needing constant supervision and guidance. The leg was healing, and her determination to find Matthew had imbued her with a new energy and sense of determination. She was perfectly capable of handling things on her own.

'If you say so,' said Liz,' She held up a stack of Tupperware. 'I'll go warm this up. I've made all your favourites.'

'You're an angel,' said Ali, calling after Liz as she made her way towards the kitchen.

'Dane,' said Ali, waiting until she heard the hum of the microwave. 'I think Matthew was here, last night.' She hurriedly told him about the mysterious intruder. 'The police think I was imagining it, but I know it was real.'

'I knew it,' said Dane, peering down the hallway. 'We need to talk, but not now. I think I may have a lead.'

'A lead – what lead?'

'Dane,' called Liz from the kitchen, 'pour us all a drink will you?'

'Later,' he whispered, leaning so close to Ali that she could feel the warmth of his lips on her cheek.

*　　*　　*

188

They sat at the dining room table sipping their drinks and nibbling on poppadoms while their dinners warmed. Ali found herself fidgeting with curiosity and anticipation. What had Dane discovered? Had he located Matthew, spoken to him? She longed to find a private space to speak, but with Liz around it was too risky.

'No Emma tonight?' asked Dane, topping up her glass of prosecco.

'She's at a friend's for the weekend.'

'Boyfriend?'

'Just an old roommate from uni,' said Ali. 'No romance on the horizon for Emma at the moment.'

'Give it time,' said Liz, always one to jump to her goddaughter's defence. 'Emma's a beautiful young woman. She'll find the right person soon enough.'

'Of course,' agreed Ali.

The smell of biryani and taka dahl drifted from the kitchen to where they were sitting. Ali was grateful for an opportunity to change the subject. 'Let's eat. I'm bloody starving.'

The night had grown cool, not yet the hint of summer in the air. Dane lit the cast-iron fire pit, and the three of them sat in the garden watching the flames flick and shimmer in the darkness.

'Do you remember that time Matty tombstoned into the sound?' Dane was starting on his second bottle of red and seemed to be growing sentimental. 'Stripped off to his shreddies and dived right in.'

'It was lucky he wasn't killed,' said Liz, laughing, 'or arrested.'

Ali, who had been slowly working her way through a bottle of prosecco, was still sober enough to wonder how being arrested could be worse than being killed.

'Didn't give a monkey's,' came Dane's voice from somewhere in the darkness.

Ali strained to see where his voice was coming from, and spotted the glow of a cigarette in the far end of the garden. 'Just liked the craic.'

'He did like a bit of fun, didn't he?' said Ali. 'Do you remember that time in Paris—'

'Don't remind me,' said Liz, now completely overcome with the giggles. 'I thought there was going to be a diplomatic incident. How on earth he got that cat through the letterbox . . .' Liz's shoulders trembled as she recalled the weekend in Paris the four of them had once spent together.

They were all laughing so raucously that they didn't hear the crunch of footsteps on gravel.

'Sounds like a right ole shindig out here.'

Emma was standing by the back gate, her overnight bag slung across her shoulder.

'Emma,' said Ali. She considered trying to get up to greet her daughter, but glancing at the half-empty bottle of prosecco, decided against it. 'I thought you weren't back until tomorrow.'

'Grace wasn't very well so I left a bit early. I didn't realise I'd come home to a bacchanalian bash though.'

'Just a bit of joyful reminiscing,' said Liz, getting up and giving Emma a hug. 'Why don't I fetch you a glass?' She shot a quick glance at Ali. 'I think your mum could do with a bit of help getting through that bottle.'

'Sounds good to me,' said Emma, and dropped into a garden seat next to her mother with a terrific sigh.

'Ems,' came a voice from the darkness, 'how great to see you.'

'Dane,' said Emma, her voice strained. 'You scared the life out of me. Hiding in the shadows again?'

'I do normally accompany my wife on dinner dates you know.' Dane approached Emma and leaned forward to kiss her, but she pulled away. 'How've you been, sunshine?'

'Fine.'

'Good, that's good.'

'Yes, all good.'

Ali watched the exchange in confusion. These weren't two strangers meeting for the first time, or exchanging some casual chit-chat at the school gates, this was Dane and Emma. They had known each other for years. What on earth was going on? Had they fallen out over something, or was this sort of tension now going to be a normal part of her existence?

'Here we go!' said Liz, returning with a champagne flute. She handed Dane the glass. 'Why don't you pour Emma a drink?'

'You're all right,' said Emma, putting a hand up in polite refusal. 'I think I'll just go to bed. I had enough to drink last night anyway.'

'Are you sure, honey?' said Ali. She had been looking forward to the four of them having a few more glasses together.

'Actually,' said Liz, plainly affected by the uneasy mood as well, 'I think we should probably be getting home ourselves.'

'But there's coffee and macaroons,' said Ali. The mood in the garden had seemed to shift. Antagonism hummed around them like fireflies, materialising one moment and fading the next. Ali couldn't help feeling like a disappointed child. She hadn't had anyone over since before the accident and was now trying to gobble up every bit of interaction and intimacy.

Dane let out a small burp. 'Whatever you say, love. I've had enough to drink anyway, and I've got a job on tomorrow.'

'You didn't tell me that,' snapped Liz.

'It's just a cash-in-hand thing for a mate.'

The cash-in-hand comment immediately made Ali think of the missing money in the strong box upstairs. She heard Liz's soft tut in the darkness.

'You should be concentrating on building your business, Dane, legitimate jobs, not cash-in-hand rubbish. That's how you build a reputation. Ask Ali.'

At some point during the *discussion*, Emma had slipped away. Ali now wished she could join her. Still struggling with the disappointment of what she'd hoped would have been a fun, relaxing evening, she tried her best to appease her friends.

'Maybe Liz is right,' she said, trying her best to defuse the situation. 'It's late and we should probably call it a night. Dane knows he can talk to me about business anytime, don't you?'

Dane stood by the fire, his face was bathed in crimson light, the shadows on his cheeks and forehead making him look oddly sinister. However, it was his eyes that disturbed Ali the most. He was staring at her with absolute hatred. The flames lifted, and his normal easy-going expression resumed.

Had Ali imagined it all?

16

Ali spent most of Sunday determinedly avoiding Graham's phone calls and texts.

Have you thought about what we discussed? I'm in Exeter again this week so could drive over after lunch one day and we could look at sorting out an independent auditor.

Yes, she had promised him she would consider how best to deal with the stolen money, but a sense of overwhelming lethargy had seemed to consume her since discovering Matthew's old business cards. The realisation that he may still have been engaged in risky trading even after he had promised to stop was just one more assault to her already fragile psyche. There had been hints, obvious now: his sudden secrecy about his business accounts; that time just before Christmas when her laptop was updating, and she had asked Matthew if she could borrow his. He had closed the lid of his Mac with such finality that she had been afraid to ask him again. Then there was the time she noticed him using an old mobile phone. *'I was just looking for some contacts I forgot to save on my SIM.'* Her thoughts had gone straight to the supposition that he had been having an affair. The older-woman, younger-man scenario was a narrative she couldn't quite free herself from, and one that she occasionally let slip into their arguments. His responses were both dismissive and defensive. *'Jesus, Ali, stop being so paranoid. I married you, didn't I?'* She just wished he had made them sound more like reassurance than regret.

As she got ready for bed that evening, she brushed her teeth, carefully washed her face, and applied Bio Oil to her scar. She studied her reflection in the mirror. She knew there were things she *should* do: let Liz know about the missing funds, call the bank, possibly the police, but that would mean exposing to everyone that her husband had stolen from her and lied to her. Humiliation swept through like a fever, and she couldn't help imagining a definite sense of schadenfreude pervading the minds of some of her less supportive business associates. *How the mighty . . .?*

It was increasingly beginning to feel as if the past was quicksand, pulling her in, and she was helpless or unwilling to resist. Rory's voice positive, energetic, undefeatable, pushed its way through her ruminations. *'Fake it till you make it, babes!'*

'Fake it till you make it,' she whispered, knowing full well she would do neither.

Monday morning, she greeted Emma with a cup of tea and a pasted-on smile, confirming a visit to the physio, and then lunch with a few old friends from the chamber of commerce. Yes, she was booking a taxi, and yes, she would promise not to overdo it. That was an understatement as she had absolutely no intention of leaving the house. This subterfuge had required some thought, including planning later that afternoon to leave her workout clothes in the laundry room and to dust her new low-heeled boots with gravel dust from the front drive.

'I guess Matthew was not the only consummate liar in this family,' she said to herself.

By the time Emma arrived home Ali already was in bed, in fact hadn't really left the bed all day, besides to get a few crackers and a swift gin from the kitchen at teatime. She listened to the sounds of her daughter moving around the kitchen and longed for the days before the accident, before Matthew, when she would throw aside work, and she and Emma would snuggle down in front of the telly with a glass of wine and a bowl of microwave popcorn. How long had it been since they did that? Three years? Four? The thought of it made her heart ache. She contemplated getting out of bed, washing her face, and joining Emma at the dining room table. But like almost everything in her life these days, fear seemed to drive her back, secluding and isolating her, keeping her prisoner.

'Tomorrow,' she muttered, and reaching for her painkillers and glass of water, gulped a couple down before switching off the bedside light and falling into an uneasy sleep.

She woke to the sound of Emma's car pulling away. The morning was bright and clear, the smell of honeysuckle drifting in through an open window. Ali lay in the sun-soaked bed, relishing the warm rays on her face. Last night she dreamt of the early days at Hope Farm with Rory, how they had lived hand to mouth and just one step away from disaster. There were hard times, and heartache, but her abiding memories were ones of laughter and love. That was all she ever really wanted. She studied the wedding band on her finger for a moment, then, slipping it off, squinted to read the faded inscription.

Rory & Ali Forever

'Not quite forever was it, Rors,' she sighed. Forcing herself from the bed, she did her physio exercises, showered, and made herself have a healthy breakfast.

She was just settling herself down at the dining room table to send some emails, when she heard her mobile go off, the caller ID displaying the letters FLO.

'Hi, Ruth.' Ali gripped the phone. 'Is everything all right?'

'Ali,' said Ruth, her voice serious. 'I need you to come down to the police station. To Torquay. Today. Can you do that?'

'What? What's happened? Is it about Matthew?'

'I'd rather not talk to you about it over the phone,' said Ruth. The was a pause and then Ruth's voice softened. 'Can you come by about one?'

'Yes of course,' she replied, wondering how on earth she would get there.

'Oh, and Ali?'

'Yes?'

'Bring someone with you?'

There was only one person to call, and when Graham didn't answer she left a tearful message on his voicemail.

'Hi, Graham. I know you're cross at me for not doing anything about the missing money, and I know I haven't replied to your text messages . . .' The tears she had been holding back since speaking to Ruth now seemed to colour every word. *'But*

something's happened and I need you.' Unable to speak further she ended the call. Within minutes her mobile buzzed.

'Ali? What's happened?'

'Ruth called. She's asked me to come to Torquay police station this afternoon at one. She wouldn't say what it was about, but it must have something to do with—'

Graham's reply cut through her growing panic. 'I'm on my way.'

The drive to Torquay seemed to take a lifetime. Graham had arrived from Exeter within an hour as promised and insisted on driving.

'Doesn't seem much like an accountant's car,' she said with false brightness, as she eased herself into the bucket seat of the Porsche.

'Ah, but it *is* a middle-aged accountant's car.' His tone was light-hearted, but she could see the worry on his face.

They made it to South Street in less than half an hour. Graham pulled up to a red brick building that seemed more like an old-fashioned schoolhouse than a police station.

'Better let you off here,' he said. 'Parking round here is atrocious, and it may be a bit of a walk.' He flicked on his hazard lights and came around to help her from the car. 'Why don't you wait inside? I'll be as quick as I can.'

The journey in the cramped sports car had taken its toll, meaning that Ali had to take the ramp up to the entrance. She was surprised to see Ruth waiting for her in the foyer.

'Thanks for coming.' She indicated to the officer behind the glass-enclosed reception desk to unlock the door into the main offices.

'I was going to wait for my brother,' said Ali. 'He's just parking his car.'

'He can join us as soon as he arrives.' Ruth led Ali down a long corridor, before stopping at a nondescript door. 'Here we are.' She inputted a keycode and pushed open the door to an interview room. Ali felt her legs begin to wobble and gripped her walking stick.

'Can I wait for my brother, please?'

'Of course,' said Ruth. She pointed to a table on which sat a laptop facing a single chair, and next to that a file folder. Opposite that were two chairs, one pulled out ready for her. 'Have a seat. Would you like a cup of tea, coffee, water?'

'No, thank you,' said Ali, too nervous to even contemplate swallowing anything. 'I'll get you both a glass of water just in case,' said Ruth and disappeared. Ali gazed around the small room with increasing anxiety. Why was Ruth being so mysterious? Why didn't she just tell her what was going on? She heard voices outside and was relieved to see Graham being led into the room.

'Everything okay?' he asked.

'I don't know what's going on,' she said, her voice weak. She pointed to the laptop on the table, the same make as Matthew's. 'Do you think that's his?'

'Here we are,' said Ruth, returning. She placed two plastic cups on the table. 'You must be Graham,' she said reaching out her hand. Graham shook her hand, and then sat down, looking as confused as Ali.

'Thank you both for coming.' There seemed to be an air of uneasy excitement in Ruth's disposition.

'What's going on?' said Ali, her anxiety now transformed into impatience. 'Why all the mystery?'

Ruth cleared her throat. 'As you know, Ali, I discussed with you how we would be tracking Matthew's credit cards via our economic crime unit?'

'Yes.'

'We've had a hit.'

'A hit?' said Ali and Graham in unison.

'We've had a notification that Matthew's Barclaycard was used to withdraw three hundred pounds from a cash machine in Crediton.'

For a moment Ali couldn't speak.

'You what?' said Graham.

'Matthew's card was used yesterday to withdraw three hundred pounds from his bank account.'

Only moments before Ali's face had been filled with shock and confusion. Now it glowed with optimism. 'Does that mean that he's still—'

Graham placed his hand on hers. 'Ali.'

'But if his card was used?'

'It doesn't necessarily mean by him,' said Graham.

'Graham's right,' said Ruth. 'Just because his card was used it doesn't mean—'

'But a bank machine in Crediton. That links up with all the recent Facebook sightings.' Both Ruth and Graham remained silent, allowing Ali to articulate her hope. 'And you said it was his Barclaycard, right? Whoever used it would have to have known the PIN.'

Graham looked at her squarely. 'It could have been cloned long before he went missing, Als. Criminals do it all the time. Steal the details and then wait a few months so that the fraud isn't immediately traced back to that online purchase or that shop.'

'But Crediton is less than an hour away.' Ruth's expression suggested that Ali may have let her expectations get out of hand. 'I mean maybe he had a memory loss or a breakdown of some sort,' she went on desperately. Here she was again, grasping at those straws. 'Maybe he had money problems nobody knew anything about.'

Graham shot her a look and Ali realised that she had gone too far. Ruth, however, zeroed in like a bloodhound.

'Were there any money troubles that you were aware of?'

'Not that I was aware of,' Ali lied. 'It's just that I've seen these kinds of stories on telly. The person gets into trouble, has some sort of breakdown, and feeling unable to cope decides to just *disappear*.'

'That's fiction, Ali.' Graham's voice a warning. 'Cheap crime drama, not real life.'

'But then how did someone get his bank card?'

'As your brother said . . .' Ruth was in police mode now '. . . it could have been cloned months before. There may even be the possibility that someone found his wallet after the accident.'

'But how would they have known the PIN code!' Ali could feel herself getting more and more exasperated at the two sceptics in the room.

'I'd like you both to have a look at this.' Ruth slid the laptop towards them. On the screen was a grainy black and white image. It was of a male figure dressed in dark trousers and a jacket; his head covered. 'It's not the best image I'm afraid, as the cameras nearest the cash machine were out of order and this is from the pub across the street.' She slid the laptop across the table closer to Ali. 'Do you think this could be Matthew?'

It took a moment for Ali to take in what Ruth had just asked her. Did the FLO really believe that the person in the CCTV footage might be her missing husband, that he was still alive? She studied the image closely. It was blurred and foggy, the figure viewable only from behind. He certainly was built like Matthew, and around the same height. If only she could see his face.

'Is that a leather jacket he's wearing over his hoodie?'

Graham, however, was having none of it. 'You can't seriously think that Matthew is still alive?'

'Just something we need to remove from our line of inquiry,' replied Ruth.

'And her,' Graham pointed to his sister. 'Is it really fair to make her think that?'

'I am still here you know,' said Ali, her attention fixed on the laptop. 'It certainly looks like him.'

'We are trying to locate additional CCTV footage,' said Ruth, 'to see if we can get a clearer image of the person's face.'

Ali slid the laptop back towards the FLO. 'What do you think?'

Ruth let out a heavy sigh. 'I've seen stranger things.'

'Do you think he might still be there?' said Ali, trying to contain her excitement.

Graham tutted. 'He was never there in the first place, Ali, and if by some extraordinary chance it was Matthew, and he didn't want to be traced, don't you think he'd be long gone by now?'

It wasn't the first time Ali was frustrated by Graham's highly developed sense of logic.

'The reason I asked you here,' said Ruth, interrupting their sibling dispute, 'is to look at this footage. Could you please have another really good look, think back to that night.' Ruth had picked up a pen and was holding it between her fingers. 'Did he say anything to you at all that might suggest he was worried, anxious, unstable?' She had a notepad in front of her but hadn't written anything on it yet. 'And has anything odd or unusual happened since?'

Ali immediately thought of the break-in, how someone had gotten into her house without any sign of forced entry, and that they only seemed interested in what had been in Matthew's bedside table. And where was the missing back door key? Asking these questions now didn't seem like such a good idea as it would only alert Ruth that she knew more than she was telling. Ruth was no fool though.

'There was a suspected break-in at Hope Farm on Friday night,' she said opening the file folder. 'Is that correct?'

'What?' said Graham. 'You never told me that.'

'False alarm,' replied Ali casually. She knew she should report the footprint on the torn business cards, and the fact that she and Dane were investigating local sightings, but she hesitated. If Matthew was going to be found she wanted it to be by her, not the police. She realised this was one more secret, one more lie. It now felt like she was drowning in them, but was also beginning to suspect that her missing husband had far more of his own.

She waited until she and Graham were in the car and on the road back to Totnes before speaking.

'Do you really think it's possible, that it might have been—'

'Don't even say it,' replied Graham tersely.

'But the missing money for the student renovations, and now this mystery person at the cash machine.' She tried to keep the hope from her voice. 'Matthew was obviously not himself at the time of the accident.'

Graham glanced her way before returning his attention to the road. 'Oh, I think he was himself all right.'

'What do you mean by that?' She could see her brother's lips tighten and then was forced to grab the armrest when he abruptly pulled into a lay-by. 'What on earth are you doing!'

Graham stopped the car and turned off the ignition.

'The thing is, Ali . . .' It was clear he was trying to contain his frustration. 'After I found out about the JDS thing, I decided to look into Matthew's finances a little further.'

'You what?'

'I know you asked me not to, but I've seen scenarios like this before.'

'You went behind my back,' said Ali, her uneasiness shifting to interest.

'He was in deep shit.' Graham sucked in a lungful of air. 'Overdrawn on his personal bank account, two credit cards maxed to the limit. There are also some serious questions about him misleading investors in his trading business he ran before you were married.'

Ali felt a mixture of dismay and unexpected excitement. 'So if what you're saying is true then he could very well have decided to go missing.'

'For fuck's sake, Ali!' Graham thumped the steering wheel. 'The truth is your wonderful, loving, successful husband was nothing more than a con man.'

Ali stared out of the car window at the lush green countryside. Somewhere in a field below a farmer was ploughing. A small spiral of dust swirled towards the sky.

'I knew about the debt.'

'You what?' Graham appeared ready to explode.

'We were sorting it out.' Ali was almost inaudible. 'I know I said I would leave him if he ever traded again, but I . . .' She couldn't bear to add *I was afraid I wouldn't be able to cope without him.*

'Oh, Ali.'

'That was what the new seaside holiday lets were for. We were going to use the rental profits to pay it off. He was going to work for it.' She decided that maybe now was not the moment to mention the forty grand that Matthew had also invested in the Salcombe property.

'Why the hell didn't you tell me this?'

Ali continued staring out the window. 'Because I knew you'd react this way.'

'Of course I'd react this way. You had me racing around trying to locate a measly twelve grand when you knew your husband was in debt for five times that.'

'I'm sorry, Graham. I just wanted to give him a chance.'

'And how did that go?' Graham was nearly apoplectic. 'He was lying to you, Ali. Stealing from you!'

Ali opened her mouth to protest, but there was no avoiding the next question. 'And this business with him misleading clients?'

'It's rumours more than anything else,' said Graham, calming down slightly, 'but serious ones. There's a very strong suggestion that he was going to be investigated by the NFIB.'

'The what?'

'The National Fraud Intelligence Bureau.'

'*No*,' said Ali feeling her heartbeat hiccup.

'They had a crime reviewer looking into it.'

'How do you know all this?'

'How do you think? I bloody work with these people!'

There was no point in arguing with Graham. Not only was he an expert in his field, but he also had contacts within the police fraud squad and the Financial Conduct Authority.

'But no criminal investigation?' she asked, hopefully.

'It was only a matter of time,' replied Graham. 'If he hadn't gone missing . . .' Realising he was playing right into Ali's narrative, Graham stopped himself saying anything further, but it was too late.

'So he really could have made himself disappear? He certainly seemed to have enough reason to.'

'Ali, please.'

'I mean if the NFBI or whatever you called it were looking into it, and the Financial Conduct Authority, then maybe . . .' her expression became oddly hopeful. 'That would be the reason why he's afraid to come home now.'

'That's a bit extreme don't you think, considering he didn't survive that crash.'

'BUT THERE'S NO BODY!' screamed Ali.

Graham reached into the glove compartment and handed Ali a small bottle of water.

'I want you to calm down, have a drink, and start trying to think rationally.'

'He was in debt, being investigated—'

'And he'd had too much to drink, lost control of the car, and crashed into the river.' He reached over and took Ali's hand. 'He's dead, Ali. I wish you would just try and accept that.'

'But there are so many unanswered questions.'

'And it may always be that way.'

Ali dipped her finger into the water bottle and tapped it against her forehead.

'How on earth did it get to this?'

'I don't know,' said Graham glumly, 'and you can try and find all the excuses and defend that man all you like, but he couldn't hold a bloody candle to Rory.'

'That's the problem,' Ali replied. 'No one could.'

17

They drove back to Hope Farm in silence, then sat in the garden sipping tea and staring at the spring buds waiting to bloom.

'Just a bit more sun,' said Ali absent-mindedly, 'and they'll be off.'

'What?' Graham too, was lost in his own thoughts.

'The blossoms,' said Ali. 'You can already see the narcissus poking through, then it will be the daffs, tulips, crocuses. Every year they come up in a different order. I anticipate one thing, and something completely different happens.'

The real issue, however, could not be avoided.

'What will you tell Emma?' asked Graham.

'I'm not sure,' Ali replied. 'The truth I suppose, but all of it. Not just how useless Matthew was when it came to money, but how I enabled it.'

'Oh, come on now—'

Ali held up her hand. 'No, Graham, it's true. I think some part of me liked the fact that Matthew was messed up, dependent. It gave me a sense of control, something I haven't felt since Rory died, and something that played into my own insecurities.' Her face was etched in pain. 'That's no way to have a marriage.'

'You're being far too hard on yourself.'

Ali smiled gratefully at her brother's championing. 'What I'm being is honest, Graham. Honest about the fact that I knew about Matthew's trading problem – well, let's call it what it really was: gambling problem – and bailed him out time and time again. That I knew he was playing fast and loose with his responsibility to my company, and I didn't stop him, and that I didn't tell anyone about it – not my daughter, not my best friend and office manager, and not you.' She had been avoiding eye contact but now stared squarely at him. 'Matthew wasn't the only one keeping secrets.'

'Hardly of the same calibre,' said Graham, but seeing his sister's face decided to change his approach. 'If that is the case, then what are you going to do about it?'

Ali took a moment to answer. 'I'll speak to Emma first, then Liz. All of this will have a direct impact on them, then I'll think about calling the bank.'

'And the police?'

'Not for the moment.'

'For goodness' sake, Ali!'

'We can't afford any more bad publicity, Graham. Our current clients, while loyal, are edgy, and the Cornwall project is still in its early stages and needs careful looking after. I also need to check those electrical and gas certifications were done, as well as sorting out the renovations to Eustace Road. This is going to take strategic thinking and discretion.'

'Sounds a bit like the old Ali is back in play,' said Graham.

'I guess so,' said Ali, feeling less than thrilled about the possibility.

'I'm proud of you sis.'

Ali turned away. 'I'm not.'

She waited until Graham left before texting Emma to ask if she would be home for tea. *I have something very important I need to talk to you about.* Then she rang Liz.

'Dartmoor Properties, can I help you?'

'Hi, Liz.'

'Ali!' Liz was her normal effervescent self. 'How are you?'

'I'm fine.'

'You don't sound it,' said Liz gently. 'What's up?'

'I need to speak to you, urgently.'

'*Urgently?*' said Liz, her voice laced with concern. 'What's it about?'

'I'd rather speak in person.'

'Sounds serious. Business I gather?'

'I'm coming into the office tomorrow.' Ali didn't want to give away anything more than she had to until she was closeted somewhere private with Liz, and not until after she had spoken to Emma.

'Oh, ah, I've got tomorrow off. It's my mother's birthday, and Dane and I are taking my parents out to lunch.'

'Of course,' said Ali, who had ordered a bouquet for Liz's mother weeks ago. 'I forgot.'

'Do you need me to cancel?'

How like Liz to consider cancelling a special family event just for Ali.

'No, of course not.' Ali felt a ripple of relief move through her. She wasn't sure she was up to dealing with both Emma and Liz in one day.

'And you're not going to tell me what it's about?'

Ali felt awful for being so ambiguous – Liz was her best friend after all. She could tell her anything, but for now it was essential that as few people as possible knew about Matthew's embezzlement.

'I'll explain it all to you when I see you.'

'If you say so,' Liz's tone was cautious. 'Do you want me to come to the house?'

'I think that would be best. I'll confirm a time with you later.' As much as Ali didn't want to pollute Hope Farm with any further talk of her husband's deception, she was determined to keep the situation private for as long as possible. Part of her discussion with Liz would be about mitigating the impact the fraud might have on a possible audit. 'And please don't mention this to anyone, for the moment anyway. Just say you're popping over for a catch-up.'

'A catch-up?'

'I'm sorry for appearing so mysterious, Liz, but it's important that I discuss this with you in person.'

'Does Emma need to come too?'

'No. I'll be speaking to her tonight.' The truth was she wanted to speak to all the necessary people involved in solving this problem individually before deciding what course of action to take. It was a business technique she had learned from Rory many years before. *'Divide and conquer, babes. Break down a larger problem into smaller, more manageable pieces. You then figure out solutions to those subproblems and combine them to solve your original problem.'* She hadn't paid much attention to it at the time but was glad it had been retained somewhere in her dented brain.

'Should I be worried?'

Ali wasn't quite sure how to respond, so defaulted to banality. 'It will be fine, Liz, I promise.'

Ali made butternut squash risotto and put a bottle of Chablis in the wine fridge. She had a feeling her conversation with Emma this evening might require it. She limped her way upstairs to the master bedroom and, going through her wardrobe, chose a favourite linen dress and pair of flats. She couldn't avoid her reflection in the wardrobe's built-in mirror. She hadn't been able to face the hairdresser's – the thought of staring at her face for two hours was unbearable – but her hair had gone wild in the last few months and needed something doing to it. She grasped the dark strands and twisted them into a chignon, which she positioned loosely at the back of her head, then pulled a few tendrils free, nicely framing her face. Maybe a messy bun would suit her too.

It was hours until Emma would return home. Even though the cleaner had been the day before, Ali still went through the lounge with a duster, and then wiped down all the kitchen countertops. She was just considering lying down for a quick nap when her mobile rang.

'Ms Penrose-Jones?'

'Yes. Who's calling please?'

'It's Tom from The Computer Shack.' Ali's brain whizzed. 'About the Surface Pro.' As hard as she tried, Ali couldn't place what he was talking about.

'The what?'

'The tablet you sent in for repair?'

Somewhere in her hippocampus a memory sparked. 'Of course, the repair.' She gave an embarrassed laugh. 'I'm so sorry I forgot. It's been a few months, hasn't it?'

Tom sounded irritated. 'I left voicemails.'

'Ah yes.' She considered telling him that she hadn't replied to his whiney messages because she was too busy trying to deal with her broken body as well as getting her head around her missing-presumed-dead husband, but that would be churlish. 'A lot going on at the moment. I'm sorry.'

'No need to apologise. I realise things have been difficult for you.' This kindness was so unexpected that Ali found herself choking back tears. 'We've completed the repairs.' He sucked air through his teeth to emphasise his next statement. 'A big job to say the least.'

'And the water damage?'

'We did our best.'

'You're not sounding too optimistic, ah . . .'

'Tom.'

'Yes, Tom.'

'We were able to restore the folders, but it took a pretty bad bashing.'

'Lots of things did that night.'

There was a long pause. 'I'd be happy to drop it by to you this afternoon.'

'That's very kind of you.'

'Well, you know . . .' There was another uncomfortable pause. 'I read about what happened and—'

'What time?' said Ali, not sure she could bear any more compassion.

'I've got a delivery in Littlehempston at three, so I could drop it by afterwards.'

Ali felt her heart soar. She had asked Emma if she could use her new tablet to store the wedding photos that would be displayed as part of a slideshow at their anniversary dinner. After Emma and Matthew had rowed, however, she had gotten a lift with Graham. It was one of the few good things that came out of the tragedy, as Ruth told her that the state the car was in meant it was unlikely that any back-seat passengers would have survived the crash. It also meant that Ali had never been able to return the tablet to Emma. Instead, it had ended up in her shoulder bag wedged under the front seat of the BMW. Emma had assumed the item lost, but Ali, in some small act of appeasement had decided to see if she could get it repaired.

'Mrs Penrose-Jones?'

'That would be great, Tom. Thank you.'

'Anything to help,' he said cheerfully. 'See you about half past three.'

She glanced out of the kitchen window. The rain had shifted, leaving the garden sparkling. A magpie sat on the fence, cocking its head, its beady eyes watching her. Ali knew that the upcoming conversations with Emma and Liz would be difficult, but also an important part of her newly revived commitment to find Matthew and sort out their marriage once and for all. She wasn't sure if she still wanted that marriage, now so weighed down by secrets, but as complex and confusing as it all was, she still had feelings for Matthew, even with the true enormity of his deception staring her in the face.

She pushed away the fury that always seemed to sit so close to the surface and tried to focus on the positives. Emma was safe, she was recovering, business was picking up, and sometime in the next few weeks Matthew would be found. She was sure of it. She reached forward and pulled the window shut, the loud thud sending the magpie fleeing into a nearby laurel bush.

She visited the wardrobe in the bedroom once again, but instead of searching for the leather jacket, reached into her bottom drawer to where she had hidden one of Rory's old jumpers. It was well worn, almost tatty, with sparse patches at the elbows. If she looked closely, she could spot one or two strands of his blond hair. She held it to her face and inhaled deeply, imagining his musky, woodsy scent, and hoping for a faint hint of sandalwood from his aftershave. Exhausted, she lay down on the bed, the jumper nestled in her arms, the soft brush of cashmere on her cheek. Her eyelids flickered and she found herself drifting into a strange half-sleep, dreaming of Matthew, the soft bristles of his beard rubbing against her cheek. Then it shifted, Rory by her side, his lithe, smooth body a contrast to her second husband's bulkier one. It was a trio of apparitions, she being one of them. The buzz of the doorbell summoned her from her ghostly stupor, and she hurried out of the bedroom and down the stairs as fast as her damaged leg would let her.

'Just a minute – I'm coming!' She opened the door and was greeted with a young man, blond, open-faced and smiling.

'One Microsoft Surface Pro,' he said, handing her a package encased in bubble wrap. 'We've repaired the cracked screen and replaced some of the components. As I mentioned on the phone it was in a pretty bad state.' The young man was in his element. 'And it's not necessarily operating at premium efficiency. I would recommend you immediately upload any data you wish to keep, photos, docs, onto a safer storage platform, whatever cloud app you use.'

'I will. That's very helpful.'

'Also,' continued Tom, 'you'll need the original password.'

'That's fine,' said Ali, and once again bamboozled by the intricacies of the human brain, even a damaged one, added, 'I remember it.'

There had been a brief argument over asking Emma to borrow her tablet that night. Ali had wanted something lightweight and portable to use as she walked amongst the guests waxing lyrical about her wonderful, loyal, and hard-working husband. What a crock that turned out to be.

After Tom left, she sat down at the kitchen table and unrolled the tablet from its cushion of bubble wrap. She knew was only her imagination, but she could swear she could detect the musty, algae smell of river water, and something about the device felt tainted, as if it were somehow still connected to the horror of that night.

When Emma was a teenager, they had watched endless horror films together, normally centred around some inanimate object becoming possessed by a demonic force. There were malevolent music boxes, cursed buttons, and of course the requisite evil doll. Ali inwardly chastised herself at her own foolishness. She didn't believe in demons or dark spirits, just the genuine impact an object could have on memories, particularly traumatic ones.

The tablet had certainly seen better days. There were dents and scratches where it had been bashed against the underside of the car seat, as well as other items in her handbag. She ran her hand across the cool smoothness of the new screen, recalling the images she had so proudly displayed to her guests the night of the anniversary dinner: a selfie of her and Matthew's first meeting at the pub, their first holiday together, and innumerable shots of their wedding.

'Lies, lies, lies,' she whispered. Part of her wanted nothing more than to delete every image from existence, but she knew she couldn't. Instead found herself searching through the desktop with the hope of finding some of the more positive memories of that night, of those few brief moments of joy she had managed to capture before her life changed forever.

She found the folder entitled *Best Night Ever!*, named before the start of the event of course, and scrolled through the shots she had taken of her guests arriving at the hotel; Matthew in the new dinner suit she'd bought for him, Liz in a colourful maxi-dress, and Dane in Matthew's old tux. She had also taken at least twenty photos of Emma looking gorgeous in a 1930s style floor length gown with stunning draped cowl back. Despite everything that she had learned over the past few days, she still beamed as she scrolled her way through the photos, stopping at one of her and Matthew arm in arm, standing in front of a large silver balloon with the number three on it. How was it she could still have such strong feelings for someone who had betrayed her so completely?

Fed up and conflicted, she tried to connect to the cloud app to upload the photographs which had been the entire point of getting the tablet fixed in the first place. For some reason she could only link to Emma's iCloud account and not hers, the message, *there is no account associated with this email address or password,* coming up time and time again. Her head began to throb, and her palms itched. She stared at the screen, noting with some interest how the letters swayed and distorted with her increasing frustration and impatience, another after-effect of her injuries. She felt a deep sinking feeling in the pit of her stomach. Once upon a time she could work until midnight and then be up at five to do her peloton session. Now she was lucky if she could make it to lunchtime without needing a nap.

'If I can't upload them then I'll just email them to myself,' she muttered. She right clicked on the folder, then on 'Send to', and 'Compressed (zipped) folder'. Then she renamed it from *Best Night Ever!* to the more mundane *Photos January,* before adding herself as the mail recipient.

Everything was going smoothly until Ali pushed send. There was a blip as if the device seemed to short-circuit and the screen went blank.

'Shit, shit, shit!' Pre-accident, the only time Ali swore or cried was when her tech went wrong. Determined to conquer at least one demon today, she shut down the tablet and then restarted it. A few seconds later the screen glowed into life. She clicked on the mail icon and then the sent folder. Nothing. She tried the outbox, but it was also empty. 'What the hell!' She scrolled down to the trash icon, hoping that maybe she had accidentally pressed delete instead of send.

That's when she saw it. Sitting in the bin folder, but not yet permanently deleted, was an email that Emma had sent from her work to personal email address. Attached was a Word document entitled *JDS*. For a moment Ali couldn't move. With shaking fingers, she opened the document, hoping it wasn't what she thought. Then the bottom fell out of her world.

It was an invoice, *the invoice*. Dated 14th December and exactly as Graham had described to her. Laid out to look exactly like one of JDS Property Management's invoice templates, it detailed maintenance work at the Eustace Road student properties to the tune of eight thousand pounds.

'She knew,' Ali whispered, her voice echoing throughout the empty room. Emma had known – all this time – what Matthew had done.

More sad than angry, Ali forwarded the invoice to her personal email account. This information didn't belong to Emma; it belonged to her and her alone. How was it that her daughter had become embroiled in the dreadfulness of her husband's secrets? Why hadn't Emma said anything to her? Ali studied the scratched and dented tablet, now well and truly haunted.

18

She spent most of the rest of the afternoon pacing anxiously around the lounge, growing more and more uneasy with each chime of the mantel clock. What was Emma thinking, keeping this from her? She must have known how damaging this would be to the company, and to their relationship. If Emma had known about Matthew's embezzlement since before the accident why hadn't she said anything? Had things really gotten so bad between them that she didn't feel she could speak to her mother openly about a very real threat to Dartmoor Properties? Ali heard the soft rumble of the approaching Audi, poured two glasses of wine, and sat down at the kitchen table.

Emma seemed to take an inordinate amount of time getting from the car to the house. Ali readjusted the freshly picked daisies in the vase on the table and waited.

'Mum.' Emma strode into the room and tossed her shoulder bag onto the kitchen island where it slid across the marble countertop, stopping only inches from the edge. 'I got your text. What's with all the mystery?' She tried to sound light-hearted, almost flippant, but there was tension in her voice.

'Sit down, darling.' She pointed to the wine glass opposite. 'Have a drink.'

Emma sat down opposite, and took a sip of wine, then glancing at her mother said, 'Must be serious if you're using the good stuff.'

'There are a few things I need to talk to you about.'

'If it's about you returning to work, I think we've had that discussion.'

Ali's lips tightened in an effort to control her anger. She had hoped this conversation would be productive, civil, but if Emma insisted on acting like a child then she would have to lay things out very clearly from the start.

'I've found some irregularities in the Dartmoor Properties accounts.'

Emma's face went blank. She had reached for her glass then stopped. It was as if everything about her had suddenly grown taut. 'What irregularities?'

'To do with Matthew's record-keeping.' There

was no point in talking around the problem. 'It appears that he had been falsifying invoices.'

'What?' said Emma, doing a poor job of looking surprised.

'The renovation work at Eustace Road?' said Ali, offering Emma an opening.

'We're working on Eustace Road now,' said Emma. 'That's what we hired the apprentice for.'

'There's an invoice for eight thousand pounds for renovation work supposedly completed before Christmas.' The distraught expression on Emma's face filled Ali with both anguish and ire. 'Only the work was never done.'

'I – I don't know what to say.'

'Don't you?' said Ali, growing increasingly frustrated with her daughter's attempt at subterfuge. 'Then there's the rerouted retainer payments to JDS.'

'Retainer payments?'

'Someone changed the monthly retainer payments on the online accounts. Instead of going to JDS Property Services it was rerouted.'

'Rerouted? To where?'

'Graham and I have been looking into it. We've even checked with the company itself. The two-hundred-pound monthly retainer to JDS Property Services was cancelled and the money rerouted to an online bank account.'

'I don't understand,' said Emma. 'It can't be.' In

one swift movement she tried to get up from the table, escape, but she moved too quickly, knocking over her glass. Wine splashed across the surface and trickled over the edge onto Ali's lap. 'Jesus, Mum, I'm sorry!'

'It's fine.' Ali grabbed a napkin and began mopping away at the spillage. Emma's face was ashen. As much as she hated doing so, Ali knew if she was going to get to any kind of truth she would have to challenge Emma. It was time to play her first card. 'I know this all must come as a huge shock.'

'I – I . . .'

And then her second. 'I just wanted to let you know before I go any further.'

'Any further?' Emma's voice strangled with panic. 'What do you mean?'

'To the bank of course, and the police. I need to find out how this happened, who knew about it, and what needs to be done next.'

'But the police?'

Ali pressed the napkin to her damp lap. 'Look, Emma, I know it's important for you to look capable, particularly in regard to your ambitions for the future, but this isn't a late payment or a problem with dodgy builders. This is fraud, a criminal offence. Everything needs to be above board. Everyone needs to be open and honest.'

'I am being honest.'

'Are you?' Emma's expression was almost the same as the one when she was three and had denied flushing a pair of socks down the toilet. 'Do you know anything about these invoices, Emma? Anything at all?'

'No, Mum. Of course not.'

'Think carefully,' said Ali, with a coolness that surprised her, 'because it's my name on the registration documents at Companies House, my reputation, and my livelihood.'

'*Mum.*'

'I know how hard you've been working while I've been out of action.' She tried to catch Emma's gaze, but her daughter kept looking away. 'I can't tell you how much I've appreciated your commitment to keeping the company going, the company your father and I built together through hard work, sacrifice, and love.'

'I told you I don't know anything!'

'Are you absolutely certain?'

'Yes, of course.'

Ali played her third and final card. Reaching into her shoulder bag she removed the tablet and slid it across the table towards her daughter. 'Because that email you sent yourself with the falsified invoice on it tells a completely different story.'

Emma started to gag. Her complexion changed from pale, to bright pink then pale again. Her forehead grew slick with sweat. 'How did you find that?'

Ali's voice was flat, dead. 'How I found it isn't important, Emma; it's the fact it happened in the first place that is so concerning.'

Emma reached for her wine glass, but it was empty. Ali slid hers across the table. Emma grabbed it and took a large gulp while Ali waited patiently. Finally she spoke.

'I was only trying to protect you.'

'Protect me?'

Emma took another gulp. 'Liz asked me to go through the electronic invoices before Christmas in preparation for the upcoming audit. I noticed some anomalies.'

'Anomalies?'

'I searched further and found the fake entry in the Xero account and then the invoice. It was stashed away in a subfolder, obviously hidden there by Matthew.'

Ali ignored Emma's accusation and got straight to the heart of the matter. 'You should have told me.'

'I know, Mum, I know, but it was the night of the staff Christmas party and you had made all these plans. You'd spent so much time and money planning it. How could I ruin it all by telling you your husband was a fraudster?'

Ali spoke slowly, struggling with her self-control. She could condemn Matthew as much as she wanted, but hearing someone else do it was another matter. 'My husband is not a fraudster.'

'Oh come on, Mum. You covered for him your entire marriage.'

She could feel her anger rising, all the fear and resentment she had harboured in the last few help-less months hardening into a small ball of fury.

'And I've covered for you your entire life!' Ali shot back before she could stop herself – her temper spilling over in one unsteady rush. Emma had known something was terribly wrong at Dartmoor Properties and hadn't told her – hadn't told her for months and months. 'You betrayed me. You're no better than him!'

'Thanks a lot, Mum,' said Emma sounding dejected. Ali wanted to reach out, to take back her hurtful words, but couldn't trust herself not to make it even worse. Instead, she could only manage one.

'Why?'

Emma's indifferent shrug made Ali spark again. 'Answer me, Emma, or believe me this is going to end badly!'

'Worse than knowing that your husband was a liar and a criminal?'

Ali pushed back her chair and struggled to her feet. 'Don't you dare!'

'Dare what!' screamed Emma. 'Speak the truth? A truth you refused to ever believe, just like you refuse to believe that Matthew is dead? He was a fraud, and something had to be done about it.'

'What do you mean "something had to be done"?' Ali demanded. 'What did you do, Emma?'

'I didn't do anything,' Emma said at once. 'I was going to—' She broke off, looking away.

It was as if Ali was seeing her daughter for the first time. 'I don't understand why you just wouldn't tell me.'

'You couldn't see the truth about Matthew even before the accident. That much was clear.'

'But it wasn't your place to make those sorts of decisions.' Ali felt distanced, detached. 'Did you really hate him so much that you were willing to sacrifice our relationship to get back at him?'

Emma seemed momentarily struck by her mother's words. 'I was trying to save you, Mum. He needed to be exposed for what he truly was, but I . . .' There was a moment of agonising silence – before the realisation hit Ali like a fist in the chest.

'You were saving it, weren't you? Saving it for later, for the audit.'

'I don't know what you're talking about.'

'Of course you do.' Ali thought about all the office-wide communications she had been party to in the last six months, reminders about deadlines for expenses, reports, estimates, the chasing down of outstanding payments. 'You knew we were bringing in external auditors as part of our expansion plan, that we were looking at a major bank loan to manage the Cornwall project and needed to demonstrate due diligence. You knew how closely our accounts would be scrutinised, and you were deliberately keeping that document hidden until the external auditors came in so that you could drop Matthew in it, weren't you?'

At first it appeared as if Emma would deny her mother's accusation, then her countenance of hurt and injustice shifted. 'He deserved it,' she said, her lips pulled back in fury. 'He was cheating the company and alienating you from everyone who cared about you, who wanted to warn you.'

Ali gripped the edge of the table, the flesh under her fingernails growing pink. 'And you were willing to lie to me for this spiteful act of revenge?'

'Spiteful?' Emma smacked her hand down on the table in fury. 'He was a crook, Mum, a con man pure and simple. He told me all about how you were going to make him a partner. He even gloated about it!'

Ali's mouth fell open. The discussions with Matthew about becoming a partner were rudimentary, confidential. How could he have told Emma?

'We were only discussing it,' said Ali, desperate to reassure both Emma and herself. 'And only about the holiday let side of the business.' Then she said something that put her entire second marriage into context. 'I would never, *ever* have made him a full partner.' She stumbled backwards as if struck, grateful for the large Welsh dresser behind her.

'That says it all,' said Emma triumphantly, 'doesn't it?'

Even though she was shocked at her own realisation, Ali wasn't going to be distracted from the real reason for their argument.

'How long were you going to keep it a secret, Emma? Were you going to wait for the auditors to find the missing money then mysteriously discover the fake invoice, or were you going to discreetly chat to them in the kitchen area or the car park? *"There's something that's been concerning me for a while, but I don't want to worry my mother."* It would have been a scandal of course, difficult for me, particularly to learn that my husband had stolen from me, but you would have been there – strong, supportive, loving.' The imagined scenario was as perverse as it was ridiculous. 'And now with Matthew missing there's no one to contest your version. No wonder you want him dead.'

'I never wanted him dead,' said Emma. 'I just didn't know what else to do!'

Ali looked at her daughter in dismay. 'So you did the worst thing possible.' Emma was cowering back in her chair, her face filled with horror. 'You not only lied and hid important information, but also deliberately misled me. All just to get your own back. Do you know how awful that sounds?'

Emma's face was beyond pale, her lips almost blue.

'I didn't mean to hurt you.'

Ali felt her heart lurch but carried on, her words driven by unbearable anger and pain.

'You've put my company at risk, my livelihood at risk, and the reputation your father and I spent our lives building at risk. That I can handle, I can fix, maybe, but what can never be undone is the complete and absolute betrayal of trust.'

'Mum, *please!*'

Ali rubbed her aching temples. 'I can't think anymore. My head feels like it's ready to crack open.' She reached across the table for her glass and gulped down the last bit of wine. 'I can't talk to you right now. I'm going to my room.' Emma opened her mouth to speak but Ali silenced her with a look. 'Graham will need to know about all this of course, and Liz.'

'No!' cried Emma. 'I don't want anyone else to know.'

Ali was finding it increasingly difficult to contain her rage. 'Do you really think you've got a choice in the matter?'

Emma stepped closer. 'Not Liz,' she begged, 'please, not Liz.'

Ali studied her daughter's face closely. 'What aren't you telling me?'

'Nothing!'

Ali felt her wounded heart sink even further. 'Was Liz in on this too?'

'No,' said Emma shaking her head fiercely. 'She had nothing to do with this, nothing!'

'Then what?'

Emma gave a long, heart-wrenching sigh. Pushing herself from the table, she got up, walked to the sink and got herself a glass of water. Sitting back down, she stared at the table for what seemed like ages, running her fingertips along the knots and grooves on the polished wooden tabletop.

'Do you remember after the Christmas party, Matthew headed home because he had that terrible cold, and you and Liz went on to the pub with the clients while I stayed back to clear up?'

'As I recall you cleared up all the leftover booze as well.'

'I was pissed off that you left me behind.'

'Pissed is the right word,' said Ali. 'But what does that have to do with anything?'

Emma swallowed hard. 'There was someone with me in the office that night. We were both drunk and, well, you know . . .'

'No, I don't.'

Emma blushed. 'We got a bit close.'

Ali scanned her hazy memory of that night, of those people left behind while she and Liz schmoozed the high-end clients in a private room at the pub down the road. There was Richard, a couple of younger developers, both female, and an estate agent.

'So you got *a bit close* with someone as you so aptly put it. Was it Damian, that young gun from Ruscombe and Layne—' and in sudden awareness added '—or was it one of the girls?'

'It was stupid, Mum, I know it was,' said Emma, avoiding the question. She sat staring at her hands for a long moment before continuing. 'But the thing is, there are some images of me from that night.' It was another one of those moments where Ali was expecting the worst. She wasn't wrong. 'With this person.'

'Images?'

'Someone got hold of some CCTV footage.'

Ali's head began to wobble.

'Jesus Christ, it's like something out of a bloody Netflix movie.'

'Except it's real life,' muttered Emma. '*My* life.'

Ali was always good in a crisis, had learned to be so, but this was pushing even her limits.

'The footage,' she said softly. 'Any idea where it came from?' Ali forced herself to stay focused. 'Was it in the car park, back alley?' Emma seemed unable to face her mother's interrogation. 'Please just tell me!'

'It wasn't from one of the outside cameras,' said Emma, 'and it's definitely not from an outside source . . .' Emma focused her attention at a point somewhere on the floor beneath her feet '. . . because we were in your office.'

'Oh, Christ, Emma.' Ali covered her face with her hands. Could this get any worse? 'So the footage of you and this someone, *getting close*, came from the security camera inside my office?'

'The one over the door,' said Emma. 'Whoever got a hold of it sent a text message to me the next day.'

'What do you mean a text message? Why would they do that?'

Emma glanced at her mother then away. 'The message is an image of me having sex, with this person. Someone has doctored it, Photoshop or something, so that there's a gag over my mouth and the words *Keep Quiet* written across the top.'

'That doesn't make sense.'

'Whoever sent it wanted me to stay quiet.'

'Quiet?' Ali's brain was spinning, and she was having trouble sticking to one train of thought. 'Quiet about what?'

'The stolen funds of course!'

'I don't—'

'You know who has access to the internal CCTV footage don't you?'

'Only senior managers,' replied Ali. 'Matthew and me.' She met Emma's pointed gaze, and saw a truth she wasn't willing to acknowledge. '*No,*' she said, her resolve failing her. 'He wouldn't do that; Matthew wouldn't do that!'

Emma grew very quiet. 'They stopped in January.'

'What?'

'The messages, the blackmail, it all stopped in January, right after the accident.'

'What exactly are you saying, Emma?'

'Matthew knew Liz had put me in charge of the internal audit,' said Emma, now directing the conversation, 'which meant he also knew it would only be a matter of time before I found out that he was stealing from the company. That's why he sent me that image, to warn me to keep quiet about the fake invoices.'

'No,' said Ali, 'that's completely absurd, ridiculous!'

'You and Matthew were the only ones with access to the CCTV footage,' continued Emma. 'And I know it wasn't you.' Her voice grew louder and more desperate with each syllable. 'Not only did Matthew have a very good reason to want to intimidate me, but I bet he enjoyed doing it as well!'

Ali reached across the table for Emma's mobile phone. 'Let me see it.' Emma grabbed the mobile from Ali's grasp, digging her fingernails into the back of her mother's hand. 'Please, Emma, let me see it.'

Emma traumatised, exhausted, helpless, relented. Sliding her thumb along the bottom of her iPhone she went to her texts. Once located, she held up the phone to show her mother a grainy black and white image taken from the CCTV footage on a computer. It showed the back of a man, trousers down, bare buttocks exposed. In front of him on the desk was Emma, her legs wrapped around his waist, chin resting on his shoulder, her face visible. The sender had added a white stripe across her mouth and the words *Keep Quiet* written across the top in dark, ominous lettering.

Ali sat back on the edge of the dresser for fear her legs would give out. 'Oh, Emma, how could you?' She felt a sickness deep in the pit of her stomach. The shock of what she had discovered over the last few minutes and hours was sitting heavily, and she was struggling. 'I can get that you had a one-off indiscretion in my office. Thoughtless, stupid, *disrespectful*—' Ali saw Emma flinch at the last word '—but to accuse Matthew of blackmailing you . . .'

'Who else hated me enough to do this?'

Ali wanted to argue, shout out another name, but she couldn't think of one. Considering what she had recently learned about Matthew, Emma's deduction wasn't as far-fetched as it seemed.

The two women stared at each other, each intractable, the distance between them a chasm. Then Emma's demeanour changed from hostile and defensive, to beaten. Her shoulders drooped and her entire body seemed to sink into itself, as if she had just been punched in the stomach. It reminded Ali of finding Liz at that bookies in Camelford.

'Why didn't you come to me with this? We could have looked into it together, and if it *was* Matthew,' said Ali, finally admitting the awful possibility, 'God knows I would have done something about it.'

'There's a good reason I couldn't tell you.' Emma paused to wipe her streaming nose with the back of her hand.

'Yes?'

'The person I was with that night,' she said, her tone pleading, desperate.

'Go on?'

'The person I was with . . . was Dane.'

Ali felt her world begin to spin, and like dominos falling, realised the inevitability of her ruin. 'Dane?' She peered across the kitchen to the fireplace mantel beyond and the tidy line-up of framed photographs. Emma as a baby being cradled in Liz's arms, as toddler being pushed on a swing, in her primary school uniform, at her high school prom. There were photos of Ali and Liz together, hiking in Snowdonia for Liz's thirtieth, their trip to Paris for Ali's hen do, the wedding photo of her, Matthew, Liz, Dane, and Emma. Bright, happy, and full of possibility – they had even managed to get Emma to smile. Now in one great, horrific swoop it was all gone. Her marriage was a sham; her husband a liar, thief, and blackmailer; her most treasured friendships compromised. She studied her daughter's face, now a picture of humiliation and despair.

'It was only that once, Mum. Honest. I was upset about what I had found out about the invoices, about Matthew stealing from you. I got drunk, tearful, emotional. Dane was there for me, a shoulder to cry on. Things got out of hand and we . . .' Emma shut her eyes as if trying to force away the memory. 'We both realised it was a mistake as soon as it happened, and promised to never, ever mention it again.'

'My best friend's husband,' said Ali still trying to get her head around it all. 'Your godmother's husband.' She scraped her fingers through her hair, wondering how on earth things had gotten so corrupt. 'She was there for you when your father died.' A sliver of lost memory, like a blocked artery being eased open, blasted Ali's frontal cortex and flooded her brain. 'That's what he told me that night in the car park.' Her throat was so tight she could barely swallow. 'He knew about what had happened that night.' Ali began to cry. 'He even laughed about it.'

'I'm so sorry.' Emma was crying too. 'I didn't plan for it to happen. It was nothing, meaningless.'

'Nothing? You say it was nothing?' Ali was on the verge of hysteria and struggling to keep control. 'Did you even think about what this would do to Liz?'

'She doesn't know about it and never will. Dane and I promised.'

Ali's voice went very quiet. 'But I do.' Then, in an act of uncontained fury she swept her arm across the table, sending the glasses crashing to the floor. There was a loud smash and slivers of glass flew through the air, momentarily reflecting the evening sun, before falling treacherously to their feet. Emma sat opposite, frozen in fear, a tiny piece of glass embedded in her arm. Ali stepped back, the crunch of broken glass beneath her feet.

'I need to think about what to do next.'

'What do you mean, do next?'

'About the missing money, Matthew's fraud, you withholding the invoices, blackmail. Jesus Christ, Emma,' she said. 'How did this all get so sordid?'

'Mum, please.'

The heavy weight of responsibility grounded her, and Ali grew calm. 'Give me your key.'

'What?'

'Your office key.' Ali held out her hand. 'I'll handle your accounts. God knows what our clients will think, how this will affect the business, but I'll manage. Give me your key.'

'You can't do this,' said Emma, with a determination that was both naïve and assured. 'I have work to do. The Assadorians.'

Ali studied her daughter – now a stranger – in amazement. 'I need some time to figure out what to do next.' And then more gently: 'I also need to protect you.'

'Protect me? From what?' said Emma. 'The black-mail stopped three months ago,' and with little sensitivity added, 'since the night of the accident.'

Ali brushed away her daughter's thoughtlessness and focused on the crisis in hand.

'I need to protect you from any further involvement in Matthew's fraud, from Dane, and assuming the person who sent you that image isn't *missing presumed dead*, a potentially dangerous blackmailer.'

'But—'

'Until then you're suspended from working at Dartmoor Properties, as much for your safety as anything else.'

'You can't do this!'

'I can do whatever I like because it is still my business.' Ali's face was stone-grey and unmoving. 'There's really no going back after what has happened, Emma, and to be honest, I'm struggling with finding a way forward.' She grabbed her crutches for support. It didn't feel as if her skeleton was capable of supporting her any longer. 'The best thing I can do now is to put some space between you and Dartmoor Properties.' Ali started to slowly make her way out of the room. 'Leave that mess,' she said indicating with a crutch to the broken glass scattered across the floor. 'I'll clear it up later, and Emma?'

'Yes, Mum.' Her daughter's voice was tiny, childlike.

Ali knew her daughter's determination to continue working would mean she would have to be uncompromising, even cruel.

'Let me make one thing absolutely clear. If you try and come into Dartmoor Properties tomorrow, I will have you removed from the premises.'

19

She spent most of the night either crying or raging at the possibility of Matthew's further and most hideous betrayal. Something about Emma's story, however, didn't ring true. As much as Ali could get her head around the fact that Matthew had stolen from her, possibly in desperation to cover a hidden debt, she could never really believe he would sink to the depravity of blackmail. She realised, of course, that the theft and blackmail were just two sides of the same coin, but the cruel act of sending Emma that text seemed completely out of character, no matter how corrupt that character had become. Stealing twelve thousand pounds was bad enough, but blackmail took things to a whole other level. That just seemed too far from the man she loved – or used to love.

The sun was just cresting the horizon when she finally stumbled from her bed and to the en suite. She studied her face in the mirror, the thin red scar prominent against the pallor of her skin. She could feel tears forming, but pushed them away. There wasn't time for self-pity, she had work to do.

She got dressed, downed a double espresso, and booked a taxi for the short journey to Dartmoor Properties.

It was still early, the office nearly empty. She had dispensed with her crutches, replacing them with an antique carved walking stick she had fallen in love with during a weekend break in Spain with Matthew, and had never, for a moment, thought she would use. It was harder work than with the two crutches, but she wanted to give everyone the impression that she was ready and able to return to work.

She limped her way past the empty reception desk and into the small main office area, which included standard desks for staff, and at the rear, just in front of the meeting room, a larger one for Liz. That desk seemed to be pristine and clear, as if it hadn't been sat at for months. Ali shifted her gaze to the managing director's office. The desk lamp gave the room a pumpkin glow, and she could see a figure seated at what was once Matthew's desk. Ali gritted her teeth and carried on. Liz heard the gentle thud of the walking stick as Ali approached.

'Ali!' She stood up to give Ali a hug but seeing her friend's puzzled expression paused.

'I thought you were on leave today, taking your parents to lunch.'

'I just popped in to check a few things,' said Liz, 'then I'm off.'

'Right.'

'And you?' said Liz.

'I'm back,' said Ali. 'Permanent and full-time.'

Liz couldn't hide her confusion. 'What? Where's Emma?'

'Emma's having a little break.' Ali's jaw tightened. 'Let's call it extended leave.'

Liz's shocked expression said it all. 'But—'

'I went through the accounts this morning.' Ali was up at four, going through the client notes, emails, payments, and thankfully she hadn't spotted anything to suggest Matthew's fraud had gone beyond the JDS payment, but she knew of course there would need to be further investigation. 'Everything looks pretty much as I left it and ticking over nicely.' She picked up a coffee mug sitting on the corner of her desk that read *Proud Gen Z* and put it back down again. Liz watched her closely, her mouth slightly ajar. Ali was determined not to drag Liz once more into the catastrophe that was her family. She had deleted the false JDS account on the system and the invoice for the renovations had been taken care of. There was still no sign of

251

the two-thousand-pound invoice for the gas and electrical checks though.

The most important thing now was that nothing could be traced back to Emma. The losses would be covered by the car insurance and money Ali had been saving for a cruise with Matthew later that year. It was beginning to look as if the entire thing had never happened, except for Dane and Emma, of course.

'Is she all right?'

Ali felt her heart sink. How could she face her best friend knowing what Emma and Dane had done? How could she not tell her? Emma could make all the excuses she liked, take all the responsibility she felt owing, but Dane was her best friend's husband, had been almost a father figure to her. His actions went beyond infidelity into something immoral.

'She's fine, just a bit overworked. I'm making her take a few weeks off.'

Ali had decided that she would keep the situation with Emma secret for as long as possible. Liz needed protecting as much as anyone else, and the more she said to her, the more risk the situation with Dane would come out. She had emailed Graham that morning asking if he would consider conducting a thorough preliminary audit in preparation for the upcoming more formal one. She had made her proviso clear. *'Whatever you discover will stay in-house. There will be no police or bank officials involved. I will sort this out myself.'* She had also arranged a phone call with Mark from JDS Property Services later that morning.

Liz picked up the phone. 'Should I call her?'

'She's not really in a position to talk to anyone, and certainly not about business.'

'Is it really that bad?' said Liz, clearly very concerned.

'I'm sorry, Liz,' she said. 'I just can't talk about it at the moment.'

'Can't talk about it?' said Liz astounded. 'I'm your best friend, Emma's godmother!'

Ali struggled with an overwhelming desire to tell her friend everything about the stolen money, the invoices, and Emma's skewed attempt to protect her. To ask for her advice, her support, but that would put her in a terribly awkward position. As acting managing director and office manager she had a responsibility to deal with any issues that could threaten the business, fraud being one of them. Telling Liz would be exposing Matthew and Emma's actions, possibly to the entire company, even to their clients. The implications could be far-reaching and damaging, and asking Liz to keep that information a secret was a request too far. Ali didn't want any of her staff, particularly Liz, compromised. This was her responsibility and hers alone. 'Emma is on a much-needed break, Liz. I'll be reassessing her situation in a few weeks, but from today I am returning as managing director, permanently.'

'But you're not ready—'

Ali felt her leg twinge as she stood up a bit straighter. 'I think that's my decision, don't you?'

'I didn't mean—'

'You're just going to have to trust me on this.' For a moment it seemed as if Liz was going to challenge her. 'I'm sorry, Liz. That's the way it's got to be, for now anyway.' There was the sound of movement in the outer office and both Ali and Liz could see Amita arriving. 'I'll tell you everything when I can.'

'And when will that be?'

Ali could see Amita heading their way, a bright smile on her face.

'As soon as I can.' More staff were arriving, and Ali was conscious of her and Liz needing to put on a united front. 'Can you come to the house tonight? Alone?'

'Of course,' said Liz, plainly still bewildered by everything that had just happened. 'Will Emma be there?'

Ali's gaze fell back to her daughter's Gen Z mug. 'I'm not sure.'

Ali sat in the office chair Emma had been using for the past two months, her heart breaking. The close circle of family and friends she had surrounded herself with, that she had worked so hard to create, was disappearing before her. First Rory, Matthew, Emma, and now Liz. Solitude was something she had always cherished. A busy working life meant she rarely had time to herself, but loneliness was what she feared. She reconsidered telling Liz about Emma's situation, but decided against it. It was her responsibility to protect her daughter, a daughter exploited by a man – a supposed friend – she now realised she had never really known. If Ali had to become a sin eater to protect her daughter, she would.

She logged onto her computer and created a team brief for nine a.m. that morning, asking if Liz could stay a little longer to attend. She messaged Darren, telling him to leave whatever site work he was doing to ensure that he and Stevie attended the briefing. Then she telephoned JDS Property Management Services.

'Mark, it's Ali Penrose-Jones.'

'Ali!' he exclaimed. 'How bloody lovely to hear from you.'

'First of all, I want to apologise about what happened with the contract.' There was silence at the other end of the line. 'You've been one of our most trusted partners for years.'

Mark cleared his throat. 'It was all a bit of a mystery to be honest. I tried to speak to you about it after we received the letter, but you know, life got in the way.'

Ali could feel her fingernails digging into her palms. 'I know full well the value of an experienced property maintenance team, particularly for an expanding company.'

'I'm very glad to hear that, Ali. I was planning to chase it up with you after Christmas, but then the accident happened, and well . . .'

'The truth is Emma had some difficulty.' Ali had no intention of discussing the car accident with Mark. 'She's been doing a fantastic job with clients, developing our portfolio, but doesn't really understand the maintenance side of things. In her eagerness to impress me, to make her mark, excuse the pun, she got it wrong.'

'I'm grateful for your honesty, Ali. That explains a lot.'

'I'm back in the office now, full-time and raring to go.' She forced herself to sound cheerful. 'I'm really looking forward to getting stuck in, but it also means clearing up some of my daughter's well-intentioned mistakes.'

'Now that I understand.'

The conversation was like a chess match. Both parties knew where they wanted to end up; it was just a question of who would get there first.

'So if you're up for it,' continued Ali, 'and in respect of our long-term business relationship and friendship, I'd like to reinstate the contract.'

Ali thought she heard the creak of an office chair as Mark leaned back.

'Well now, that's an interesting prospect. Our books are pretty full at the moment, so any new contracts, or renewal of old ones,' he corrected himself, 'will incur some costs.'

Ali rolled her eyes. Her research that morning, including a few phone calls to people in the know, had brought to light the fact that Mark had recently lost a large contract to a national franchise. He needed the business.

'Bottom line, Mark.' Now that she was back in the office she could feel her sense of power returning. She would not be hustled.

'We'd be looking at a fifteen per cent increase at a minimum.'

'Five.'

'Pardon?'

'I'll give you five, plus a courtesy payment of the cancelled six-month retainer fee for your troubles. Take it or leave it.'

There was a long pause. 'Including guaranteeing we'll be managing any further property developments?'

Ali wasn't the only one who had done her research. Mark had obviously heard about the Cornwall project. 'Our contract for large-scale maintenance projects and out-of-hours work will be exclusive to JDS—' she frowned at being reminded of the false account name Matthew had created as part of his deceit '—including any future developments. Smaller work we'll try to keep in-house.'

Her gaze shifted to the outer office where the rest of the staff had arrived. There were worried glances as they each read the email instructing them to attend the team briefing, and hushed conversations with Liz shortly afterwards as they tried to determine what it was all about. *Why didn't Liz know about the retainer payments being stopped? The fake invoices?* Ali scribbled on the notepad in front of her. Then she remembered Matthew's insistence on handling his own paperwork. *You really had it all covered, you bastard, didn't you?*

'I guess we have a deal then.' Mark's soft chuckle focused Ali's attention back to their conversation. 'You drive a hard bargain, Ali, always have.'

'Give me a couple of weeks to get myself back into the swing of things, and then I'll take you out to lunch to celebrate.'

'I'll hold you to that,' said Mark. 'I must say, it's nice to have you back in the driver's seat.'

'It's nice to be back,' she replied brightly, though beneath the bravado, her voice was laced with sadness. 'I may even have one quick job for you right now.'

'Sounds urgent.'

'It could be. I just need to check.'

'Was something missed?' Mark appeared to be excited to be back in the thick of things.

Ali thought to the false invoice for the gas and electrical checks. 'It might have been.'

Ali was just preparing for the meeting when she heard the ping of a text message. She saw the sender's name and felt her stomach turn.

No luck in Bideford yesterday, but off for lunch with Liz and the outlaws, so a bit of a pause for now.

Dane had added a grinning emoji to his message, which only sickened Ali further.

Lack of new sightings suggests he might be lying low for a while. If he's got that money he might even have found some digs in Crediton. I've got a few jobs on the next couple of days so won't be able to get there straight away. Can you keep up the FB posts focusing on that area? See if there are any further sightings?

Ali threw her phone on the desk in revulsion. How could she have ever trusted him?

There was a knock on the clear glass of the office

door, Amita mouthing the words: *'We're waiting for you.'* Picking up her notebook, she straightened her skirt and put on a slick of lip gloss. She was ready.

The team briefing was as awkward as she had expected.

'I wanted to let you all know that Emma is currently on a leave of absence and will be for the foreseeable future.' There were shocked expressions all around. 'She's absolutely fine by the way.'

'She will be back though?' asked Amita, looking teary.

'Of course,' Ali lied. 'She just needs a bit of a break. But *I'm* back now, full-time, and will be picking up all Emma's excellent work and taking it forward. I just want to reassure you that all your jobs are secure. As you're aware we have a few large jobs coming up and I'll be needing all your help and support to ensure those customers know that we're still on track.' She smiled at the worried faces. 'And if all goes well you should be expecting another bonus, a considerable one at the end of the year.' Ali could see the faces light up around the table. It was amazing how easily Emma's situation was forgotten. 'Now let's get back to work.'

Her Apple Watch buzzed to remind her she had a meeting scheduled with Darren.

* * *

'Come in, Darren, sit down.' Ali was sitting at the small meeting table in her office with two cups of coffee in front of her. 'You take yours black, don't you?'

Darren nodded and took the seat opposite. Ali slid a cup his way. He was a large man, over six feet, handsome and broad-shouldered from his years playing rugby, and no nonsense. He had the sort of pale, freckled skin that would burn, never tan, and a shock of thick salt-and-pepper hair that was only ever just contained under a paint-flecked baseball cap.

'Nothing to worry about,' said Ali with forced brightness. 'I just wanted to catch up on a few things.'

'Fire away.'

'Before I start, I wanted to refer to a few company policies.' She deliberately shifted the papers on her desk so that Darren could see she had his HR file. 'The most important being confidentiality.'

'What exactly do you mean by that?' said Darren, living up to his straightforward reputation.

'What is said in here, stays in here.'

'Of course.'

'If it doesn't—'

Darren sat up, his large frame jostling the table and creating tiny swells in their coffee. 'I've worked for you for ten years, Ali. To suggest that I—'

'I know,' interrupted Ali, 'and I'm sorry for even

261

suggesting it, but I imagine you can gather from recent events that there is a need for me to be very cautious at the moment.'

Darren leaned forward, his large hand nearly touching hers. There had been a time not long before she and Matthew met that they might have been a couple. They had flirted good-naturedly during staff meetings, stood just that little bit too close to each other on site visits, and even had a drunken kiss at one of the staff Christmas parties. Everyone in the office was certain they were *going to be a thing*, but then she'd met Matthew – younger, exciting, unpredictable – and the stalwart, dependable Darren faded into obscurity.

'Is this to do with Emma?'

'She's done some amazing work in the last two years.'

'But?'

'I put too much pressure on her, should have kept a closer eye on things.' Her voice wavered and she struggled not to cry. 'Some mistakes were made. Mostly to do with the maintenance side of things.'

'I know,' said Darren softly.

'She told you?'

'She said she'd messed up on some contract stuff and asked me for help with the gas and electrical safety checks.'

'But you're not—'

'I brought a mate in. He's fully certified.'

'When was this?'

'Just after Christmas.'

Ali felt a rush of relief and gratitude to know that the student flats had been properly checked and certified, otherwise it could have left her open to legal actions, insurance penalties, reputational risk, ruin.

'And the payment?'

'He owed me a favour.'

'*Darren.*'

'Friends have got to stick together, haven't they, especially in hard times.'

For a brief moment, Ali wondered if she had got involved with the wrong man. 'I don't want you to worry about the renovations at Eustace Road. I'll be getting Mark back on it.'

'Well, now there's a thing,' said Darren. 'Stevie is showing a lot of potential, and even though I always said this job was just a bit of a side-line, the thought of taking on a bigger project is rather exciting.'

'What are you saying?'

'I'm saying Stevie and I have started the kitchen refit, ordered the windows, and are waiting for a costing on flooring.'

'You want to do it?'

'It would save the company some money, and there would be no need to have to explain anything to the people at JDS.' Darren dropped his voice. 'People say they'll be discreet, but you know, word gets around.'

Once again, Ali struggled to fight back tears.

'Thanks, Darren. I really appreciate everything you're doing for the business.'

'I'm doing it for you, Ali.'

'Jesus, Darren, you're going to make me cry.'

'If there's anything you need, *ever*, you just let me know.'

'I will, and thank you.' She took a file entitled *Eustace Road* from the stack on the desk in front of her. 'I know we've got electronic files of everything,' she said, 'but there's something nice about talking over a piece of paper don't you think?'

Darren leaned back. 'Let me tell you exactly how we're doing.'

By late afternoon Ali was exhausted but pleased with her progress. She had started working on the contract for the Cornwall project and was already planning out the workflow schedule for Darren, Stevie, and JDS Services. Maybe she would even take on another apprentice. She had spoken to Yusef Assadorian and had agreed a provisional date to begin looking for a suitable commercial site for him, and finally after everyone had left, checked the CCTV file footage for any evidence of the recording of Emma and Dane, but as suspected, the digital data had been wiped.

Her leg ached but she resisted taking any painkillers. It was odd, but even in the midst of all her anguish and heartache, things seemed to be looking up. Had it always been this way? Throughout most of her life Ali had learned the hard way to succeed under pressure, and more often than not rose to it. Had Emma's questionable behaviour over the last few months been a response to what she had learned at home? Had she inadvertently trained Emma in the same coping mechanism?

She reached into her shoulder bag for her purse. Tucked into one of the side pockets was a small piece of folded-up paper, one of Rory's Post-its she hadn't delegated to the drawer. He had given it to her after her father had shown up at her project in St Ives with his placard, protesting the development of holiday properties.

'The locals have nowhere to live!' he had shouted at the builders, a local news reporter at his side. Ali had arrived in her Range Rover with the tinted windows and had not even glanced his way. Within an hour a private security firm had removed him from the site. That night she had ranted, raged, and wept. Rory had tried to comfort her, but she had been distraught, inconsolable. 'Just one more betrayal,' she sobbed.

The next morning, she found the small square of paper on the pillow next to her.

Forgive them even if they are not sorry. Holding on to anger only hurts you, not them.

20

Ali arrived home just before six and was relieved to see Emma's Audi still in the drive. While she was still unsure how and when her daughter might be able to return to Dartmoor Properties, if ever, she did hope to find some sort of middle ground, both personally and professionally, so that they could at least try and rebuild their fractured relationship. The fact that Emma had ensured the gas and electrical certifications had been done, and was arranging the Eustace Road renovations with Darren meant her focus was still solid, and that she did care. The wider issue of whether Ali could trust her again still weighed heavy though. She stood in the front drive, frozen, unmoving, her walking stick embedded in the gravel like the proverbial sword in the stone.

'How did I get it all so wrong?' she muttered to herself. She had tried so hard after Rory's death to support her daughter: counselling, bereavement groups, retreats. Anything to give Emma the support she – overwhelmed with grief and the worry of running Dartmoor Properties on her own – didn't have the time or strength to do. Whatever the reason for the disaster that was now her life, her reality, Ali, always the survivor, was determined to help her daughter avoid the same outcome.

Even though she had resolved to try and sort things out as positively as possible, she still approached the house with caution. After what had been said last night she was worried Emma might not be open to discussion. She would start by telling Emma she could stay at Hope Farm for as long as she liked. It was still her home after all, then they could discuss moving forward someway, perhaps working part-time with the company, or even setting her up on her own.

She slipped her key into the front door with a cautious optimism. In a few days, weeks, or months they might actually be able to become close again. It was something to work towards at least. She felt the key stick and jiggled it to no effect. Emma had obviously left hers in the lock on the other side.

'Emma?' Ali knocked gently, not wishing her daughter to think she was still angry. She was, but not *as* angry. 'Emma, are you there?' Another few knocks and even ringing the bell offered no reply. 'Probably has her bloody headphones on again,' muttered Ali, as she made her way around the side of the house to the back garden.

There was a strange stillness in the air, a feeling of disquiet that made Ali quicken her footsteps. The side gate, which she had always been able to open with ease, now seemed stubbornly unco-operative. As Ali struggled with the latch, she felt her panic begin to grow.

'Emma,' she called, rattling the wrought-iron latch. 'I can't open the gate. Can you come and help me?'

She waited for the sound of the French doors being opened, but there was none, just the weak drone of a tractor in the distance.

'Damn thing!' With one final effort she felt the faulty latch give. 'There's a bloody lifetime guarantee on that.' She worked her way through the crunchy gravel, the walking stick of little use. Her crutches had been relegated to a downstairs cupboard but right now she could have used them. Ali rounded the corner to the patio.

An empty bottle of Grey Goose vodka sat on the ceramic bistro table and there was a shattered glass on the flagstones. 'Jesus, Emma,' she muttered, 'what have you been doing?' All hopes of a conciliatory discussion now seemed out of the question if her daughter had decided to drown her sorrows. It wouldn't be the first time Emma's kamikaze approach to conflict resolution had ended up in a serious hangover either.

The evening sun, iridescent gold, ricocheted off the polished glass. The back door was open, and inside, just spilling over the edge of the settee Ali could see two bare feet. Resting her cane against the table, she eased open the door. A soft breeze ruffled her hair, now damp and lank from her recent efforts, and the smell of vomit assaulted her senses.

'Oh, Ems,' she sighed. 'Take it from me. Getting pissed won't help anything.'

As she moved into the dining area and towards the open-plan living area, the stench grew stronger. Ali braced herself for an evening of wet flannels and sick buckets, not the carefully managed conversation she had hoped for.

Emma lay on the settee, a large pool of vomit on the floor beneath her.

'Oh, Ems,' whispered Ali. As she moved closer, however, she could see her daughter's complexion was waxy, her stillness unnerving. A fear so instinctive, so profound, gripped her, and Ali felt her legs weaken. 'Emma?'

Ali shifted Emma onto her side, and tilting her head backwards ever so slightly, gently coaxed a finger between her lips. Her jaw dropped, mouth opened, and with that came a subtle, welcome intake of air. 'Emma, wake up!' She gently tapped her daughter's cheek, and Emma began to stir.

'Mum?' she mumbled, and then promptly threw up all over her.

Ali stared at her sick-sodden shoes in dismay. The smell of vodka and bile made her want to gag but like any good mum, she got on with it.

'Come on then, sunshine.' Carefully positioning herself so as not to jar her leg, Ali gently eased Emma from the settee and towards the wet room downstairs. Her daughter's legs were shaky, and she leaned heavily on Ali, causing little spasms of pain throughout her body. 'Let's get you to the loo, love, and then maybe a shower.'

'I love you,' Emma slurred. 'You're the best mum in the world.'

'Shush now, darling. Everything will be all right.' They made their way to the downstairs bedroom and into the wet room, Ali grabbing a handful of towels along the way. 'Here you go.' Ali placed a towel on the floor, then gently helped Emma down so that she was positioned over the toilet. Then she soaked a flannel in cold water and went to kneel down beside her. 'Easy now, sweetheart,' she said, wiping the sick from around her chin. 'Everything will be fine.'

'No it won't,' sobbed Emma, between retches. 'I lied t'you, betrayed you. You hate me, don't you?'

'Oh, Emma, no.' Ali grabbed her daughter in her

271

arms and held her tightly, oblivious to the putrid-smelling sick. 'I could never hate you, never. You are the most important person in my life.'

Emma began to cry, great heart-wrenching sobs that shook her body and resonated through Ali's own.

'I'm so, so sorry—'

'It's all right, honey; everything will be all right.'

'I love you, Mum.'

Ali pushed back a lock of sweaty hair that had fallen across Emma's face and gently cupped her cheek. 'I love you too, honey, and always will.'

Emma gave a wonky smile and then grimaced. 'I'm gonna be sick again.'

Ali was only aware of Liz's arrival when she saw her standing in the bathroom doorway.

'What on earth?'

Ali glanced up from where she had been kneeling beside Emma. 'She's had a bit too much to drink.'

'I saw the bottle outside.' Liz frowned. 'And the lounge. That bottle wasn't full was it?'

Ali gave a nod of confirmation. It had been a Christmas present to Matthew and hadn't even been taken out of the box.

'For goodness' sake.' Liz stepped forward and gently rubbed Emma's back. 'You could have made yourself really ill.'

'I *am* really ill,' replied Emma, her voice echoing in the toilet bowl.

'Kneeling like that can't be good for you, Ali.' Liz reached down and gently helped Ali to her feet. 'Why don't you go change and I'll sit with Emma for a bit.' Ali was grateful for the opportunity to get up from the floor and stretch her aching leg.

'Just strip off in here,' Liz instructed, 'and throw your clothes in the corner. We're going to have to do a right old wash and clear-up after Emma is settled.'

Ali slipped off her loafers, socks, trousers, and blouse and threw then in the corner of the wet room, then she took a fresh wet flannel and began wiping down her legs.

'Let me,' said Liz. Ali handed her the flannel, and Liz gently wiped her feet. 'Now go change into something warm. You're shivering.'

Ali put on a clean pair of joggers and jumper and then headed to the kitchen to make them all a cup of tea.

'Don't worry about us,' called Liz. 'I think it will be a while yet before Emma will be able to hold anything down. You just go and have a warm drink and a sit down.'

Ali avoided the rancid-smelling lounge and went into the kitchen. It was nearly an hour before Liz emerged.

'I've put her in your bed,' she said, referring to the downstairs bedroom, 'with plenty of towels around her.' She made her way to the utility room and emerged with a bucket. 'I think she'll need this as well.'

Liz came back a moment later and went straight back to the utility room. 'Mop?' she called. 'And I hope you've got another bucket. Where's the Dettol . . . ah found it.'

Ali heard the squeak of the taps and then the hollow sound of water filling a bucket. Seconds later Liz emerged with a steaming container of bubbles.

'I can't let you—'

'Of course you can,' interrupted Liz. 'It'll only take a minute.'

A half hour and two more buckets of soapy water later and Liz was done. She made herself a cup of tea and sat down beside Ali on one of the bar stools at the kitchen island.

'Well,' she said with surprising cheer, 'that's not how I was expecting to spend my evening.'

'Oh, Liz,' said Ali, staring into her untouched cup of tea. 'I'm so sorry about this.'

'What's to be sorry about?'

'What a mess my family has turned out to be.'

'Not a mess,' said Liz gently, 'just a family.'

Ali wondered if Liz was thinking of her own parents now living happily in Jersey, or of her brother with his Swedish wife and four children living on a farm in Somerset. As close as the two women were, they had never really discussed Liz's childlessness. Ali knew there had been one unsuccessful attempt at IVF some years before, but nothing more. Instead it seemed as if she had put all her energy into being the best possible godmother to Emma. The sordid text image of her daughter and Dane having sex, flooded Ali's brain like a poison. She looked away, unable to face Liz's kindness.

'Matthew was stealing from me.' It was the first time Ali had admitted it properly – but she could no longer deny what was now an irrefutable fact. 'He created false invoices and redirected company payments to a secret online bank account, all to the tune of over twelve grand.' Liz jolted slightly. 'The signs were all there: the previous money problems, secrecy, and absolute insistence on doing his own paperwork. Jesus, how could I be so naïve?'

'You weren't naïve,' said Liz fiercely, 'just trusting.'

'I was a fool.'

Liz shifted uneasily on the bar stool. 'How did you find out?'

'Emma came across some anomalies when she was doing some preliminary work for the big audit.'

'I thought she might . . .' Liz stopped speaking mid-sentence, her hand creeping up to her face to cover her mouth.

'Thought she might what?'

'Nothing.'

'Did you know?' asked Ali, wondering if her

daughter's earlier protestations about not telling Liz were untrue. 'Did Emma tell you?'

'Emma was the model of discretion,' said Liz. 'Matthew, however, wasn't.'

'But if you knew—'

'I didn't know anything, Ali, only suspected.' Liz pulled nervously at a strand of her hair. 'I remembered what he was like before when he was trading,' she continued, 'and losing. Energetic, almost hyper, and intensely, intensely secretive.' Ali opened her mouth to speak, but Liz carried on. 'We all knew Matthew was pretty terrible with his paperwork. Normally he would just hand me rough costings and say, *"Be a good girl, Liz, and knock up an invoice for me."* It was only when he stopped asking for help that I began to wonder what was going on.'

Ali wasn't certain if she was reassured or worried by Liz's statement.

'But why didn't you tell me about your concerns?'

'I did try.' Liz kept her attention fixed on the veining patterns of the marble countertop. 'But you told me to leave it, said that you would handle it.'

Ali had vague recollections of a conversation about Matthew's admin problems sometime before Christmas.

'I spoke to Matthew about it the night of your anniversary party. We had just agreed to that big audit and I was a bit worried. I told him that I'd be happy to help him get all his paperwork in order.'

'Is that what you rowed about?'

A look of fury passed across Liz's face. 'He just laughed at me and said not to ruin the evening with business talk.'

Suddenly Ali felt frightened, and terribly alone. 'Too many secrets have been kept,' she said, 'too many lies told.' If ever there was a time for absolute truth, thought Ali, this was it. 'There's something I need to tell you, Liz.'

'*Mum!*' Emma's terrified scream came spiralling out of the bedroom.

Liz jumped up. 'What on earth?'

Ali forced herself up as quickly as possible. 'You stay here and finish your tea. I'll sort it.'

Liz, plainly unnerved by their conversation, didn't argue. Ali hurried to the bedroom, aware she hadn't needed her crutches or walking stick. *In a crisis comes strength . . .*

Oh fuck off, Rory!

'What is it, Ems?' Ali sat down on the bed beside her daughter.

'Just a bad dream. About that night.' Ali knew she wasn't the only person who had bad dreams about the accident. 'You were in the water, and I was trying to reach you, but I couldn't.' Tears trickled down Emma's cheeks and onto the pillow.

'It's all right, Ems; everything will be all right.'

Ali wasn't certain how many times she had said that phrase already, but she was determined to keep on repeating it for as long as necessary. 'Now go back to sleep, honey.'

'I love you, Mum.'

'I love you too.' Ali paused. 'Ems?'

'Yes?'

Ali dropped her voice to a whisper. 'Did you think Liz knows about what happened, between you and Dane?'

'No!' cried Emma, evidently horrified at the prospect. 'Absolutely not, and we must make sure she never finds out either.' She reached out from under the bedclothes and grasped Ali's hand. 'You must promise me on your life that you'll never tell her. Promise me!'

Ali leaned forward and kissed Emma on the forehead. 'I promise.'

When she came back to the kitchen Liz was looking through the refrigerator.

'There's miso soup, eggs, rice. Do you think Emma will be able to manage any of that?'

'I think it will be toast and tea,' replied Ali. 'Maybe a bacon sandwich in the morning.'

Liz nodded, and taking the mugs from the island began washing up.

'There was something you were going to tell me before Emma called.'

'It's nothing,' said Ali, handing her a teaspoon, 'nothing at all.'

'Would you like me to stay tonight?' asked Liz, drying her hands on a tea towel. 'Dane won't mind.'

The mention of Dane sent a small shiver through Ali's body. He had texted Ali only that morning asking for a bit more cash for the search. Ali hadn't replied.

'You've been an absolute gem, Liz. I don't know what I'd have done without you, but I think I'll be all right on my own.'

Liz's expression grew serious. 'You *will* be back at work on Monday won't you?'

'Of course.'

'And Emma?'

'I think you can see from what's been going on that Emma and I still have a few things to work through before there's any more thoughts about her returning to work.'

'Maybe it's all just caught up with her,' said Liz sadly.

'Maybe.'

Liz reached forward and enveloped Ali in a warm hug. 'I love you, Ali.'

'I love you too, Liz.'

Ali waited for Liz to leave before calling Graham.

'Ali?' He sounded as if he had been expecting more drama. 'What is it?'

In the background she could hear a soft gong, and then the muffled sound of a tannoy announcement.

'Where are you?'

'At Paddington waiting for my train to Bristol.'

'Do you have any plans for next week?'

Graham's voice grew serious. 'Why? What's going on?'

'Do you think you could come and stay with us for a few days?'

21

It was nearly noon before Emma emerged from her cocoon duvet and finally managed to shuffle her way into the kitchen. Showered and shampooed, she still looked somewhat worse for wear. Ali had a glass of water and a paracetamol waiting for her.

'Fancy something to eat? Toast? A boiled egg?'

Emma looked at her with tired, hungover eyes, then walked towards the opened French doors and gazed out at the lush, green countryside. In the distance they could hear the soft baying of cattle.

'Yesterday,' whispered Emma, the blush of morning sun tinting her pallid cheeks, 'losing this view was all I could think of.'

Ali went to stand beside her. 'I hope I didn't make you feel that you couldn't stay. I was angry, but more than that I was frightened.'

Emma looked at her mother in surprise. 'Frightened?'

'You're a good person, Emma. You made a bad decision, but for what you thought were the right reasons.' She put an arm around her daughter's shoulders. 'I was very hard on you. I really should have considered everything that you've gone through over the last few years. The impact that has had. How it made you so . . .' Ali trailed off, unable to express her feelings of deep concern.

'Crazy.'

'I was going to say vulnerable.'

'Crazy works,' said Emma staring into some invisible distance. 'I was thoughtless, destructive, and hurtful.' She gave a bitter snort. 'I tried to convince myself that I was keeping the invoice hidden to protect you, but maybe a part of me did want to drop Matthew in it, maybe a part of me was jealous.'

'Jealous?'

'After Dad died it was just you and me for a while, wasn't it? It was hard, but we stuck together, we got through it, were a team. Then Matthew shows up, all bells and whistles, and the photographs start disappearing from the mantelpiece.'

'Just a few,' said Ali sadly. 'I only thought it might be time for us to stop living with a ghost.'

'Not a ghost,' said Emma softly, 'my dad.'

'I got that bit wrong, didn't I?'

'I know Matthew didn't like them there.'

'I just found it so hard to navigate sometimes. My past with your father, the present with Matthew.'

'I didn't make it any easier.'

'You were hurting too.'

Emma rested her head on her mother's shoulder.

'It was like I was in some kind of haze?' Emma needed to talk, and as painful as it might be for Ali to hear, she didn't want to stop her. 'After Dad. Then things went wrong with uni, and now work.'

'I put too much pressure on you.'

'That's the thing, Mum,' replied Emma. 'You didn't. I loved it. I loved working for you – the problem solving, the negotiating, the clients.' Her voice was filled with vigour. 'I loved every single minute of it.'

Ali felt a tremor of relief. 'I was worried that I tried to impose my aspirations on you, just like my father tried to do to me, and that along with everything else that's happened over the last few years is—'

'Why I did what I did?' said Emma. Something in her tone spoke of honesty and reconciliation. 'Why I kept the truth from you?' She gave a small tut of self-reproach. 'Let's be honest about it, shall we? Why I lied to you about something so integral to your safety and wellbeing, as well as the wellbeing of Dartmoor Properties. Why I behaved like a spoiled child.'

'You did it to protect me.'

'So I said,' replied Emma, 'but if I really wanted to protect you I should have told you what I had discovered, not kept it a secret.' Ali had never heard her daughter speak with such candour. 'You were right about what you said the other day, that maybe part of me wanted to get back at Matthew, punish him for taking you away from me.'

'You weren't the only one keeping secrets,' said Ali. 'I knew about his ongoing money problems, his compulsion for trading even after he promised me he had stopped. I hid that knowledge from everyone, even myself.'

'None of us is blameless,' muttered Emma.

'But I should have stopped it.'

'Why always you?'

'Pardon?'

'I could have stopped it. Liz, who from what you told me clearly suspected something was up, could have stopped it.' Her face hardened and for a moment she looked truly unkind. 'But most of all Matthew could have stopped it.'

'But he didn't,' said Ali.

'Maybe it's time for us to just stop blaming ourselves, accept what has happened, and move on.'

Ali beamed at her daughter. 'When did you get so smart?'

'Something to do with what my parents taught me maybe.'

Ali took a moment to let Emma's words settle before speaking. 'I know there's still a lot to work out, but if you're interested I'd like you to consider coming back to work at Dartmoor Properties.' She watched Emma's expression change from confusion to delight and then back again in the few seconds it took her to process her mother's words. 'You don't have to answer now.'

'It's something to consider.'

'Maybe after a little break?' said Ali, conscious she might be overwhelming her. 'I could use your help, particularly if Matthew does come back—'

'You still believe that?'

'I've been looking for him, Emma.' She refrained from adding that Dane had been looking too. 'And have a number of strong leads about where he might be.'

'Where he might be hiding, you mean,' said Emma, and clarifying further added: 'considering what he's done and all.'

'I suppose you're right about that,' said Ali, Emma's words adding more fuel to her fire of belief that Matthew was still alive. 'It certainly explains why he hasn't gotten in touch.'

'And what will you do if he does come back?'

In the field beyond, Ali watched a sparrow hawk swoop down and snatch a grey tit from the sky. The drama was over in a moment, leaving the sky clear once more.

'Talk to him,' was all she could offer. 'Ask why he did it. How things could have gotten so bad that he couldn't come to me for help.'

'And you'll forgive him?'

Ali hugged her daughter closer and inhaled the fresh scent of her shampoo.

'Of that I'm not sure.' Ali carefully considered her next question. 'What about Dane?'

Emma sighed. 'Not a day goes by that I don't regret it.'

'He should have known better.'

'I'm an adult, Mum.'

'You're twenty-two. He's nearly forty.'

'I'm still accountable.'

'Accountability goes both ways.'

'Dane is just a dick.' Emma said the phrase with such dismissal that Ali knew with certainty her daughter would be able to move on from that terrible mistake. 'Self-centred, deluded, jealous of Matthew, and sliding towards middle age with not much going for him.' She suddenly looked ashamed. 'Except for Liz of course.'

'Oh God, Liz.'

'You promised you wouldn't tell her.'

Ali felt as if she was standing alone on a mountain top, the wind swirling at her feet.

'And I won't.' She kissed her daughter's cheek. 'Maybe the best thing for both of us would be to start again.'

'I think we are, aren't we?'

'I mean really start again, move on.'

'I'm not sure I—'

'Sell up, find a new place to live.'

'You're not serious.'

'It struck me last night as I was lying next to you in bed thinking. This house is so weighed down with memories, not all of them good.'

'I never thought you'd leave Hope Farm.'

'Fighting, always fighting.' Ali's voice was calm, but she could feel her pulse throbbing in her throat. 'First for this place, then the business. Never giving an inch. Always pushing. If only I stopped to think a bit more, had been more open, more kind, you wouldn't have been so vulnerable to someone like Dane.'

Emma responded to Ali's calmness with her own. 'You're a good mum, always have been.'

'Not as good as I should have been,' she said sadly. 'I'm not saying this for sympathy, Ems, or from self-pity, but because I want to understand.' She took her daughter's hand, held it to her lips, then let it go.

'Do you still miss Dad?'

'Of course, honey, always.' Ali crossed the threshold and stepped into the garden. 'But I'm not so sure this is the best place for us anymore.' She held her hand out for Emma to join her. 'There's lots to talk about, but maybe right now all we need to do is sit outside and enjoy the sunshine.' They walked to the far edge of the garden where the ancient willow took pride of place. Rory had thought it large and unruly, but Ali had refused to let him cut it down. She ran her fingertips across the coarse bark, remembering reading something once about its natural healing properties.

'Did you really mean what you said about selling up?' asked Emma.

'It just feels like it might be time for a change.' She cleared her throat. 'I was also thinking of selling off the holiday let side of the business.'

'You what?'

'It was always Matthew's baby.' There was a sense of finality in her tone. 'And a lot more work than seemed worth it.'

'Are you sure? I was under the impression it was quite lucrative.'

'I'm not quite sure of anything at the moment, honey, but it would certainly improve the company's current cash flow.'

'Which would be good news for the audit?' Emma tilted her head, studying her mother closely. 'And Matthew?'

Ali's response was uncategorical. 'What about him?'

'If he comes home?'

'*If* he comes home,' said Ali, becoming more convinced than ever that she would have to be the one to find him, 'there'll be a lot of questions.'

'About the blackmail you mean?'

'I want answers, Emma. Definitive ones.'

'And the house in Salcombe?'

Emma was proving to be very astute this morning. 'Well, that's the thing,' she said. 'I've always wanted to live by the sea.'

'You're not actually thinking of moving to Salcombe, are you?'

'Why not?' Ali felt momentarily buoyed by Emma's interest. 'I could do with a change of scenery. You could come too.' Ali couldn't think of a better place for them both to recuperate and rebuild, and having Emma further away from Dane would be an added bonus. She felt a desperate sadness when she thought about Liz though. How could she possibly keep Emma safe and still not let Liz know about her daughter's affair with Dane? One of her relationships was going to have to give and it broke her heart to know which one.

Emma exhaled a sigh of relief. 'So it's all working out.'

Ali was tempted to reply with: *Well, I wouldn't say commercial fraud, a missing husband, blackmail, and an excruciating leg injury is exactly working out,* but instead just said, 'I think it's starting to. What do you think? Would you like to come too?'

For a moment Ali could see a spark of genuine interest in her daughter's face, but almost as quickly it faded.

'Actually . . . after everything that's happened, I was thinking of maybe going back to uni in September, finishing my degree.'

'*Oh.*'

'That might give me the distance I need, you know, to get myself together.'

Ali forced herself to sound cheerful. 'That sounds like a great idea.'

'And maybe when I'm done you might still need a good project manager?'

'I'll always need a good project manager.'

They walked the few metres towards a wrought-iron bench that sat next to the small fishpond. Ali followed, negotiating her way through the dewy grass, grateful at last for the solid support of the metal bench. The sun slipped behind a cloud and for a moment they were bathed in a strange half-light.

'I'm sorry this all happened, Emma.' Ali wasn't certain if it was the effects of the car accident or her obsessive need for closure, but these days things just seemed to go from her brain and out her mouth with little filtration.

'What for?'

'Not listening to you about Matthew. Leaving you to feel so alone.'

Ali thought back to her discovery of Matthew's business cards, of her suspicion that he had started trading again. Her knowledge that at the time of their wedding he had tens of thousands of pounds in his account, yet only a few years before that had been seriously in debt. God she was a fool. A lonely, trusting, desperate fool. A new emotion crept into her consciousness, one that she had yet to experience regarding her missing husband, hatred. She hated Matthew, hated him with all her heart, and there was only one thing that might allow her to put those feelings to rest. She had to find him and get the answers she so rightly deserved.

A plan started to form. One that might allow her to find out the truth once and for all. She thought back to her meeting with the FLO a few days ago, about a possible sighting of Matthew in Crediton, and then to where her Range Rover, unused and dust-covered since her accident, was parked out the front. She was never more pleased than now that she had opted for an automatic.

22

Monday morning Ali was in the office early checking that everything was in order for the Easter bookings, and consulting with the realtor about a sales brochure for the holiday lets. She had checked the Facebook page for any further sightings, but since the report of his bank card being used things had gone very quiet. Maybe Dane was right. Maybe Matthew was lying low.

'And we all know why that is, you bastard,' muttered Ali, as she worked her way through the accounts.

She heard a gentle knock and looked to see Liz entering the office with two cups of coffee.

'And I thought I got in early.' She handed Ali a mug. 'I've got a spare blueberry muffin if you're hungry. I don't suppose you've had anything to eat yet.'

'Not a morsel,' said Ali, who had been at her desk since five-thirty and hadn't even thought about breakfast.

'How's Emma?' said Liz, taking a seat at Matthew's old desk. Before everything went crazy and Ali's life had slowly started to disintegrate they used to regularly have a conflab over coffee and whatever breakfast pastries Liz had brought in that morning.

'Good, she's good.'

'And the situation with the invoice?' Ali knew Liz was as eager as her for some sort of resolution to the problem that had been haunting them both.

'I've sorted it. As far as I'm concerned the entire thing is closed. If we're going to go for that business development loan, it's going to have to stay that way too.'

'I understand,' said Liz quietly.

'I'm going to be out for the afternoon,' said Ali, negating any further discussion about the fake invoice. It wasn't that she wanted to distance herself from Liz, but rather protect her from any more involvement in Matthew's questionable actions. She also didn't want to risk letting slip what she knew about Dane and Emma. She suspected when Emma first disclosed her affair with Dane that it might change their friendship, but was now feeling it profoundly. 'I thought I'd pop by the house in Salcombe. See how things are before the new tenants move in.'

Liz brushed a muffin crumb from her lap. 'I could go with you if you like. It would sort of be like old times, you and me on a day trip.'

Ali tried to smile. 'Probably best if I go on my own. I don't know what time I'll be back, and you've probably got—'

'Loads to do,' said Liz, with forced cheerfulness. 'You're right. In fact, I've got a to-do list as long as my arm. End of month is coming up and all.'

'Well I guess it's sorted then,' said Ali. She pressed the space bar on her keyboard and her computer screen glowed into life. 'Better get back to it.'

'Me too!' said Liz. She stood up and pointed to Ali's empty mug. 'You all done?' Ali nodded. 'Guess I'll go and wash these up then.'

'Thanks, Liz.'

'Not a problem.' Liz collected the mugs and left. Ali watched her go, feeling deflated – try as she might to solve everything, keep everyone safe – here was one thing that couldn't easily be remedied. She knew Liz was hurt by the distance Ali was putting between them – but how could Ali act normally when she was keeping such a terrible secret from her best friend?

Ali took the A385, and instead of turning left at Western Bypass for Salcombe, carried on past the community college, over Shinner's Bridge, and followed the road that ran alongside the river until she reached the turn-off for the motorway and the hour-long journey to Crediton. She was damned if she was going to let Dane find Matthew, especially now that she knew what had happened between him and Emma. There had been numerous sightings of her husband, or someone resembling her husband, but Crediton was the first location that had included the solid evidence of his bank card being used, and the CCTV image that Ruth had shown her, of a man who looked remarkably like Matthew.

She hadn't visited the town since she was a child and had come on a school visit to see the birthplace of local favourite St Boniface. She remembered the town as being one long, main street dotted with the standard shops and cafés. As she entered the main shopping district, it appeared that not much had changed. She parked near the Old Town Hall and walked the short distance to the high street. It was late afternoon on a Monday, and the streets were quiet. It didn't take her long to find the bank machine at the local Tesco Express, and the pub opposite where the CCTV footage Ruth showed them had come from.

She walked back and forth along the street for at least an hour, wondering if Matthew might be living in one of the shabby flats on top of the shops.

Three hundred pounds from the cash machine wouldn't go that far, however. Maybe he was using the twelve grand he'd stolen from the company. Maybe that's why things had gone so quiet. Finally, and with shops closing, she walked back to her car. She wasn't certain what she'd expected to find. Matthew walking up to her and giving her a big hug seemed pretty unlikely.

She drove home in a haze of disappointment. Why hadn't she gone into the shops and asked the storekeepers if they had seen someone matching Matthew's description? Why hadn't she shown the traffic warden or *The Big Issue* vendor a photo of Matthew? *'Have you seen him? He's my husband. He's gone missing. I'm very worried about him.'* But she did none of those things, only trudged gormlessly up and down, up and down, hoping for some sort of miracle to take place.

She arrived at Hope Farm to the sound of The Stone Roses playing on the kitchen music system and the smell of garlic. As she made her way into the kitchen she could see Emma dancing around Graham, a glass of rosé in her hand.

'Come on, Uncle Graham,' she called. 'You remember how to dance don't you?'

Graham laughed, put down the spoon he was using to stir his home-made puttanesca sauce, and began swinging his arms and shaking his hips in what only could be described as the worst dad dancing ever.

'Mum!' She had been spotted and Emma was now dancing her way towards her. 'Uncle Graham's come over for a surprise visit.'

Ali pointed to her glass. 'Should you be drinking?'

'I promised Uncle Graham I'd only have one.' Emma put down her glass and took her mother's hands in hers. 'You can hold on to me.'

Ali glanced over to see Graham watching her with a happy, hopeful expression that said, *Just do it, Ali. Dance with your daughter!*

'It'll have to be Faithless or nothing,' said Ali, gripping Emma's hands to help keep her balance.

'Siri,' Emma called, 'play *Insomnia*.'

The heavy thump of synth and bass filled the kitchen. Emma began bobbing up and down to the beat, forcing Ali to do the same.

'Come on, Uncle Graham,' Emma called, and a second later Ali found herself in the middle of her kitchen in a small circle holding hands with her brother and daughter and bobbing up and down to a Nineties dance tune like a fool.

They ate their pasta in the garden as dusk settled in, watched as a pipistrelle bat dipped and dived around the garden, hunting for insects that had been drawn to the garden light.

'I spoke to my old tutor today,' said Emma, her voice as soft as the night. As eager as she was to hear more, Ali forced herself to wait. 'I'll have to do some revision before the term starts at the end of September, but he sees no reason why I can't resume my third-year studies. He said my year working in business is a big plus.'

'That's fantastic news,' said Ali, with a mixture of pride and sadness. 'I guess you'll be looking for a flat in Plymouth then?'

Emma shifted in her seat. 'Uncle Graham said I could spend a couple of months working with him over the summer.'

'In Bristol?'

'Just until September. You'll be busy with work, and with Amita promoted to junior project manager you won't be short-staffed.'

'You've thought of everything, Ems, haven't you?'

'Well it's not like I'm going to leave you high and dry, am I?'

'And come September?'

'A student house would be nice,' she said, 'but I'll come to stay at weekends, and when you eventually move to Salcombe—'

Graham, who had been dozing in his garden chair, sat up nearly knocking over his wine glass.

'Salcombe? Who's moving to Salcombe?'

'I was considering it, maybe renting out this place for a bit and living by the coast.'

'Maybe you could move in too, Uncle Graham,' teased Emma.

'How about just visiting?' said Ali pointing to the empty plates on the table in front of them. 'If

Uncle Graham lived with me I think I'd end up being the size of a house.' She kept her voice light and cheerful. She didn't want to spoil the mood by reminding Emma that her uncle would be returning home to Bristol in a few days.

Ali watched her daughter's face in the flickering firelight. If the situation with Emma and Dane hung heavily in Ali's heart, she could only imagine what her daughter was feeling. Maybe time away from the pressure cooker of that dilemma would be good for everyone. It would protect Emma from any further engagement with that diabolical man, and also might allow Ali to try and re-establish some sort of neutral relationship with Liz. Their friendship may never be quite the same, but Ali sure as hell needed her as a trusted office manager, and if somewhere down the line things got awkward or difficult with Dane, Ali would be there for her.

She looked up at the starry night sky. Emma seemed to be coping, Graham had agreed to keep his knowledge about the missing money a secret as long as the full audit went ahead, and Matthew – her darling, lying bastard of a husband – might still be alive and living less than an hour away. All she had to do was find him.

23

Ali spent most of the week catching up on work, meeting with clients and brushing up on her knowledge of building and renovation regs for the Cornwall build. The luxury holiday home project for Matthew's millionaire client would secure their future, and maybe even allow Ali to step back a little. The situation with Matthew certainly had made her start to re-evaluate things. If her husband was alive and living in Crediton then she wanted answers. Answers to the business cards, the stolen money, and the blackmail, and if he really ever was the man she thought he was. She also wanted her bloody twelve thousand pounds back.

By Friday lunchtime she was exhausted but pleased with what she had achieved. She heard the ping of a text. It was from Graham.

*Liz rung Emma to say the Woolacombe holiday
apartment has become free this weekend. We
were going to pack up and head off after tea.
Fancy a few days by the sea before the place
is sold?*

Ali read the text with a mixture of pleasure and
regret. It was just like Liz to think of ways to support
Emma. A jolt of sadness struck her when she realised
that on any other occasion Liz and Dane would have
been invited too. She knew she had made a promise
never to tell Liz about what had happened, but she
was finding it more and more difficult to keep it a
secret.

Only yesterday Dane had popped into the office
to drop off Liz's lunch. Seeing his Mercedes pull
up in the car park, Ali had hid in the toilets until
he was gone. She had avoided replying to any of
his texts, but had a terrible feeling this situation
wasn't going to go away. Pushing those troubling
thoughts aside, she replied to her brother's text.

*I'm in! but I'll have to meet you there tomorrow
afternoon. I still have one or two things to do.*

By the time she arrived home Graham and Emma
had already left for Woolacombe. *Frittata for you
in the fridge,* said the note from Emma on the
kitchen table. *And we're expecting you no later*

than 2 p.m. tomorrow! Ali opened the refrigerator, removed the frittata, and stuck it in the microwave. She avoided the bottle of red sitting seductively on the countertop, and stuck to sparkling water instead. She had a busy day tomorrow.

She slept fitfully, dreaming of dark-clad, hooded figures, their faces blank, indistinguishable, as if somehow their features had been wiped clean. She woke gasping, grateful for the relief of her alarm.

She showered, dressed, packed something for the weekend, and headed towards Crediton.

It was still early when she arrived, but the car parks were nearly full, the streets bustling with people. As she walked towards the town centre she heard voices and the sound of fiddler music. Ahead of her was the market square. Small marquees and garden parasols were set up around the plaza selling everything from locally sourced meat and cheeses to hand-carved wooden toadstools. A large sign read:

Crediton Farmers Market every first and third Saturday of the month

'Shit,' muttered Ali, 'just what I need.' And then she reconsidered. If Matthew was in a bad place, concealing himself from her and what he had done, then maybe having a crowd to hide behind would be a good thing.

She started at the bank machine.

'Where did you come from, Matthew?' she muttered. 'And where did you go?'

She went into the Tesco Express, the chemist's next door, the pub opposite, ready with a photo of Matthew on her mobile, and a hopeful expression on her face. *'Couldn't say.' 'Never seen 'im.' 'Looks like a lot of blokes round 'ere.'* were the only responses. By eleven o'clock she was feeling discouraged. She must have spoken to fifty people but not one of them could recall seeing Matthew. Maybe he was living out of the area and had come in to get some money. Maybe he was only passing through. Maybe he'd never been here at all. All they had to go on were some dodgy Facebook sightings, and that CCTV footage. She was heading back towards the market square, her path hindered by hand-holding couples and dog walkers, when she spotted a man a few metres away. He was Matthew's height, wearing a dark hoodie even in this heat, and had a medium-length beard. He was heading for the teeming market square.

'Matthew?' she whispered in disbelief, and then unable to contain her excitement began to scream, 'Matthew!' Heads spun and bodies reluctantly stepped aside as Ali pushed her way through the crowd. He was moving fast and her being less than sure-footed meant she struggled to keep up with him. Finally, he stopped in front of a stall selling vapes and bongs.

'*Matthew.*' Ali forced her way forwards and, grabbing his arm, pulled him towards her. 'Where have you been?'

'What the fuck?'

The figure turned and Ali could see that it wasn't Matthew. Of course it wasn't him. He was too tall, his hair too dark, beard too full. He also had a large tattoo of a spider's web on his neck. Was she that desperate to find Matthew that she had lost all common sense?

'I'm s-sorry,' she stuttered. 'I thought you were my husband.' She felt her courage desert her. 'He's missing, you see.' The man stared at her with a mixture of pity and irritation. Ali felt her legs begin to wobble. 'I'm so sorry,' she repeated and, backing away, nearly fell over a rheumy-eyed Shih Tzu that was licking ice cream off the pavement.

'Careful!' screeched the owner, an enormous woman in a floral dress, cookies and cream dripping down her arm.

Ali fled as fast as her injured leg would take her. She had no idea where she was going, but such was her embarrassment and humiliation, that she was determined to walk until her body gave out. Finally, after what seemed like an eternity, she found a small leafy alcove next to the Methodist church, not even big enough to call a park. It was cool and dark, and she found herself retreating to a bench covered in graffiti. She wanted to sit and sob, but after the spectacle in the town square, more than anything wanted to disappear. What was she thinking, chasing after some stranger? She tried to erase the image of people staring at her, and of that man, definitely not Matthew, pulling away and saying, 'Have you lost your fucking mind, lady?'

She thought she must have.

'Can't be that bad can it, missus?' She searched the area to see where the voice had come from. In the far corner of the tiny square, just a few metres away, next to what she had thought was a binbag full of rubbish, was a man. He was sitting cross-legged with his back up against the wall, rolling a cigarette. His piercing blue eyes emerged from the shade-soaked corner like a jaguar in the jungle, and his long straggly hair, and worn and weathered face, spoke of someone who had spent many years sleeping rough. He could have been twenty-six or sixty. 'No need to be afraid, love,' he said, spotting her startled expression. 'I won't hurt ya. Just getting meself out of the midday sun.'

'Mad dogs and Englishmen,' replied Ali.

'Sommat like that.' He lit his cigarette, and the rich, pungent scent of Turkish tobacco drifted her way. 'You okay?'

Ali was touched by his concern. 'Tough morning.'

The man took a long drag and exhaled, the smoke drifting around his face. 'I experience that,

306

sometimes,' he said. He was studying her closely, picking up every detail. Could he see her red-rimmed eyes and the scar on her cheek? What did he make of this woman crying alone on a park bench in the middle of the day?

'I was trying to find someone,' she said finally.

'Aren't we all, love?'

She gave a weary smile. He obviously considered himself a bit of a comedian, or maybe it was just his naturally irreverent take on life. She imagined someone who kept all of his worldly possessions in a couple of binbags must have one.

'My husband,' she continued. 'He went missing after a car accident nearly three months ago.'

'Missing,' said the man.

'The police thought he was dead—' she wasn't sure why she was telling him all this '—but then his bank card was used last week, here in Crediton.'

'So you fancy yourself a bit of a detective?'

'Something like that,' said Ali, 'only not a very good one.'

The man started to cough, a deep rattling sound that made Ali wince.

'Thing is . . .' he said his voice gentle, 'if someone wants to go missing, really wants to, you ain't going to find them.'

'But he might be hurt, confused.' The man raised an eyebrow. 'I thought I saw him in the market square.' An involuntary sob escaped her lips. 'But it wasn't him, just some bloke who thought I was a complete and total nutter.'

The man chuckled. 'Welcome to the club.'

'I've been an idiot thinking I could find him, thinking he's still alive.'

'I've seen stranger things,' said the man. 'One bloke I hung out with in London was a businessman. Made millions of pounds a week, then—' he snapped his fingers dramatically '—lost it all in one go. Wife left him; kids wanted nothing to do with him,' he shrugged glumly. 'You know the story.' For a moment Ali felt as if he was reaching into her soul, but then another coughing fit overtook him, and the moment was lost. 'You're a loving wife looking for a missing husband.' He cleared his throat, and his voice became bright and resonant. 'If thou remember'st not the slightest folly that ever love did make thee run into, thou hast not loved.'

'*A Midsummer Night's Dream?*' asked Ali.

'*As You Like it.*' The man stood up and walked towards her. Ali gripped her handbag a little bit tighter but didn't move. As he grew closer she could smell him. A mixture of sweat and unwashed clothes. She tried not to gag. 'Do you have a photo?'

'Yes,' she said, her hope renewed, and taking her mobile from her pocket held it out for him to see. 'This is from our anniversary dinner a few months ago. His beard is probably a bit longer by now.'

'And you think he'd still have it, the beard I mean?'

Ali stared at the man in surprise. She had never considered Matthew might have shaved off his beard. It would certainly make him less recognisable. She thought about the grainy CCTV image, of the face covered by the hoodie. 'I really don't know.'

The man studied the image and made a small *hmm* sound.

'What?' said Ali, intrigued.

'There's this bloke who comes into The Ship sometimes.'

She forced herself to remain calm. 'The Ship?'

'Pub just round the corner from the market square.'

'And this bloke?'

'Strange sort of fella.' The man chuckled. 'I know that sounds odd coming from me, but a quiet sort of chap; buys himself a pint or two and sits in the corner.'

Ali lifted her mobile so that it was closer to his face. 'And he looks like him?'

'A lot like him.'

'*Oh God.*' Her hands were shaking so much she had to rest them on her lap.

'Now, don't get carried away,' said the man. 'I said it looked a lot like him; I didn't say it *was* him.'

'But there's a chance it could be?'

'I'd say so.' The man placed his hand on her shoulder. The fingers were long and finely shaped, though yellow-stained by tobacco, the fingernails cracked and dirty. Ali didn't pull away. She was grateful for the support. 'Thinking back, it was always on a Tuesday night,' he continued. 'Two for one on Stella.'

'Tuesday night you said?'

'Tuesday night.'

Ali reached into her bag, opened her purse, and handed him a ten-pound note. He glanced at it, scowled, and then waved it away.

'Didn't do it for the money.' He sounded offended. 'Just to help.'

'I know,' said Ali, 'but you did more than just help. You gave me hope.' She held the note out again. 'Please take it.' The man's face was an image of conflicting emotions: pride, desire, hunger. Ali folded it and placed it in the front pocket of his grubby shirt. She held out her hand. 'My name's Ali.'

The man took his hand in hers. It was rough, strong, and felt oddly reassuring.

'Nice to meet you, Ali,' he replied. 'I'm Jed.'

Ali held his gaze. 'See you on Tuesday, Jed.'

24

She made good time to Woolacombe, buoyed by
the prospect of a relaxing day by the sea before
her return to Crediton to finally find Matthew. She
pulled into the apartment car park, then got out
to gaze out at the sea. Even though it was only
April, the wide expanse of beach was dotted with
windbreakers and beach tents. The unseasonable
warm weather also meant that beachgoers were
out in force: dog walkers, surfers, and wetsuit-clad
swimmers. She heard the sound of a newly arrived
text to discover it was a message from Emma.

*Where are you? I'm about to go bodyboarding
and Uncle Graham has headed to the beachside
café for fish and chips!*

She found Graham digging into a plate of fish and chips.

'Get everything done?' he asked in between mouthfuls of mushy peas.

'Just about.'

'Hungry?'

Ali gazed out at the long expanse of golden sand that led to blue water and frothy, white-tipped waves.

'She's fine,' said Graham, reading her mind. 'Not long gone out with a bodyboard and a huge smile on her face. I don't think I've seen her look so happy in ages.'

'Do you think she'll be all right?'

'We're doing everything we can to ensure that.'

Ali spotted a notification on her mobile, a text from Dane, suggesting he move further south into Cornwall and asking for more money. That deep ache in the pit of her stomach that had started when she first learned of his terrible betrayal was back again, inescapable no matter how beautiful the setting. She grabbed the mobile from the table and resting it on her lap, blocked Dane, and removed him from all her contact lists. She didn't want his help anymore, didn't need it. She knew at some point she would have to confront him, but until then would just try and do her best to keep avoiding him. The knowledge of his exploitation, no matter how hard Emma had tried to rationalise it, would not leave her. When her daughter was safely away with Graham in Bristol, she would speak to him, Liz too. She gazed out to where she spotted Emma was riding the waves, happy and carefree. As terrible as it would be to betray her daughter's trust, some promises were too damaging to keep.

Even though it was spring and still cool, Ali spent the afternoon on a sun lounger, while Emma and Graham played cricket with a plastic ball and bat they'd found in the apartment. By teatime they were all famished.

'I've booked us a table at a really nice seafood restaurant with great views of the bay,' said Graham.

'And puddings?' asked Emma grinning.

'Choice of three different kinds of cheesecake,' he said, sounding the most excited he had all day.

They shared mussels and calamari, drank pitchers of ice-cold beer, and ordered one of each flavour of cheesecake so that Graham could try them all. They walked back to the flat, cheerful and full, and played Scrabble until none of them could keep their eyes open any longer.

She and Emma shared the king-size bed in the master bedroom, while Graham made do with the bottom bunk in the second bedroom. As she lay waiting for sleep, Ali snuggled up to her daughter.

Emma's breathing was deep and even, her face peaceful. When she finally found Matthew there would be a lot of questions, particularly about the blackmail, something she still wasn't convinced he was capable of. There were still so many issues to be addressed, and many, if not all of them, would determine whether or not she would stay married to him.

She halted her wayward thoughts and inwardly berated herself for her betrayal. Her loyalty first and foremost should be to Emma, but the truth was that no matter how much she tried to rationalise it all, close off her heart, she still had feelings for Matthew.

She woke to the smell of bacon frying and Graham singing about being as easy as a Sunday morning. Emma was making oohing and aahing sounds like a background singer, periodically collapsing into laughter.

'Don't give up the day job,' said Ali, as she entered the kitchen.

'She doesn't like The Commodores,' said Graham feigning indignation. 'Who doesn't like The Commodores?'

Ali mouthed the words '*I don't*' when Graham wasn't looking, sending Emma off into another fit of giggles.

They sat on the balcony, ate bacon butties, and drank strong coffee. After a quick walk on

314

the beach, they packed up their cars to return home.

'You don't mind if I ride home with Mum, do you, Uncle Graham?' asked Emma.

'Of course not, sweetheart,' he said, and then grinning broadly added: 'There's a nice pub on the way that does a smashing Sunday roast.'

They stopped for lunch in a picturesque village, then drove the remaining hour home to Totnes, Graham speeding ahead in his Porsche. The conversation between Ali and Emma was open and easy. Emma spoke excitedly about restarting university in September, and doing some work experience with her uncle over the summer. When she asked about her mother's plans for the future, however, Ali hesitated. It would all depend on what happened on Tuesday when she went back to Crediton.

As they exited the A385 and onto the single-lane road that led to Hope Farm, Ali felt her heart soar. She had her family back, well most of them, and was beginning to look forward to the future again. There was only one last piece of the puzzle.

As she pulled into the drive, she spotted a flash of neon yellow and blue. A Devon and Cornwall police car. She glanced at Emma. Her daughter's expression only moments before had been relaxed, easy; now it was clouded with uncertainty. Ali pulled up next to Graham's Carrera. He was standing by the front door. On one side of him was a uniformed PC, and on the other, Ruth.

'They've found him!' exclaimed Ali. 'They've found Matthew!' She forced her way out of the car as quickly as her body would let her, and half ran, half limped her way over to where Graham and Ruth were waiting.

'You've found him, haven't you?' she said to Ruth. 'Was it in Crediton? At The Ship?'

Ruth looked at her with kindness, and then pity. 'I think we'd better go inside.'

'What? No.'

Graham reached out his hand. 'Ali.'

A sense of sudden dread swept over her. 'For God's sake, just tell me what's going on!'

The FLO's face was calm. 'We've found a body, Ali. We think it's Matthew's.'

25

They had to carry Ali into the house, Graham on one side of her and Ruth on the other. They sat her on the settee – her face blank – while Emma poured whisky and made tea.

'It's not possible,' she said, shaking her head. 'He's in Crediton. Someone's seen him in Crediton.' She thought of Jed waiting for her on Tuesday night outside The Ship.

Ruth sat down beside her, a picture of quiet determination.

'The Dartmoor Search and Rescue team were doing some air-scenting dog training near Dartmeet when they came across the body. It was in some thick undergrowth at the very edge of the river.'

'Had it been there long?' asked Graham. 'I mean, had it been there all along?'

'I couldn't say for certain,' replied Ruth, 'but the river flow forecasting from the period suggests it's a strong possibility.' Ruth took a sip of tea. It was clear she was upset too. 'The forensics team are doing a full investigation and we should know more in a few days.'

'But he's in Crediton.'

'*Mum.*'

Ruth, as always, knew how to handle the situation.

'There is one way to categorically confirm or deny that it's him,' she said.

'Dental records,' said Graham, trying to keep his voice low, but Ali heard. She began to cry.

'Graham's right,' said Ruth, 'we're going to have to access his dental records.'

'I don't—'

'It's standard procedure,' she continued, 'and the truth is, I'd rather work alongside you than against you.'

'Of course,' said Ali, biting back more tears.

Sunlight glinted off the liquid in her whisky glass, creating amber shadows on the tabletop in front of her.

Ruth cleared her throat. 'And we're going to need some samples of his DNA.'

The funeral was on a sunny day in late spring. Ali and Matthew had never really talked about dying because they had always enjoyed living too much. In the end she defied convention and decided on a natural burial high on a wildflower meadow overlooking the very same river that had taken his life. They lit a fire in the centre of an ornate stone circle, the smell of applewood and sage infusing the air around them. She glanced at the wicker coffin settled on the grass, bees feeding on the casket spray of white lilies, and felt an odd sense of release. Maybe it was the shot of whisky from Graham's flask, or the warmth of Emma's arm one side and Liz's on the other, but she finally felt ready to step forward. Into what she hadn't a clue, but she had done it before and would do it again.

She left the small group of mourners by the burial mound and was making her way through the long meadow grass when she heard someone fall into step beside her.

'Ali,' said Dane, leaning forward to kiss her.

'Don't!'

'I've been trying to reach you. Why haven't you replied to any of my texts, why won't you talk to me?'

A fury so consuming, so overpowering tore through her like an infection. 'You never really believed he was alive, did you?' she said, trying hard to contain her vitriol. 'You were just leading me along in some sort of perverse game.'

'What?' said Dane, looking bewildered. 'Of course I believed it. I've spent the last month searching for him, haven't I?'

'What were you planning, Dane? Trying to keep my hopes up for as long as possible so that you could keep tapping me for more money? Continue to be my friend, my confidant?'

'What the hell are you talking about?'

A waft of his citrus-and-leather-infused cologne drifted her way, and a devastating revelation swept over her.

'It was you in my house that night, wasn't it? What were you looking for, money?' Her expression darkened. 'Ah, of course, I see it now. You were after his laptop, weren't you?'

'Jesus, Ali, this is crazy!'

'You and Liz kept on and on about the bloody laptop. How important it was to find it. How all his passwords and login details were stored on it.' Fuelled by her knowledge about what he had done to Emma, her common sense deserted her. She leaned a little closer. 'He had everything you wanted didn't he, Dane? Money, status, power.' The whisky had loosened her inhibitions as well as her tongue. 'And there's you with a failing business and a predilection for younger women.'

Dane's face went blank. 'What are you talking about?'

Ali had promised her daughter she would keep

her terrible secret, but the anger that now consumed her was like a cancer eating through everything she held dear. Her body felt poisoned by the weight of lies that had been forced on her, her heart hardened to the point that she couldn't even cry as Matthew's coffin was lowered into the ground. But now with Dane standing next to her, the scent of his aftershave, the creak of his expensive leather shoes, she felt an overwhelming desire to lift her walking stick and strike him, strike him again and again until he was nothing but a bloody pulp seeping away into the long grass. She would never have believed she could have become so brutal, but the last few months had changed her, distorted her into something dark and different.

'I know you resented Matthew, were jealous of him.'

Dane couldn't hide his unease at her apt accusation. 'You're upset, Ali, not yourself.'

'I know you used him, manipulated him, and when he was out of the picture you tried to do the same to me.' Ali also almost added, *as well as my daughter*, but stopped herself.

'This is mad, Ali.'

'I know what you are,' spat Ali. In her peripheral vision, she could see Liz approaching. 'A predator, and a pathetic one at that. It's only a matter of time before Liz knows it too.'

*   *   *

The wake was held in The Bull, the large back room filled to the brim. Ali sipped her red wine and made her way from one sympathetic face to another, accepting words of condolence with a smile and a few quiet words of thanks. Dane stood in a far corner, drinking brandy and glaring, while Liz hovered between them looking both confused and heartbroken. By three p.m. the remaining sandwiches were hardening at the edges, and by five Ali was drunk, woozy, and secluded at a table in a far corner of the room, Graham and Emma at her side. The afternoon was easing into evening, the high street quiet. A breeze blew in from the large picture window, bringing with it the earthy autumn aromas of woodfires, compost, and decay.

'S'pose we should go,' said Ali, not making the slightest move to get up.

Graham pointed to a young man polishing glasses behind the bar. 'Dev says he'll drop us home whenever you're ready.'

There was the thud of footsteps, and the trio looked up to see Dane standing in front of them.

'*Shit*,' whispered Emma, who had managed to avoid him for most of the afternoon.

'Stay where you are.' Ali placed a reassuring hand on her daughter's arm.

'Lovely ceremony, Ali,' said Dane who was obviously very drunk himself. 'Who would have thought a fire pit would be a place to hold a funeral?'

'Exactly,' said Graham, not catching the sarcasm. 'I thought it was one of the most beautiful ceremonies I have ever attended.'

'You did him proud, Mum,' said Emma, staring at the table.

Graham thumped the table with his fist, sending the glasses jangling.

'We can't send the young man off without a good old singsong can we?' He coughed once or twice, and in his deep, clear, baritone, began to sing an old Irish hymn their mother used to sing to them as children. The room fell pin-drop silent. Ali reached for a tissue from her bag. When she looked up again, Dane was gone.

26

The next few months were a blur. There was the death certificate to collect, probate to sort, and the certainty of a coroner's inquest. 'Standard for an accidental, violent or unexplained death,' Ruth had said. She had come to the house one afternoon not long after the funeral to explain what was happening with the investigation.

'What I'm about to tell you, Ali, is upsetting,' she began. 'Are you sure you want me to continue?'

'Of course,' replied Ali. 'I want to know everything.'

Ruth's expression grew serious. 'The post-mortem has revealed that while the injuries Matthew sustained in the car accident were serious, they may not have been fatal.'

'What does that mean?' said Ali, unable to grasp the FLO's meaning.

Ruth shifted a little closer to where Ali was sitting. 'The post-mortem report determined there was an amount of water in Matthew's lungs.'

'Of course,' said Ali. 'He was in the river for a long time.'

'It's more complex than that.'

Ali was growing impatient. 'Please just tell me.'

'The aspiration of fluid into the lungs, as well as changes to some of the lung tissue, suggests Matthew was alive when he went into the water.'

Ali sat mutely for what seemed like an eternity before finally being able to speak. 'Are you telling me that he drowned?'

'I can't really confirm anything conclusively, Ali. That decision will be made formally at the inquest in a few months' time.'

'But he was alive when he went into the water.'

'There *were* traumatic injuries,' replied Ruth, 'but yes he was.'

'So he drowned?'

Ruth held her gaze. 'He drowned.'

Ali took a few moments to take in her words.

'And if he'd gotten out of the car, would he have survived?'

'Hard to say for sure,' replied Ruth, plainly uneasy at this level of speculation. 'His injuries were extensive, but the emergency services did arrive soon after . . .' She stopped mid sentence perhaps realising she was treading on dangerous ground.

'So he may have survived?'

'Yes, he may have.'

For a while after that time seemed to slow, and Ali – unable to process the information – put all her energies into work. She went in early and stayed late, filling all the time in between with committees, associations, and anything else that distracted her from dealing with both the reality surrounding Matthew's death, and the fiction that had been their lives together. Her friendship with Liz, while still intact, became increasingly formal. Workdays were fine – they could chat about business, the weather – but any mention from Liz of getting together socially was met with a polite refusal.

There was no way Ali would ever be in the same room with Dane again; this meant spending most weekends with her brother and daughter in Bristol to avoid any possibility of a dinner invitation or surprise visit from the couple. As far as she could tell Dane had kept quiet about their confrontation at Matthew's funeral, but Liz was undoubtedly aware something serious had gone on between them.

'Maybe you just need a little bit more time on your own,' she had said at one point, clearly desperate to rationalise Ali's growing estrangement.

Summer was easing its way gently into autumn. The Cornwall project had kicked off and was progressing nicely, and Emma was happily temping for Graham until she resumed her studies at Plymouth University in a few weeks' time. Life, or a half-life, as Ali now thought of it, went on.

She was returning home one evening after another chamber of commerce meeting when she spotted her brother's Porsche in the drive.

'Sis.' He held up a large takeaway bag as she approached. 'I brought Chinese!'

They ate crispy chilli beef, Kung Pao chicken, and salt and pepper prawns. They talked about Emma restarting university, about Ali putting off moving to Salcombe until the spring, and buoyed by the Cornwall project, and news of the Assadorian deal, how business was booming. They also talked about Graham's new partner.

'Met him on a dating website.'

'What?' Ali looked at her brother with a mixture of curiosity and delight. 'You, on a dating website?'

Graham's cheerful expression became serious. 'After everything that's happened—' he took a sip of wine '—well it made me think how important it is to have someone in your life.'

'You have me.'

Graham held his glass up in salute. 'I know that, and you'll always have me too, but maybe it's time for me to try again.' He frowned. 'I hope that doesn't sound insensitive?'

'Don't be silly,' said Ali. 'What happened to me happened. I can't change it.' She touched her glass against his, the chiming of crystal echoing through the room. 'I'm happy for you, Graham; I really am. I hope you've found someone who deserves you.'

He smiled broadly, showing dimples in his cheeks very similar to his niece's. 'He's a chef.'

Later, drinking their coffee in the lounge, Ali broached the subject that had been niggling her all evening.

'So,' she said to her brother her tone light, 'why are you really here?'

'Sis . . .'

'It's okay, Graham, I know you're just looking out for me, and I appreciate it, but I can tell there's something on your mind and has been all evening.'

Graham gave a weary sigh. 'Busted.'

'So?'

'Emma's worried about you.'

'What?'

'About Matthew's estate.'

'What estate?' said Ali, now unable to hide the bitterness. 'A few designer clothes and a joint credit card with nearly two grand on it?'

'And the mortgage?' asked Graham. 'For the Salcombe house?' Ali didn't reply. 'You need to let them know, Ali. It's been nearly three months.'

'I'll get around to it. I'm still paying it aren't I?'

'And the executor of Matthew's will?'

'Some solicitor in Truro, taking his bloody time with it too.'

'Anyway, what's going on with you and Dane? The atmosphere at the funeral was frankly Nordic between you two.'

'He's not the person I thought he was, Graham.'

'And Liz?'

'We see each other.'

'Outside of the office?'

'We're both busy.'

Graham sighed deeply.

'It's not enough that Matthew lied and stole from you, but it now appears he also was responsible for destroying the best friendships you've ever had.'

'We'll get through it,' said Ali, happy to let Graham think Matthew's actions were the cause of the animosity between her and Dane.

'Whatever's going on in your personal life,' he continued, 'you still need to go to the mortgage company with a copy of Matthew's death certificate. As a joint mortgage holder, you get the property after Matthew's death, but you need to have that recorded formally.'

'I know, I know.'

'Sooner rather than later, Ali.' His face was thoughtful. 'I know a good family lawyer.'

'I don't need—'

'Of course you do!' Graham's patience had worn thin. 'There are things that need to be done, Ali; must be done, to protect you, Emma, and everything you've worked for.'

Ali rubbed her forehead, allowing her finger to follow the thin train of her scar from cheekbone to chin.

'I have been avoiding it,' she confessed. Ali tipped the last of her decaf into her mouth. 'It's just that Matthew dealt with everything for the Salcombe house. It was his baby.'

'But your name is on the mortgage too, isn't it?'

'Yes.'

'Then it's time for you to deal with it.'

'Okay,' said Ali. 'I'll call the broker in the morning and arrange a meeting.'

'Promise?' asked Graham, still unconvinced.

'I promise,' said Ali, the weight of the pledge hanging heavy on her head.

With work and other commitments, it was a week later before Ali booked an appointment with Mike at The Mortgage Place in Plymouth. It was a Friday afternoon, and the streets were filled with students preparing for freshers' week at the university. She wondered if Emma would be walking along this road soon, and glanced eagerly at the passing faces. On impulse she sent her daughter a text inviting her to lunch, and knowing how busy she was added the key words, *sometime soon?*

The Mortgage Place office on Mutley Plain was just one more in a long row of estate agents and lenders. Ali quickened her pace. Even though she had been putting it off for ages, there was something comforting about finally sorting this all out. She couldn't give a toss about Matthew's estate, what there was of it. The charity shop could have his designer suits and limited-edition Nikes; the business was secure, now all she wanted now was to keep the house in Salcombe safe.

She entered the glass-fronted, open-plan office searching for a receptionist. Ahead of her were four desks, two on either side. They were spaced closely together, clearly no need for confidentiality at The Mortgage Place. At the far end two people were eating their lunches and staring at their mobile phones. Ali cleared her throat.

'Excuse me,' she said finally. A man in his thirties in a too-tight, too-cheap suit and slicked-back hair, looked up. 'I'm looking for Mike.'

'That's me,' he said with little enthusiasm.

Ali walked down the centre aisle towards him, noting the first two desks on either side were unoccupied.

'Why aren't you sitting at the front,' she asked, 'where everyone can see you?'

'It's lunchtime,' he replied feebly.

She remembered coming here with Matthew four years before. They'd had a boozy lunch to celebrate finding the property in Salcombe, and he had convinced her to forgo the traditional bank mortgage – *'with my credit history Als'* – for a brokered deal. *'A friend of mine works there.'*

Their skilled adviser back then wasn't Mike, but could have been – same hair, same cheap suit, same attitude.

'Is there somewhere we can speak privately?' she asked.

Mike gazed around as if suddenly aware of the minuscule space. 'Umm, not really.'

'Then you'd better find one, hadn't you?'

They ended up in the small staff room, not much bigger than Ali's en suite. Mike had brought his laptop with him, and they sat side by side on plastic chairs, surrounded by boxes of old brochures.

'So, Mrs Penrose-Jones,' he said putting on his brightest customer service smile. 'How can I help?'

Ali handed him a photocopy of Matthew's death certificate. 'I just wanted to inform you that my husband died three months ago.'

Mike's smile faded. 'Oh gosh, I'm sorry.'

'Me too.'

Mike seemed inordinately confused. 'And?'

'And I'm supposed to inform you, and you are supposed to change the details of the mortgage to reflect the fact that I will now be the sole mortgagee.'

Mike was staring at her, his mouth slightly agape. 'What? Oh yes, of course.' He tapped a few keys on his laptop and studied the screen. 'That's no problem, we can sort that immediately.'

'While I'm here,' said Ali, 'I was wondering if we could look at possibly renegotiating the mortgage itself. I won't need a fixed rate.'

'Of course!' said Mike, coming to life at the prospect of a potential commission. He scrolled down the page, his brow furrowing slightly. 'It might be a bit more difficult with the recent remortgage of course, but let's see what we can do.'

For a moment Ali thought her hearing had failed. 'Remortgage, what remortgage?'

Mike shifted the laptop closer towards her. 'January of this year. The property was remortgaged to fund your renovation work.'

Ali scanned the document settling on the two signatures at the bottom of the page.

'That's not my signature,' she said, her voice shaky, 'and I've never seen this document before in my life.'

Mike's face went blank.

'Who was responsible for this?' she said her voice rising. 'Who witnessed it?'

Mike scrolled down a bit further. 'Someone called Alex Davison.'

'And where is this Alex Davison person?'

Mike was like a fish gasping for air. 'Alex was two, maybe three before me.'

'What the hell are you talking about?'

'He left the company just after Easter.'

'What?'

'There was Alex, then Simone, and then Liam who lasted less than a week.' Mike gave her a sheepish look. 'There's not much training and our monthly targets are ridiculous.'

Ali stared at the man before her in horror. 'I don't give a fuck what your working conditions are! What I do care about is the fact this remortgage is fraudulent. I never signed that document. That is not my signature!'

'I – I . . .' stuttered Mike. 'I don't know what to do.'

'You can start with finding the original paperwork. And get your manager on the phone *right now*!'

27

She had to stop for a drink at a grotty Wetherspoons a few shops down from The Mortgage Place to calm her nerves, which seemed to be vibrating at a hundred miles per hour. The manager had been useless, saying they'd have to get someone from head office to look at it, and there was a strong indication from Mike that maybe mortgage brokerage was no longer for him.

She limped her way to the car, closed the door, and even though it was autumn put on the air conditioning. Then she rang Graham.

'Jesus Christ, Ali!'

'I know, I know.'

'One hundred and fifty thousand pounds – that's a quarter of the entire property value!'

'He said it was for renovations.'

'And the signature?'

'Looks a bit like mine, but not mine.'

'What about the witness signature?'

'Some wide-boy adviser, supposedly Matthew's friend who's long gone.'

'This is going to be tough,' said Graham. She had never been more grateful for her brother's expertise than now. 'And you, as co-owner, are bound by that document, and by creating the circumstances in which the fraud was able to occur—'

'I didn't *create* anything!'

'By knowingly allowing Matthew to manage the original mortgage means it may be very difficult to deny the validity of the remortgage.'

'You're saying the money's gone? Lost?'

'I'm saying we're going to need to get in a hand-writing expert.' Graham was deep into problem-solving mode. 'And a very good lawyer.'

She drove home with extreme caution, checking her speedometer, and being especially careful around corners. When she arrived, she went straight to the bedroom and removed the photo album box from the drawer. It was nearing dusk and dark clouds had started to roll in, but she took the album to the garden, lit the cast-iron fire bowl, and removed the photos from their plastic sheaths.

'You dirty rotten bastard!' she screamed, tearing up a photo of her and Matthew holding hands at the beachside altar. 'How could you do this!' Next came an image of them cutting the wedding cake, and then of him toasting the bride. 'What the fuck have you done with my money?'

One by one the images were torn up and tossed into the fire, the flames bursting into colourful infernos as the dioxins in the glossy paper ignited. Tucked in at the back of the album was an A4 envelope. Inside were printed mobile phone photos of her and Matthew before the wedding, at dinner parties and romantic walks by the seaside, and a lovely image Liz had taken on her iPhone of them cuddling on the settee. She had been saving them all to create another album and had even come up with a theme: *Past, Present, and Future.* Matthew had thought her idea charming.

Ali peeled open the seal and shook the contents into the fire, watching as they settled and slightly dampened the flames. It wasn't long before they rekindled, licking around the images, blackening their edges. She spotted something in the centre of the quickening fire and picked it up, waving it in the cool night air to extinguish the smouldering paper. Squinting to see it in the encroaching gloom, she walked towards the house. Once inside she switched on the overhead light and studied it more closely. It was an analogue photo, probably taken on a cheap disposable camera. It was of Matthew as a teenager and standing next to him a man, clearly his father. It was the only photograph he had of the man, as his late mother, in an act similar to the one Ali was performing right now, had burned all photographs of Matthew's father following his abandoning the family.

'Apple doesn't fall far from the tree,' she murmured, as she held the scorched image up closer to the light. They were both standing by the coast as she could just see breaking waves in the background. Next to them was a small holiday chalet, more like a shed, and on it a hand-carved sign that read *Taran*.

'Hi, Liz.'

'Ali.' Liz sounded surprised to hear from her as they rarely had conversations outside of the office these days. 'Are you okay? Do you need anything?'

Sadness filled Ali's heart. The situation with Dane had meant that she had been forced to step back from Liz, leaving her feeling as if she was grieving one more loss.

'I've just been sorting out some old photos—' well that wasn't a lie, was it '—and I came across one of Matthew with his dad.' The was a pause on the other end of the line as Liz waited to hear more. 'They were by the coast somewhere, a holiday chalet, I think. Do you know where it might be?'

'A holiday chalet?' said Liz sounding mystified.

'Oh yes, of course,' she said happy once again to be of assistance. 'I remember him telling us once that his dad had a place near Freathy.'

'Freathy?'

'Freathy Beach, near Portwrinkle. In Cornwall.'

Ali revisited the linen cupboard, to where still hidden behind the laundry basket, was the plastic carrier bag containing the contents from Matthew's bedside table drawer. She opened it, pushing aside the detritus of his unremarkable life before finding what she was looking for: the keychain with the black and white flag and the word *Kernow* written across it in white. She ran her fingertips across the cuts, weighed it in her hand. 'It's not possible, is it?'

She knew it was ridiculous to travel south at this time of night, and with the rain coming in, but she couldn't wait. With little to go on except a name and a grainy photo, she put on her mac and wellies and headed out.

Poor weather meant little holiday traffic, and she made it over the Tamar Bridge and into Cornwall in half an hour. Then she followed the A38 through the rolling darkness until she reached Portwrinkle and the B3247.

The road was narrow in places with passing points that seemed to be balanced on the very edge of the clifftop. It was pitch-black aside from a few lights along the hillside. Most of the properties along this stretch of coast were holiday homes, empty during the autumn and winter months. The bright lights of an approaching bus momentarily blinded her, forcing Ali to squeeze into one of the precarious passing points. Her headlights disappeared into darkness, but she knew just over the tiny lip of green, the steep, grassy hillside plummeted to the cliff face, and a fifty-foot drop to the beach below. She hoped it wasn't much further to Freathy.

She stopped to collect her thoughts and courage in the car park of the Freathy Inn. She had googled Taran Chalet before leaving home, but all that came up were a list of holiday properties in the area. If the shed was anything like the one in the photo, she doubted anyone would be interested in renting it. In the end she decided to have a quick glass of something and hoped the landlord might be helpful.

Inside the pub was warm and welcoming, with low ceilings and a fire burning in the hearth. She placed her coat on a deep leather chair by the fire and went to the bar.

'Glass of red please,' she said to the bartender.

He took a bottle of Merlot from the bar and poured her a glass. She took the photo out of her pocket and slid it across the bar towards him along with a ten-pound note.

'I know this is a long shot,' she said in her

friendliest voice, 'but I'm trying to find a holiday chalet nearby. It's called Taran.'

The bartender, a shaven-headed man in his late forties, glanced at the photo. 'Don't know it.'

Ali pushed it closer. 'Are you sure?'

'Love, there are hundreds of holiday homes and chalets around here.' He sounded annoyed. 'You think I know the names of all of them?'

'It's just that . . .' Ali felt that familiar, over-whelming sensation of panic that invariably caused her to prattle on. 'It's to do with my late husband – Matthew. I think he may have been running his business from there and I really need to find it.' The bartender, unmoved by her ramblings, said nothing. 'The thing is he died three months ago – well, before then actually; his body was missing for ages. You probably saw it in the news. Our car crashed on the moors in Devon, and ended up in the river?' The bartender regarded her sceptically, one eyebrow cocked.

Letting out a mournful sigh she reached for her wine glass. 'Never mind, just forget it.'

'It you stopped talking long enough to let me get a word in edgeways maybe I could help.' The bartender slid the photograph back towards her. 'Course I knows what happened to Matt, poor bugger, read it in the *Herald* didn't I?'

'You knew him?' said Ali.

'Used to stop in for a pint every other Thursday

he did.' Every other Thursday Ali was under the impression that Matthew went to visit an old friend in Bodmin, and then to the gym. 'Nice fella,' continued the bartender. 'We was wondering what might have happened to the chalet, you know, after he was gone.'

'The chalet,' repeated Ali, grabbing the wooden stool next to her for support. 'Taran?'

He rode in the car with her the half mile down a narrow path dotted with holiday homes, chalets and bungalows, most of them empty.

'There!' The barman, an ex-Royal Marine named Kenny, pointed to a small, shared drive. Ali pulled in. The car headlights glowed bright, reflected in the sliding door directly opposite. 'It's nothing like in that picture you've got, love,' he said. 'After his dad died about ten years back and left it to him, Matt started doing it up. Nice little place it is now.' He got out of the car then went around to Ali's side to help her out. The wind had picked up and the air was heavy with the promise of rain. Ali reached into the glove compartment for a torch.

The white-blue glow of the LED torch beamed ahead, offering her first proper look at Taran. The chalet was about the width and depth of a double garage. There was a step up to a small decking area and then a glass sliding door that led inside. She glanced at Kenny. 'You want to come in?'

'Nah,' he replied. 'I should be getting back to the bar.'

'I can drop you back.'

'I'm pretty used to walks in bad weather, love.' Kenny zipped up his puffa jacket. 'You just be careful driving back along that road now. It can be treacherous in the rain, and if you go over the edge, well, there's not much stopping you from rolling straight into a ditch, or even worse over the edge.'

She waited until Kenny was out of sight before walking across the short expanse of decking. The key slipped into the lock with ease, and then she slid open the door and stepped into Taran.

It was as small inside as it seemed from out – a single room – on one side a kitchen with cooker, two cabinets and an undercounter fridge, and on the other a settee/sofa bed, coffee table and, in the corner, next to the tiny wet room, was a desk. It felt cold and damp, as if the heating hadn't been on in months. Well of course it hadn't. Ali found the light switch and flicked it hopefully, but wasn't surprised to be met with continued darkness.

Using the torch from her glovebox, she started with the desk, opening the single drawer, and even running her hands underneath it, like she had seen in the movies. She opened the kitchen cupboards, just two plates, a mug, and cutlery for one. It was clear Matthew didn't receive visitors. The fridge was empty except for a half-empty bottle of Evian, and under the sink were just the standard cleaning items and binbags. There was nowhere else to look. Her attention fell to the settee, and she rushed over, throwing aside the cushions and even pulling it away from the wall, but Matthew's laptop, the thing that she had come searching for, was nowhere to be found. She thought back to Liz's words of six months before. *He kept everything on that laptop, Ali – bank account details, financial records.* Maybe even the stolen remortgage money?

'It must be here!' In a fit of temper she stomped her foot down hard on the wooden floor. There was a hollow sound, audible through the faux sheepskin rug. Holding the torch in her mouth, Ali pushed the settee aside and rolled back the rug. There, in the centre of the floor, just underneath where the settee had been, was a hatch. Fixed within it was a small metal handle. Ali snatched a cushion and eased herself down onto it, then grabbed the handle and lifted.

She had imagined finding a secret vault or winding staircase leading to an underground labyrinth, but instead was greeted with a small metal-lined compartment about the size of an apple crate. Nestled inside and safely encased in bubble wrap was Matthew's MacBook Pro, and sitting directly on top of that, a cheap pay-as-you-go phone and charger.

Outside the wind grew fierce, rattling the windows and blowing debris across the decking. Rain splattered against the small skylight, and the room was momentarily suffused in phosphorescence as lightning struck. Ali reached into the recess and grabbed the phone and bubble-wrapped relic, toppling backwards onto the floor as she lifted it out. She lay flat out for a moment, her leg in spasm, the precious MacBook Pro nestled against her chest.

She considered unwrapping it straight away but realised after all this time it would probably be out of battery. It would be pointless trying to charge it here. Instead, she did a final double check of the room, locked up, and stumbled her way across the slippery decking to her car. The freezing rain pelted against her skin, and a violent gust nearly knocked her over, but she didn't stop moving until she was safely inside.

'Bloody hell!' Rain ran down her face and soaked the collar of her jumper. It was a few minutes before her hands were steady enough for her to drive.

She pulled out and drove her way along the single-lane road that ran parallel to the clifftop. What felt like hurricane-force winds jostled the car, and Ali felt her fingers cramp as she gripped the wheel. The inside of the vehicle was flooded with light, and Ali glanced into her rear-view mirror to see another car's headlights directly behind her.

'Gimme a break,' she mumbled, and kept her speed steady. The driver behind, perhaps a local fed up with slow-moving tourists, pulled even closer. Ali tapped the brakes, hoping to offer a gentle reminder to the driver to keep their distance. Behind her headlights flickered and Ali's car was once again flooded with light, this time much brighter. She instinctively returned her gaze to the rear-view mirror and was momentarily blinded by the car's high beams. Some idiot on the road was the last thing she needed. She just wanted to get home safely.

She squinted into the darkness hoping to find a lay-by or passing point ahead where the impatient asshole could overtake her. There was a loud thump and Ali felt her head shoot back as the car behind knocked into her. 'What the fuck are you doing?' she screamed, but the driver wouldn't relent, bumping against her again and again, apparently trying to force her into a lay-by, or into one of the deep ditches along the hillside. Her heart was thumping ferociously, and she could feel her left leg beginning to tingle as sciatica set in from the repeated impacts.

'Stay calm, stay calm.' It was too dark to see what make of car the psycho behind her was driving, but it seemed tiny. It would take a lot to run her two-and-a-half-ton Range Rover off the road. She felt the car skid slightly as she oversteered on a sharp bend and let out a sob of relief when she managed to steady it. She caught sight of a sign indicating the road ahead was widening and terror gripped her. She would have to try and pull away before the road broadened and the nutter behind her could pull up alongside her.

'Oh God, oh God.' she cried, desperately trying to keep her thinking straight. A flash of memory fizzled across her brain, of Emma in the driver's seat having just passed her provisional licence, and Ali talking her through all the features on their very first Range Rover. *'There's an automatic lighting system so you don't have to worry about forgetting to put your headlights on. No, Emma, don't twist that – it's for the rear fog lights . . .'* Ali slid her fingers along the lighting control stalk and twisted the middle section downwards, activating the rear fogs. Bright orange light filled the darkness behind her, and she tapped on her brakes again to intensify the glare.

The car dropped back slightly, and for a moment Ali thought to try and make out a few blurry letters on the licence plate. But there wasn't time. The car was picking up speed and heading towards her. Throwing aside indecision, Ali shifted the car into first, put her foot down and sped away, her rear end fishtailing on the muddy road. Terrified that the maniac might still be following her, she sped along the winding road, repeatedly glancing in her rear-view mirror, desperately hoping not to see the glare of headlights behind her.

28

It was after midnight when she finally arrived home. The first thing she did was to go into her bedroom, lock the door, plug in the Mac, and type in the password Chiefs123. There had been a faint *boing* sound and the laptop screen juddered. Ali tried again.

'No, no, no!' she screamed. 'The one bloody time I need it to be!' Afraid she would lock out the laptop with further failed attempts, she reluctantly closed the lid and fell into an exhausted sleep. She woke the next morning fully clothed, and with the laptop still on the bed next to her.

She dressed quickly and didn't bother with breakfast. The crisp October morning was bright and clear, the air heavy with the acrid scent of burning leaves. Ali unlocked the passenger door, put Matthew's laptop safely in the footwell, and then walked around to check the damage to the rear of the Range Rover. The Carpathian Grey was now sullied with scrapes of mustard yellow paint.

'I still can't believe it,' she mumbled, getting into the driver's seat. She had contemplated calling the police, but after her experience with the break-in wasn't sure they would take her seriously, even with the obvious damage to the car. There was no CCTV along the coastal road, so no way to check who the other driver had been.

She followed the road for Ashprington, the small village nestled not far from where the Harbourne River met the Dart. She passed the stone cross opposite the Durant Arms and pulled onto a dusty road with a cracked pavement and grass growing up the middle. When she reached the two large brick pillars she was nearly there.

She drove over the cattle grid and down a long drive until she reached a large manor house. She parked up next to a dilapidated old jeep and studied the landscape around her. The manor, once a grand structure that had housed five generations of well-off wool merchants, had long since been converted into flats and small cottages. Behind the building was a walled garden where the residents grew organic fruit and vegetables. Cows and goats grazed happily in a nearby field. It was an idyll that had inspired city dwellers for over thirty years to leave their hurried lives behind and seek something new. Ali despised it. She collected the laptop and walked the short distance to the front door. She knew it would be unlocked and didn't bother to knock. Inside it smelled of woodsmoke, home-made soup and scented candles. She made her way down the hallway and into the large communal kitchen where a woman in her early sixties, hair piled loosely on her head, was kneading bread dough.

'Alice,' she said, her voice rich with surprise. 'Is that you? How are you?'

'Hi, Molly.' Ali didn't want any reason to have to stay longer than necessary, so avoided any chit-chat. 'Do you know where my father is?'

Sensing Ali's discomfort the woman smiled serenely. 'He was out earlier doing the composting, but I expect he is back in the office by now. We're designing a new website. We even have an Instagram page.' She seemed thrilled by the modern amenities she had once so eagerly spurned. Seeing the questioning look on Ali's face she explained further. 'It promotes our open days, workshops and fund-raisers. All the money we need for expansion.'

'Of course,' said Ali, realising once again that no matter how noble the thinking, it always came down to the same old thing. She gave a bow out of habit and went back down the hallway and up the large staircase to the second floor. As hard as she tried, she couldn't shut out the painful memories that flooded her brain, of her dying mother's face, pallid and sunken like wet crepe paper.

She found the office, knocked twice, and entered.

Her father was sitting in a far corner. On the desk in front of him were two laptops side by side. He was busily working back and forth between them.

'Instagram, eh?' she said.

He gave her a surprised look. 'Got to keep up with the times, Alice.'

'Everyone calls me Ali now.'

'You look tired,' he said, 'and unwell. Have you been eating properly?'

'I've been eating.'

He made a small *hmm* sound. 'And how's my granddaughter?'

'Emma's fine.'

'Back at uni I hear?'

'How do you know that?'

He pulled a chair up and beckoned for her to sit. She hesitated.

'Come on, Alice,' he said, returning his attention to the dual screens, 'you're still recovering, and those stairs are a killer.'

Exhausted from the events of the previous night, she sat down and removed Matthew's laptop from her shoulder bag.

'I gathered this wasn't a social visit. Forgotten

your password? Lost a file? I'm sorry, love, but just because I once worked in IT—'

'Looks like you still do.'

'For a good cause, Alice, a good cause.'

'So is this,' she said laying the laptop on the desk next to him. Maybe it was something about her tone, or the fact that she was so unusually calm, but her father stopped what he was doing and gave her his full attention. 'I need you to get into it.'

'What do you mean, "get into it"?'

Ali opened the laptop lid. 'I need you to hack into this computer.'

'Now just a—'

'I know you've done it before,' she said, intercepting any possible refusal. 'Graham told me about the battery farm. How you hacked into their system and hijacked their website.'

Her father blushed with pride. 'We got our message to nearly a half a million people before they shut it down.'

'Lucky *you* weren't shut down.'

He shrugged. 'Every step towards the goal of justice requires struggle, suffering, and sacrifice.'

'Did that include your wife?'

Her father sighed sadly. When Ali was sixteen, her mother developed early-stage breast cancer. There had been long discussions in the communal household about alternative approaches. In the end she had decided to forgo chemotherapy in favour of massage, meditation, and music, in order to *think herself well.* She died a year later. 'Can you get into it or not?'

'I'm not sure I should,' her father replied, 'or want to for that matter.'

'Matthew stole one hundred and fifty thousand pounds from me.' Ali's voice was fraught. She hadn't believed she'd be able to say those words without being physically sick. Her father stared at her in astonishment. 'I need you to help me get it back.'

He pointed to the laptop. 'In there?'

'I think so.'

It took her father less than five minutes to hack into Matthew's Mac. He restarted it, and then held down the command and S keys to open it in single-user mode. Text scrolled down on the screen, and when done loading, he typed in three simple commands, pressed return, and waited for the computer to shut down.

'I'm creating a new administrator,' he said, turning the computer on again. 'This will give me access to change the password on any other account associated with this device. Once I change the password we can get in.'

He did a few more steps to complete the registration, and now as the administrator went into Matthew's original account, changed the password, and logged into that account with the new password.

'That easy?' said Ali, dumbfounded.

'Sadly so,' he replied. 'Now what are you after?'

Matthew's home screen was populated with links to online gambling sites, the Exeter Chiefs homepage, and one called *Beard Care for Boys*. In the top right-hand corner was a folder entitled *Taran*, inside two hyperlinks, one to an online bank account Ali had never seen before, and one to a forex trading site.

'That,' said Ali, pointing to the bank account. 'I want to get into that.'

'You're kidding me, right?' said her father. 'Hacking into the Mac is one thing, but getting into his bank account? That requires a whole other skill level.'

'But you can try, can't you?'

'Alice,' said her father. 'There's two-factor authentication, unique login codes—'

'But I need to get in!'

'What you need, love, is help from your brother, a solicitor, and the police.' Her father stood up and walked towards the window where he stood staring out into the orchard, hands clasped behind his back. 'Hacking into a dead man's computer is bad enough, but then into his bank account?'

'It's my money!' Ali was now nearing hysteria. 'All my assets are currently tied up in property deals which means my cash flow is nearly non-existent. I'm in the final stages of securing a bank loan to complete a major building project and start on another, but if it gets out that the Salcombe property was remortgaged, it could sabotage the whole thing.' She stifled a sob. 'If I lose these jobs it will destroy the business, ruin me. I'll lose everything.'

'I knew that bloody man was no good,' her father muttered. He resumed his seat and clicked the desktop link to the online bank account. 'See,' he said pointing to the screen. 'Two-factor authentication, text only. Without his mobile we won't be able to log in.'

'His mobile is rotting away at the bottom of a river somewhere,' said Ali before remembering what was sitting in her coat pocket. If Matthew had a secret bank account with stolen money in it, he wouldn't use his iPhone to access it, would he?

Ali held out the burner phone. 'Can you get into this too?'

It took less time for her father to hack into the cheap Samsung than it did Matthew's laptop. Then they tried the password.

'200784?' said her father in amazement. 'He used his own birthday as his mobile pin? Are you certain?'

'He used a version of it for his bank card too.' She watched transfixed, as her father typed in the numbers. A few seconds later the mobile buzzed, indicating a newly arrived text.

Her father shook his head. 'He really *was* crap with online security, wasn't he?'

He entered the authentication code and the online bank homepage came into view. She heard him stifle a gasp as he pointed to the screen.

'Check out the balance.'

'One hundred and fifty thousand four hundred and eighty-nine pounds.'

Her father's face was like thunder. 'Where do you want it?'

Ali gave him her bank account details and watched as the account balance changed from over one hundred and fifty thousand pounds to nothing within a matter of seconds.

'Done,' said her father, and then with great sadness added, 'It never ceases to amaze me the length people will stoop to for money.'

'Nothing amazes me anymore,' said Ali.

He was just about to log off when Ali stopped him. 'Can we check for any additional transactions please,' she said, her throat almost too tight to speak, 'specifically eight thousand pounds?'

Her father went back to the transaction screen and scrolled down, studying it closely. Ali stepped away, unable to face any further anguish.

Her father gave a furious growl. 'You're going to want to see this.'

Still unable to face the damning evidence on the screen, she forced herself to focus on her father's profile instead. 'The eight thousand pounds was in there wasn't it?'

'It *was*,' replied her father, 'but it's where it went that might interest you.' He took her hand and pulled her closer. 'Ali, look.' He was pointing the cursor to the named recipient of the stolen eight thousand pounds. Ali felt the colour drain from her face. Then, without asking he clicked on the forex desktop shortcut.

'It's Chiefs123,' said Ali without prompting, and watched her father search through the site.

'He definitely was trading again?' she asked, but already knew the answer.

'Indeed he was,' replied her father with barely contained fury. He clicked once more, and a document entitled *joint dealing application form* came into view, 'only this time it wasn't on his own.'

29

Ali drove the twenty minutes back to Totnes, to the modest house on the corner with the dark blue Mercedes parked outside.

'Ali.' Dane didn't bother to hide his look of aversion. 'Here to tell me more about what a complete asshole I am?'

They hadn't spoken since Matthew's funeral two months before. Ali had discreetly asked Darren to stop employing Dane as a subcontractor, and had come up with innumerable reasons not to socialise with the couple anymore. She knew it had been acutely painful for Liz, but she couldn't face being anywhere near Dane. What most worried her was that her anger would be such that it would only be a matter of time before she would have to tell her best friend what had happened. For the moment staying away meant keeping Liz safe from the terrible truth. As contradictory as it might sound, she had begun to realise that sometimes there was a good reason for keeping secrets.

'I guess you'd better come in,' he said, stepping back to let her pass. Ali made her way along the hallway and into the lounge.

She sat and folded her hands on her lap.

'How's business?'

'Ticking over, just,' he said, 'after you stopped employing me. Got a couple of jobs coming up down the line.'

'I didn't mean on the building.' She reached into her bag, removed Matthew's Mac and placed it on the seat next to her. As hard as he tried, Dane couldn't hide his surprise.

'Is that what I think it is?' he said, trying to control the eagerness in his voice. 'Where did you find it?'

'I think you know that don't you, considering you were following me on the road back from Freathy last night.'

'What the hell are you talking about?' His attempt at feigned innocence was laughable.

'I rang Liz yesterday to ask if she knew if Matthew's father had a holiday chalet, if she knew where it was. I expect she told you all that.' Ali indicating past a window towards the garage where Dane kept an old Triumph Dolomite he was restoring. 'Did you follow me in that all the way from Totnes?'

'You're out of your mind,' he said, laughing dismissively.

'I wondered at first about the odd coloured scrapes of paint on the back of the Range Rover, then I remembered Liz telling me how hard it was for you to find a particular shade of yellow for your bodywork.' She watched his smile fade. 'Inca, wasn't it? I wonder if there are one or two scrapes of Carpathian Grey on your front bumper as well? Shall we go check?'

Dane reached for the laptop. Ali did nothing to stop him.

'The new password is Fraud123,' she said, her voice hard. 'Go on, type it in.' Unable to resist, Dane typed in the password and the homepage came into view. 'I wouldn't bother logging into Matthew's online bank account, the *secret one*,' she hissed, no longer able to hide her bitterness. 'The one hundred and fifty thousand pounds Matthew stole from me when he remortgaged the Salcombe house is already safely back where it belongs.'

Dane's expression was unreadable.

Ali took a breath and carried on. 'So the thing is we all know Matthew's admin skills were pretty lax, but he was good at securing a deal.' She glanced around at the modest lounge. 'Dartmoor Properties is due to make over two hundred thousand pounds in the next year or so thanks to him.'

'What the hell are you getting at?' said Dane, tossing the laptop onto the seat next to him.

Ali picked it up. 'Maybe I *will* log into the account after all.' She tapped in the password and clicked on the header entitled *transactions*. 'This account, like most others, not only details money transferred in, but money transferred out as well.'

'So?' said Dane, looking increasingly uneasy.

Ali pointed to the screen. 'On the 14th of December, 6.49 a.m., eight thousand pounds was stolen from Dartmoor Properties and transferred into an online account—' she didn't try to hide the look of triumph from her face '—and a short time afterwards transferred into yours.'

Dane's expression froze. 'I don't know what you're—'

'It's the same account we paid your subcontracting wages into.' She gave a huff of disbelief. 'You and Matthew didn't bother hiding it because you never thought you'd be found out. And when that money, *and* the four grand you got Matthew to redirect from the retainer fees didn't earn you a result—' she clicked on another link and Matthew's forex account came into view '—and you were both seriously in the shit in terms of your losses, you decided to go for something more substantial.'

'How dare you . . .'

Ali's scorn was palpable. 'That's why you were so desperate to find the laptop, wasn't it?' Her memory, once so sketchy, now seemed as clear as a summer sunrise. '"*Oh, Ali, we need to think about stopping his direct debits, standing orders.*" What a load of bullshit that was.'

'I think you'd better—'

'Let me finish!' she shouted, and was surprised to see Dane accede. 'You knew that if I found the laptop I would go through it to see if there were any clues as to why Matthew might have gone missing, including the fact that you and he had opened a joint trading account.' She glared at him in absolute abhorrence. 'I let you go through my bedroom looking for that thing!'

Dane's voice was deep, feral. 'He owed me.'

'You're pathetic.'

Dane shifted to a new tack. 'He begged me to be a joint account holder, Ali. To help keep an eye on his losses so they wouldn't get out of hand like before.'

'Oh, aren't you the noble one.'

'You can't seriously hold me responsible for Matthew stealing from you?'

'You had a lot of influence over him,' Ali growled, 'always have.' She took her mobile phone out of her pocket and held it up for him to see. On it were screenshots of the texts she and her father had discovered on Matthew's burner phone, texts from Dane.

Just one last pop, Matty, and we're out. We'll roll over that 150K, pay off those blokes, stash a little away. No one will be any the wiser.

'You convinced him to go for a final win, one last trip to the moon.' Her voice shook with fury. 'I noticed there was no mention in your text of paying the stolen money back into the mortgage account.'

She watched as a vein in Dane's temple began to throb. Maybe it was the stress of knowing that with Matthew being dead he was solely responsible for nearly ninety thousand pounds of trading debt, and for a moment he appeared defeated. Almost as quickly, however, his countenance changed back to that of the confident conman.

'We were going to use that investment to cover our losses, make a profit.'

'*Investment!*' Ali screamed. 'It wasn't an investment; it was money stolen from me!'

'We could have done it, Ali, made it all up, made things right again.'

'That's what all the losers say,' said Ali in disgust. 'And I'm sure once you'd paid off your losses and taken a good chunk of the profit for yourself, you were going to put the 150K back into the mortgage account, right?'

'You'd never need know.'

'Except that the car accident and Matthew going missing meant that the money never made it into your joint trading account, did it? It stayed in Matthew's online bank account, which you couldn't access unless you had his laptop.'

'We were going to fix it, Ali, really we were.'

'You coerced him into stealing that money! From the company and from me!'

Dane held her gaze. 'Not quite so sure that'll stand up in court, sunshine.'

Ali longed to shut him up, shove the facts so far down his deceitful throat that he would choke on them. Instead she held up her phone and swiped to another screenshot. Another text to Matthew.

Don't panic. I said I'd handle the situation with Emma.

'It was *you* who was blackmailing Emma,' said Ali, 'not Matthew. He was trying to protect her.'

'I wouldn't go as far as saying "protect".' Dane seemed to be enjoying this opportunity to torment her. 'Matty was happy to sit back and let me do the dirty work, always was. He talked a big show, how great he was at negotiating those property deals, but I was the one who made them happen.'

'Intimidating those people into selling them cheap you mean.'

'Call it what you like, *sweetheart,* it still made

your darling Dartmoor Properties a pretty hefty profit.'

'And you were behind it all? The stealing, the remortgaging?'

'Let's just say Matty and I were probably closer partners than you were.'

'And Liz?' Ali couldn't bear the thought that her best friend might be involved. 'Where does she fit in all this?'

'Nowhere!' For the first time in their exchange Dane seemed to be genuinely frightened. 'Liz doesn't know anything about all this and never will!' In a sudden, unexpected motion, he stood up, grabbed the laptop from Ali's lap, and raising it high above his head, smashed it to the floor. There was the agonising crunch of plastic and metal, and Ali watched a dislodged *delete* key skid across the floor and underneath the coffee table. 'The bank transfers, text messages,' continued Dane, his attempt to contain his growing panic palpable, 'can all be easily explained away. After all, I was just trying to help out my best mate – a man who'd had already had a history of poor investments – get himself out of trouble.'

'You're kidding me, right?'

'He was terrified Ali,' Dane's attempt at justifying his manipulation of Matthew was infuriating, 'with the prenup and all, and your clear diktat that if he ever traded again, you'd leave him.' He gave a smile so false it made Ali feel ill. 'Matty loved you and didn't want to lose you. When he suggested putting the twelve grand into my bank account so that he wouldn't be tempted to trade it, I had to support him. How was I to know it was stolen from your company?'

'You don't seriously think anyone will believe that do you?'

'Where's the evidence?' replied Dane. 'Where's the evidence that the 150K *investment* – because that's what Matty called it – came from anywhere else but you, that it was okay'd by you?' He held his hands up as if innocent. 'I had absolutely no idea Matthew had remortaged your property without your knowledge. And my message to him about Emma was simply an offer to speak to her about improving their relationship.'

'Because you are so selfless and caring,' spat Ali. She stood up to face him. 'Your lame excuses won't get you anywhere. Matthew's laptop and the pay-as-you-go phone are on their way to Torquay police station even as we speak.' She recalled her father's cheek against hers as he had gotten into his car a few hours before, Matthew's laptop and mobile phone carefully enclosed in bubble wrap on the seat next to him. She pointed to the crushed laptop on the floor in front of them. 'I loaded his profile onto my old Mac to see how'd you'd react. They'll trace the stolen money from Dartmoor Properties to you, and if that isn't enough to get you arrested, I'll make sure they get you for harassing and blackmailing Emma.' She looked him up and down. 'You disgust me.'

His hand was around her throat before she could stop him. Slowly he lifted her from the ground, her arms flailing. She tried to claw at him, but he was too strong. Her throat felt as if it was in a vice, her windpipe crushed, lungs screaming.

'Stop,' she rasped, pinpricks of light dancing in front of her eyes. 'Please stop.'

'It should have been you who died that night,' he snarled. 'Would have made everything so much easier.'

Ali heard a sound behind her. Dane paused, gazed over her shoulder, and suddenly released his grip. She fell to the floor, landing on her right side, her leg throbbing. It took her a moment to right herself, clear her head, and when she finally had regained her senses, could see Dane standing next to her, dead still. She followed his line of vision towards the front door.

'Honey,' he whispered, 'what are you doing?'

Liz was standing in the hallway a pistol in her hand.

'You didn't think I knew you had it, did you?' she said to Dane, her lower lip trembling. 'It's a Stechkin, Russian,' she said to Ali. 'Memento from the war,' then returned her attention to her husband:

'You're not really supposed to have it, are you, darling?'

'Put the gun down, Liz.'

'Is it true, what she said?' Liz indicated towards Ali, inadvertently pointing the gun in her direction. 'That you made Matthew steal that money?'

Dane took a step forward. 'I didn't make Matthew do anything.'

Liz raised the gun and pointed it at her husband's head. 'Did you or did you not make Matthew steal from Ali?'

'Matthew was a big boy; he could have said no.'

Liz shook her head back and forth. 'No. I thought he did it because he was selfish, greedy.'

'He was,' said Dane. 'Now give me the fucking gun!'

She kept the gun pointing at Dane but focused her attention to Ali.

'I couldn't bear the thought of you being hurt, Ali – not then, not ever.'

'I know, Liz, I know.' Ali forced her panicked breathing to slow, 'but it's okay now. I know what really happened.'

'What really happened,' said Liz, in a wistful way of someone deep in shock. 'How could you possibly know what really happened?'

Dane stepped forward another inch. 'Liz, honey, please.'

'Shut up, Dane, just shut up!'

Ali forced herself into a sitting position, her bad leg stretched out in front of her. 'I know you were trying to protect me,' she said, 'both you and Emma, from the truth about Matthew—'

'He hurt her,' Liz shouted, 'abused her!'

Ali blinked in bewilderment. 'Hurt who? Who did he hurt?'

'She left her mobile on the bed and I saw the photo.' Liz began to sob uncontrollably. 'I saw that awful photo!'

Ali knew at once what she was referring to.

'It was a mistake, Liz, a foolish mistake. Emma feels terrible about it.'

'Why should Emma feel terrible?' Liz seemed to be teetering dangerously back and forth between hysteria and calm. 'Matthew was supposed to look after her, not take advantage of her.'

It came to Ali then, as clear as it was heart breaking. 'It wasn't Matthew in the photo, Liz, it was Dane.'

'Shut up, Ali!' yelled Dane. 'Shut the fuck up!'

'She needs to know!' roared Ali in reply. 'He had sex with Emma, Liz. He manipulated and exploited her.' There was no hiding the truth anymore. The secrets that had polluted their lives for so long needed purging. 'It was you who sent that CCTV image of you both having sex to Emma in order to blackmail her into keeping quiet about the fake invoices.' Ali, crammed full of secrets for so long now, seemed unable to stop divulging them. 'And about the money he stole from Dartmoor Properties and gave to you.'

'*No*,' whispered Liz, 'please no.' Her hand flew to her throat as if she couldn't breathe. 'I thought it was Matthew in the photo. I was certain it was him.'

Ali thought back to the grainy image on Emma's phone, only the back of the person she was having sex with visible – tall, broad-shouldered, dark-haired – it could have been either man.

'It wasn't Matthew,' said Ali. 'It was Dane. Ask him.'

'Please tell me it wasn't you, Dane,' said Liz, her face ghostlike.

'Liz honey.' Dane stepped past Ali and continued slowly moving towards his wife. 'It was a mistake, okay, a stupid mistake. We were drunk. We never meant for it to happen.'

'Of course you did!' screamed Ali, now aware of what really happened that night. 'Emma told you about what she had discovered, didn't she, about Matthew and the fake invoices? She was upset, vulnerable, drunk, and you took advantage of her, all with a view to blackmailing her in order to keep her quiet!' All the pieces of the puzzle were slowly fitting into place. 'You knew how to access the CCTV footage,' said Ali in horrific understanding, 'because you had helped to install it.'

Liz tilted her head slowly sideways, like an animal trying to make sense of the unexpected.

'It was *you*?' she said in disbelief, then she frowned. 'Of course it was. I remember thinking when you came home that night that you smelled different, like someone else.'

Now truly exposed and with nowhere to go Dane stumbled his way to the settee and sat down.

'Matty and I got ourselves into a bit trouble, serious money trouble with some pretty nasty blokes.' He ran his hand across his sweat-stained forehead. 'We managed to keep them at bay for a little while with the eight grand, but I suggested to Matty that we needed a bigger score to sort things out. At first he wouldn't go for the remortgage thing.' He looked at Ali, his face was filled with ferocity. 'The stupid bastard really loved you, but by then those assholes we owed money to weren't just threatening us, but threatening our families as well. We came up with a plan,' he continued, sounding increasingly desperate, 'but then Emma found the fake invoice—'

'Which would have slowed everything down for you,' said Liz, now haunted with the knowing, 'and with the prenup and Ali's vow to end the marriage if she discovered Matthew trading again, you had to keep it a secret.'

'And with Matthew and me no longer together,' said Ali, picking up on Liz's train of thought, 'you

374

wouldn't have had access to the mortgage money, or any money for that matter. You weren't drunk that night,' she said, now forced to accept the indefensible. 'You deliberately seduced Emma. Got hold of the CCTV footage, and used it to blackmail her into keeping quiet.' She stared at Dane, unable to comprehend the depth of his depravity. 'And after the accident when Matthew went missing? You stopped sending the texts to Emma so it would look like he did it, like he had been the one blackmailing her.'

'It wasn't Matthew in the photo?' repeated Liz, who had seemed to have fallen into a sort of stupor. It was as if she was seeing her husband for the first time. 'It was you?'

Dane hung his head. 'It was me.'

Liz moved closer, her hand shaking fiercely. 'I knew something was wrong with Emma not long after she started that internal audit. She became quiet, secretive, not like herself at all. I thought it might just have been the pressure, or maybe that Christmas was approaching. She always gets down that time of year because she misses her dad.' Next to her, Ali gave a sigh of acknowledgement. 'I waited until she went to lunch and checked the document history on her computer. That's when I found the false invoices. It didn't take long to trace them to Matthew.' She glared at her husband, 'I never for one moment thought you would be involved.'

'Liz, please listen,' said Dane, but there were no more lies to be told.

'I was going to tell you, Ali, I really was,' said Liz, 'but it was the night of the Christmas party, then the holidays. I thought Emma would have done it, but then we returned to work after Christmas,' she shook her head in self-reproach, 'then your anniversary party.'

'It's not your fault Liz,' said Ali. 'None of this is . . .'

'That poor, poor girl having to shoulder that burden all on her own.' Liz didn't seem to have heard Ali's words. 'I just didn't know what to do. If I told Emma I knew about her keeping quiet about the invoices it would only upset her more. God knows she was trying hard enough to earn my respect. More than that, I knew after everything you had been through in the last few years, finding out the truth about Matthew would destroy you.'

'The truth always comes out,' Ali murmured. 'One way or another.'

'I decided I would wait until after the anniversary party to tell you. You had spent so much time and money in the planning, seemed so happy about it all that I didn't want to ruin it for you.' She gave a dejected smile. 'Your very special night you called it. Do you remember?'

'I remember.'

'You and Matthew had already gone to the hotel

to set up for your presentation,' continued Liz, 'and I went to yours to help Emma with her hair and make-up. She'd been on Instagram posting pictures of herself.' Liz chuckled, the sound eerie and unfitting. 'When she went to the loo I thought I'd post a photo of myself as a laugh. But I got it all wrong of course. Couldn't find out where the photo had gone.' Ali was beginning to recognise a terrifying similarity between her and Liz's experience. 'So I just started searching.' Liz began to cry, a slow, steady wail that sounded like a tortured animal. 'That's when I saw it, the picture and that horrible message.' Her face was distorted in loathing and disgust. 'I thought it was Matthew, not you!'

'Put down the gun Liz,' said Dane, 'please put it down.'

'I decided I would tell you everything I knew the day after the party,' she said, 'but then the accident happened.' Liz reached forward and touched the scar on Ali's cheek. 'When I saw the car in the river, I thought you must be dead.'

Ali felt as if she was walking through fog, like the time she and Rory got lost on the moors.

'You were beside me,' she said, the mist in her head slowly lifting. 'You pressed your scarf against my cheek and told me to hold it there while you undid my seatbelt.' Ali gave a tiny gasp. 'You undid my seatbelt.' She pressed a hand to her cheek as memory after memory slotted into place. 'Then

Matthew started screaming that the river was coming, that his legs were wet. The car started shifting.' She stared at Liz, her face twisted in dreadful realisation. 'You undid his seatbelt too, Liz, didn't you? You reached past me and undid his seatbelt.'

Liz's voice was barely a whisper. 'I had to get you out.'

'You pulled me out and laid me on the bank.' Ali felt her heart rate begin to race. 'Where was everyone?'

'I went to get some torches,' said Dane numbly, 'and Liz sent Emma to the car for the first aid kit.'

'I could hear sirens.'

'The ambulance,' said Dane. 'Graham was waiting for it.'

'But Matthew,' said Ali, already beginning to become aware that something terrible was about to be revealed. 'What happened to Matthew?'

Liz placed the gun on the floor next to her.

'All those things he did,' she said, 'the stealing, lying.' Beside them Dane groaned. 'The water was rising.' Liz's expression was unforgiving. 'In the car now, lifting him.'

'Liz . . . what in God's name did you do?'

Liz sat back on her heels. 'Nothing,' she said. 'I did absolutely nothing.'

'No,' said Ali, the truth slowly dawning.

'I watched the water take him, let nature decide.'

'But he was screaming, pleading for help. All you had to do was pull him out of the car like you did me. You could have saved him,' Ali implored. 'Why didn't you save him?'

Liz's voice had an eerie calmness. 'The judgement was clear.'

'You let him go into the water.' The words felt impossible on Ali's tongue. 'Didn't even *try*.' She thought back to one of her earlier conversations with Ruth. 'And the dashcam?' she asked, remembering her earlier conviction that it may have recorded the events of that night. 'Did you let the water take that too?'

Liz smiled, and for a moment her face was oddly serene. 'I had to protect you, Ali, like I've always done.'

The two friends' eyes met.

'Instead you've destroyed me.' Ali pushed herself further back against the settee in order to be as far away from Liz as possible. Her best friend, advocate, soulmate, bridesmaid, godmother to her daughter, was now just one more keeper of terrible secrets. 'You might as well have killed him.'

'No,' said Liz calmly, 'I just let justice take its course.'

'Justice! What do you know about justice?'

'I didn't let him drive when he was over the limit,' said Liz, now with a slight edge to her voice, 'argue with him in the car park, fight with him in the car.'

'Are you saying this is my fault?'

'I'm saying that we all hold some level of responsibility for your husband's death.'

'And Matthew?' said Ali, unmoved by Liz's words.

Liz bowed her head. 'Matthew was as accountable as any of us for what happened, if not more.' Liz's face was filled with sorrow and regret. 'Only he paid the ultimate price for it.'

There was a moment of silence, so absolute and complete they could have all been kneeling at a church pew.

Ali took her mobile phone from her coat pocket. 'I'm calling Ruth.'

There was a shuffling sound and both women turned to see Dane creeping towards them.

'You're not contacting anyone,' he said, pointing the gun at Ali.

'Put it down, Dane,' said Liz, 'I think we've had enough of all that for today, don't you?' She smiled forlornly. 'Ring Ruth if you like, I'll tell her everything.'

'They can't charge her,' cried Dane frantically, 'because there was no crime.'

'No *actual* crime,' replied Ali, 'but the damage has been done.'

'And what's done cannot be undone,' Liz mumbled, lost once again in her faraway world.

Outside the sound of builders at work, a passing

car, the bark of a dog, hinted that the world was carrying on as usual; inside the three people sat, silent, unmoving, their lives, friendships, futures, irrevocably changed. Finally Liz stood up, straightened her skirt, and reaching down gripped Ali by the arm and gently lifted her to her feet, the two women standing so close they could have embraced.

Liz held out her hand.

'Give me the phone. I'll do it.'

Epilogue

Ali made her way along the beach, her new spaniel puppy bouncing alongside her. The tide was coming in, and it wouldn't be long before it was completely submerged. She stopped for a moment, digging her toes into the soft, golden sand, relishing the sunlight on her face. On days like today she could almost begin to believe things would be all right again.

'We'd better hurry, Sprocket,' she said to the energetic bundle nipping at her feet. 'Emma and Graham are coming over for tea tonight.'

She took the steps up to the cliff road with ease, her right leg only niggling her slightly. She stopped at the greengrocers on the high street for fresh asparagus, and then walked the ten minutes to Haven Close, to her beautiful flagstone-fronted home built out of the ruins of a former Baptist Chapel. It sat high on the hillside overlooking the estuary, just a few minutes' walk from the town centre.

'Perfect,' she sighed, as she approached. Sunlight glistened off the stepping stones, washed clean from a brief shower earlier that morning.

The move to Salcombe was both as easy and as difficult as she had expected. The sale of Hope Farm was unnervingly quick, forcing her to face the reality of leaving that sacred space and finding another, but she had persevered, and with most of her family photographs now lined up on the dresser by the window, and Rory's old jumper in the drawer by the bed, it felt her own.

She took a deep breath before climbing the steep hill that led to the house. Her daily walks with Sprocket had improved her mobility as well as her wellbeing. There was still a strong element of Rory's old 'fake it till you make it' in her disposition, but if that got her through the day, so be it.

The building, with its tall windows and sturdy silhouette, still spoke of Sunday sermons even though it had been redesigned and upgraded to a slick specification.

She hesitated, resting her hand on the heavy oak door, before slipping her key into the lock. Sprocket raced past her and into the kitchen where he knew a bowl of water would be waiting. She gazed down at the floormat in troubled expectation. Lying there, facedown, was an envelope. She knew that when she picked it up and turned it over there would be no stamp. It, like all the others, had been delivered by hand.

The handwriting was as familiar as it was heart breaking. Immaculately tidy, with delicate loops on the letter 'l'. She looked out of the front door to the street beyond, wondering how long ago it may have been slipped through the letter box, and if its sender was still nearby. Then she closed the door and locked it, slipping on the chain for added measure.

The letters had been arriving almost weekly since her move to Salcombe, always on beautiful headed paper, and always hand delivered. She considered opening it, knowing that inside would be another message from Liz, another plea for forgiveness.

'I'm sorry Ali, forgive me. It was all a terrible mistake. I'll do anything to win you back. We said friends forever, remember?'

Dane had been absolutely correct when he had said Liz wouldn't be charged.

'Police officers take an oath to preserve life,' Ruth had explained to her, 'but it's not the same for members of the public I'm afraid. There's no way we can prove culpability, and without culpability, there is no crime.' By the time a proper interview had taken place, Dane had convinced Liz to change her story, to say she simply couldn't get to Matthew in time. Emma had also implored her mother not to tell the police about the blackmail, and when Ali discreetly asked Ruth about it, the FLO's response had been unequivocal. 'From what it sounds like to me, there is no clear evidence to connect Dane to the offence. While I'm no barrister, it's very doubtful it will stand up in court,' she said, echoing Dane's words, 'and off the record, Ali, the defence team will run Emma through the ringer, believe me.'

In the end Ali had closed the door on it all – her past, her friendships and even Hope Farm – deciding instead to start afresh in Salcombe. Or so she had thought.

There had been rumours of Dane and Liz heading up north to start afresh too, but Ali hadn't followed them, determined to extricate them from her life forever. However, when the letters started arriving she had no choice but to be pulled back into that terrible ordeal.

She balanced the envelope in her hand, contemplated peeling open the seal and reading it, but the words would only be the same, pleading, desperate, deceitful. Instead she opened the drawer to the alcove cabinet and added it to the pile of others. She heard Sprocket's impatient bark as he awaited his familiar post-walk treat, and glancing up at the arched doorway that had once led to the church pulpit, she stepped through and into the sun-filled kitchen beyond.

Acknowledgements

Thanks to my friends and family who supported me throughout the exceptional learning journey of writing my second novel:

My daughter, Danielle, for being such a great listener and offering great insight. My son, Dom, for his clear thinking, and of course my husband, Nick, who pretty much hasn't seen me for the past eight months.

I would also like to thank Karen Taylor and Ann Pelletier-Topping for offering quiet spaces for me to escape to and write.

Thanks as well to my good mate and excellent writer Finn Clarke for her words of wisdom, Laura

Fraser-Crewes for keeping me fit and well, Charlotte Taylor for her expertise on old buildings and barn conversions, David Horspool for plot development, and Dr Mark JP Kerrigan for helping me to secure the time to write.

Very special thanks goes to Tony Shaw for his procedural knowledge, and the wonderful Antony Dunford for proofreading a very sketchy first draft in a day.

Grateful thanks also goes to friends and colleagues at Plymouth College of Art for their time, their ears, and thoughts: the excellent library staff including Donna Gundry, Leesa Westlake, Emily Watkins and Jonah Garner, and other valued colleagues including Adam Levi, Rachel Gipetti, Nick Crawley, Karen Weston and Wendi Smith.

I'd also like to thank all those kind strangers who replied to my odd emails – *How long can a body go missing on the moors?* – with enthusiasm: Bob Harrison and Julian Setterington of Dartmoor Search and Rescue, as well as Physiotherapist Alice Brelsford for her guidance on injuries and recovery, and Shaun Walbridge for his advice on forensic accountancy.

Thank you to Lisa Moylett and Zoë Apostolides at Moylett McLean Literary Agency for sticking with me while I worked on this novel and prepare for the next.

And finally, my sincere thanks goes to the wonderful team at Avon Books. Publicist Becci Mansell, freelance editors Sophie Burks, Helena Newton, and Anne Rieley, and most of all to Molly Walker-Sharp for her superhuman knowledge, patience and support – you really made this all possible!

The truth lies just beneath the surface . . .

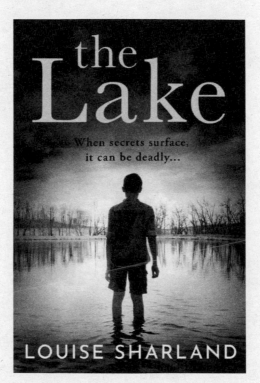